LEGION'S LAWYERS

By VINCE AIELLO

Published by SarEth Publishing House
SarEth Publishing House
Carlsbad, California

First Edition: November 2014

Printed in the United States of America

ISBN 978-0-9883413-5-7

SPHN 14-0730198826

SarEth Publishing House

Also by Vince Aiello

LEGAL DETRIMENT
THE LITIGATION GUY

*For **Sarah Rose** & **Ethan** – It would be impossible to imagine life without either of you.*

If someone needs a lawyer and they have a choice between one who's the nicest guy in the world or one who's a ruthless, no-holds-barred, blood-thirsty SOB, which one are they gonna choose? Don't blame me because you don't like the answer.

-Roger Legion
The Litigation Guy

PROLOGUE

AMERICA'S FINEST CITY BUILDING, 24TH FLOOR
SAN DIEGO, CALIFORNIA

Time. To an attorney, it is a blessing and a curse. It is a unit of measurement that allows an hourly rate to appear less offensive when broken down into smaller pieces. It is key to success for research and the honing of an argument or pleading. When ignored, it has the ability to leave an attorney with nothing but malpractice. Its power is never fully appreciated.

Roger Legion sat at his desk in his corner office trying to capture every moment of every billing event of that day. After thirty-eight years, billing time is almost second nature. You just have to make sure that your memory remains sharp and your ability to write must evidence that your three years of law school were not wasted.

Roger was in his mid-60s, nearly six feet tall, and if you didn't know his age, you would easily be persuaded to believe that he was twenty years younger. He had a full head of coifed, black hair that was accented by a band of gray. His suits were tailor-made with fine, Italian fabric and his executive, white shirt with gold cuff links underscored his position as the eminent leader of Legion and Associates, a premier insurance defense law firm. He wore custom-made ties of silk and his shoes were constructed of the finest, imported, Italian leather. His suit was more than a statement of success. He never removed his suit coat in the office. To Roger Legion, it was part of a uniform proudly worn by a warrior. The courtroom was an arena where the goal was annihilation, destruction, and carnage. Civility was left for the idealist lawyer, who never took a case to verdict. As Roger would often say at Legion and Associates, he taught his lawyers to weaponize the facts and then bludgeon their adversaries with them.

Legion would never advertise it, but he was a father figure to all of the fifteen lawyers in the firm. He would tell his attorneys that no one stands alone at the firm. He would defend them, physically if necessary, if anyone dared to besmirch them or lay a hand on them. To his attorneys, he could be a caustic taskmaster. But he also possessed the qualities of a military leader, who was on the front lines with his men. They all knew that he would take a bullet for them and when he gave an order, it was never questioned, simply carried out regardless of right or wrong.

The America's Finest City Building was a downtown landmark. It was one of the newer skyscrapers, thirty stories high, and two blocks from the San Diego Bay. Legion's corner office on the 24th floor, consisted of two walls of floor-to-ceiling glass. The other walls were mahogany and covered with various photos and awards, testifying to a lifetime of success. His desk was grand and made of mahogany with burl inlay. It was not cluttered; it contained a flat screen monitor, a keyboard, the law firm's landline telephone, and his cell phone.

He considered clutter to be a reflection of what was going on in a person's mind. Roger considered himself a master in the art of reading people: jurors, opposing attorneys, judges, and anyone, as Roger would say, that could "fog a mirror." If he could not read a person, then he believed that they were laboring under a mental disease or defect.

Roger desisted from his task recapture exercise to peer out at the Pacific Ocean. The sun was in the process of setting and it displayed a magnificent panoply of colors. The sun's rays were muted by the skyscraper's tinted windows. Roger Legion never took anything for granted, including the San Diego weather.

For some reason, he noticed that the time display in the corner of his computer monitor exhibited '3:21 pm.' It was at that moment his cell phone came to life. He picked it up and the Caller ID simply stated 'UNAVAILABLE.'

Normally, he would not have answered that type of call, but today would prove to be different on every level.

"Hello," Legion's baritone voice announced.

"Mr. Legion," answered a voice that he did not recognize. "In two minutes, a helicopter will land on the top of your building. The men inside that helicopter are coming to slaughter you and everyone in your law firm. Guide your actions accordingly."

"Who is this?" Legion asked with rushed, serious articulation.

Before he could finish his sentence, the call was disconnected. Legion's mind scrambled to comprehend the caller's message as he glanced out the window.

Legion suddenly stood from his chair with his countenance displaying bewildered awe. From the south heading north, in the distance, he saw a Bell 429 Global Ranger helicopter. This helicopter was large enough to hold eight people, including the pilot.

He knew that everyone at the law firm was now in danger. Roger tore out of his office like a Kenyan sprinter. Time was about to challenge Roger Legion.

Part 1

CHAPTER 1

8 DAYS EARLIER

Roger Legion boarded an elevator in the lobby of the America's Finest City Building for a non-stop ride to the 24th floor. He donned a dark, gray custom-made suit that had a light pinstripe. He wore a gray tie that had a pattern of small, black fleur-de-lis. The whiteness of his shirt was bright and accented with gold cufflinks. His Bruno Magli, black calf, classic lace-up shoes completed his attire.

As the elevator ascended, he took a fleeting look at his Rolex watch to note that it was 8:45 am.

Roger stepped off the elevator into the 24th floor command center of his insurance defense law firm that was Legion & Associates. The reception area floor was black marble with a center inlaid design of a lion's head. The sofas were made of brown, Italian buffalo leather. Above the receptionist's head, behind the raised, granite countertop, in large letters proclaimed the words, 'Legion & Associates.'

On the left side of the reception area, when you exited an elevator, was a large conference room. There was a glass door at each end of the conference room that opened into the reception area and an alabaster trimmed glass wall that separated the conference room from the lobby. Two smaller conference rooms were found on the opposite side of the reception area.

Roger Legion's name was immediately uttered.

"Mr. Legion, Don Howard from Commonwealth Franklin Insurance is on the phone. He's been on hold for quite a while. I told him you weren't here, but he said that he wanted to wait on hold for you," explained Nina, the law firm receptionist.

Legion rolled his eyes and his face displayed annoyance.

"I offered him your cell phone number and he wouldn't take it," Nina conveyed. "He seems to get angry if I ask him if he wants to continue to hold."

"How long?" Legion asked.

"Forty minutes," she told him.

Legion walked quickly toward Nina and raised the three middle fingers of his left hand back and forth twice. She knew that his motion was requesting her telephone receiver.

Nina wore a cordless headset and a black and white knit Jacquard pleat dress with a white sweater. She was in her early 40s and her brunette, wavy hair was layered and perfectly showcased her china doll complexion.

She handed the phone to Legion and connected the call.

"Don," Roger exclaimed in an ebullient voice.

"Roger, how are ya?" Don answered, not sounding upset at all, but rather excited to speak.

"You should call me on my cell," Legion expressed.

"No. I don't wanna bother ya. I figure you're probably in trial or something."

"You call me anytime. I've always got time for you. What can I do for you today?"

"Larry Larkin from your office is down at a settlement conference in Judge Jeckson's department with one of my claim reps, Nancy Barton. That settlement conference is going into its third day. They're the only ones there. The judge wants three thousand dollars more, but we've been sticking to our guns. I need her back here in an hour for a conference call with the home office. Now, I think it's extortion, but if you say to pay it, we'll pay it."

"No." Roger's response was decisive and distinct. "I will go over there right now and clear this up."

"Thanks, Roger. You're really savin' my butt from the fire," Don sounded relieved.

"Anything for you my friend. Next time, call me on my cell. I always look forward to talking with you."

"Okay, gotta go," he quickly responded and the call was disconnected.

Legion slowly lowered the phone from his face and handed it to Nina.

"Good morning, Nina." His voice was stern, but friendly.

"Good morning, Mr. Legion," she voiced with a warm, bright smile.

All non-attorneys at Legion & Associates were required to address the attorneys as 'Mister' and their last name. Nina was the only non-attorney on the 24th floor. All the support staff, including secretaries, law clerks, typists, paralegals, and the accounting department would be found on the 23rd floor. No employee from the 23rd floor was allowed on the 24th floor unless they had a business-related reason. If an attorney needed anything from the 23rd floor, like a file or office supplies, a runner would bring it to them.

"I am going back to the courthouse," Legion advised. "I'll be back shortly."

Legion returned to the elevator bank and pushed the call button. He kept his back to Nina until an elevator bell rang announcing its arrival and he entered it. He turned and his eyes locked with Nina's eyes as the doors closed, but his face never changed expression.

Nina had been working at Legion & Associates for the past thirteen years. As she stared at the closed elevator doors, she wondered for a moment why his mere presence caused her such panic. To her, Roger Legion was a bête noire, or black beast, something that a person particularly dreads.

CHAPTER 2

Javier Jimenez stepped off an Aeromexico flight at the Mar de Cortés International Airport located in Puerto Peñasco, in the State of Sonora, Mexico. The City of Puerto Peñasco is located on the Gulf of California, approximately 430 miles from downtown San Diego. Like San Diego, this resort town was built on a desert situated next to the ocean. The climate was arid, but comfortable when the wind blew. Summer rains were short and heavy with temperatures ranging from 80 to 105 degrees. Monsoons had the ability to wash out desert roads and uproot trees.

Inside the airport, it was a comfortable, air-conditioned, 72 degrees. The sounds of mariachi music filled the air and like every other airport in the world, everyone seemed to be in a hurry. Outside, it was 82 degrees and expected to climb.

Javier was 66 years old, 5 feet 7 inches, with a full head of wavy, gray hair and a gray goatee. He wore blue jeans, worn-leather boots, and a flannel, patterned, long-sleeve shirt. Around his neck hung a bolo tie with an ornamental slide formed in the shape of a steer's head. His skin was weathered by constant sun exposure, due to his work in the landscaping business. He carried no bags and donned a San Diego Padres baseball hat.

He was officially the owner and operator of Jimenez Landscaping, a meager 'mow & go' grass cutting operation and tree pruning business located in the Bay Park section of San Diego.

His real occupation was as a *Capo de la Droga* or drug lord for the Barranca Drug Cartel in San Diego. He was responsible for supervision of all activities involving methamphetamines, heroin, cocaine, and any other street drug that had a monetary value. Javier was obligated to appoint territorial leaders, make alliances, and order the occasional execution when an individual interfered with business.

It was the making of alliances that brought him to Puerto Peñasco this day. San Diego was also infiltrated by an Italian, organized crime figure named Vincenzo Fiorito or 'Jimmy Flowers.' He was not from Italy, but was a first generation American, born to Sicilian parents. He was a graduate of Stanford University with a Master's in Business Administration and operated a restaurant in the Little Italy section of San Diego called the Bagheria Bedda. He was rather unique for a gangster, because the profile he kept was beyond low. It was negligible. He had never been arrested, his picture never appeared in the newspaper relating to any crime, and he had been married to the same woman for nearly forty-one years.

Jimmy's 'golden goose' was prescription drugs. He wanted nothing to do with the street drug transactions that Javier Jimenez dominated. Rather, he had developed a sophisticated distribution system and preferred the clientele in the trendy neighborhoods of Rancho Santa Fe, Del Mar, and La Jolla. People in those areas could afford exorbitant prices and high-powered attorneys, if necessary.

Jimmy's drug business and Javier's business never interfered with each other. They each respected the other's business acumen and any problems were always resolved amicably. They considered each other friends.

As Javier walked down the airport hallway, he heard a voice call out. He saw two men awaiting his arrival.

"*Jefe* (Boss)," called one of the men, approximately 5 feet 10 inches tall, thin, wearing a green t-shirt with a denim vest. He wore sunglasses, a thick, black moustache, and four days of beard growth.

The other man was slightly heavyset, also with black hair, clean-shaven, with blue, Dockers pants and a crème color golf shirt. Both men were in their late 30s.

These men were *Lugartenientes*, or Lieutenants, in the Barranca Drug Cartel. The Lieutenant was the second highest position in the cartel organization and they were responsible for supervision of the *Halcons* or Falcons in their territory. The Falcons were the eyes and ears of the street.

Javier's gait did not change as he continued toward them at a normal pace.

"*Hola* (Hello)," Javier said when he was within six feet of them.

The heavier man simply nodded an acknowledgement of Javier's presence and said in a calm voice, "*¡Vamonos!* (Let's go!).

The three men walked out of the airport and into the desert sun of the parking lot. None of them would speak another word until they reached their destination.

CHAPTER 3

Roger Legion entered the Hall of Justice and swiftly made his way through to the escalators. He proceeded to the third floor, home of Department 63 with presiding Judge Daniel Jeckson.

In addition to courtrooms on the third floor, rooms were available for settlement conferences, mediations, or just to allow lawyers and their clients to discuss their case. In the second room that he checked, Legion found Larry Larkin and Nancy Barton. They were both viewing Larry's smartphone and laughing at a video. When Roger Legion entered the room a pall of silence enveloped it. Both Larry and Nancy stared at him as if he was about to say "You're under arrest."

Larry was in his early 30s, 5 feet 10 inches tall, with reddish brown hair, and a face full of fading freckles. Larry had two children, both under the age of five, and was recently divorced. This day, he wore a blue suit, his tie was loosened, and the top button of his shirt was undone.

Larry had been at Legion & Associates for nearly three years. He was a former non-equity partner at the law firm of Kenview Polaris. The firm had nearly one thousand lawyers throughout the country when it imploded. The work did not generate the type of salaries that the firm had come to expect. At the end, it became a Ponzi scheme and was crushed by its own weight.

Larry was known as a premier rainmaker and he was always searching for new leads. He read three newspapers every morning and devoted a portion of each day to hunting down leads and determining what person within an organization either selected or recommended their defense counsel. That person was known as the 'trigger' in the organization and that was the person Larry wanted to know.

Roger realized early on that Larry's talents had value, but he should have been a full-time rainmaker and not a lawyer. He had no 'fire in the belly' or passion for the profession. What he wanted was the big payday, but he didn't want to work to get it.

Nancy Barton was in her early 60s and began her career in insurance after her two children were out of college. She was 5 feet 7 inches tall, slightly heavyset, and very buxom. She wore a tulip-printed hem dress from Lane Bryant with a lilac-colored sweater.

Nancy was divorced and always smiling. She had a passion for horses. In the insurance world, she preferred to stay in the background at a settlement conference and allow the lawyers to talk. When you spoke to her, you learned that her refinement was tempered with a party streak.

Larry and Nancy rose to their feet and Roger spoke the first word.

"Nancy, how are you? It's been too long."

"Roger, this Judge," Larry began a hurried explanation when he was cut off.

"Still riding horses?" Roger asked her in a raised voice to shut down Larry.

"No riding anymore," she answered. "The bones are creaking too much. What about you? Been doin' anything fun?"

"Just working," he replied.

"You going to Del Mar this year?" Nancy inquired.

"Only if you go with me," Roger told her.

Nancy was referring to the Del Mar Racetrack located in the northern section of San Diego County.

"You're kiddin'?" she wondered with shocked jubilation.

"No. I'll get some box seats. You give me some tips and we'll play the ponies."

"You've got a date, Roger. Now, I know you're married, but feel free to invite any of your single friends. Age doesn't matter. I won't hold it against them. As long as they can stand vertical and do the hokey-pokey. You know what I'm sayin'!"

As she uttered the last line, she wagged her finger at Roger. Roger and Larry both looked at her and smiled.

"We'll make it happen. You've got to get back to your office for a conference call. They need you there in less than an hour," Roger told her.

"What are we gonna do about King Pissy in Department 63?" she asked.

"Larry and I will take care of it."

"Okay," Nancy said, picking up her bag. "Oh, what about the authority? Are we gonna pay the extra money?"

"No," Roger answered in a calm tone.

"All right," she said and turned to Larry. "Larry, let me know what happens." She then turned to Roger, "Roger, always a pleasure. Now, don't forget about Del Mar."

"I won't," Legion replied.

Nancy proceeded through the door heading to the down escalator.

Larry immediately wanted to plead his case surrounding the events involving the settlement conference.

"Roger, what I wanted to tell you was," he spoke fast, but was again halted.

"SHUT UP!" Legion snapped. Larry was taken aback by his vociferous tone. "Fix your tie!" he demanded. Roger masked a brewing anger. His visage now displayed it.

As Larry buttoned his top button and adjusted his tie, Roger began his discourse.

"How many times have I told you not to take shit off anybody? The only people who can tell us what to pay is a jury. Anybody else can go to hell. Not a guy, like a judge, who sits in a chair all day and wears a black dress. If he doesn't like it – tough. The insurance company is not a party to the action. Therefore, the Judge has no jurisdiction over them. He can order them to a settlement conference, but he can't hold them hostage for three days. That's bullshit! And the insurance company is gonna think all you wanna do is milk the file and not shut it down. You have to do more than talk about being tough. Actions, not words. Let's go."

Larry started to walk toward Roger to exit the room.

"One other thing:," Roger asserted with his steel-blue eyes locked on Larry's eyes with a laser focus, "As long as you work for me, whenever you step in this building, you make sure your shirt is buttoned and your tie is on properly. You understand?"

"Yes," Larry uttered in a calm, subdued inflection.

"Don't forget it. If I ever see it that way again, I'm gonna rip it off your throat."

Legion walked out of the room like a sport's team manager in total disgust. Larry realized that Roger was more upset about his tie than he was about the events involving the settlement conference.

CHAPTER 4

Javier Jimenez and the two lieutenants spent slightly over ninety minutes heading southeast over desolate, desert roads of the State of Sonora in a black, 2008 GMC Yukon Denali. To the east, the desert landscape appeared endless. To the west, the beauty of Puerto Peñasco was now a faded memory.

Javier sat in the passenger seat and simply admired the natural scenery. The other passengers remained stoic and looking forward to the conclusion of their escort assignment.

After they had traveled approximately forty miles, they turned off onto a desert road that was marked only with a large windsock, which appeared ready to be blown over at any moment. Within a half mile on this road, appeared a guard shack.

The geographic location was approximately five miles northwest of a little town, just a speck of dirt, called Ejido Juan Alvarez.

A guard emerged from the small building, dressed in fatigues, with a wool hat and a scarf over his face. In his hand, he held an AK-47 machine gun. He recognized the driver of the Yukon and waived them passed the guard shack.

The strong winds were causing sand to whirl up, like a thick fog in the morning. The driver knew exactly where he was going. Even in the fog-type sandstorm, the building could not be missed. The perimeter walls were twenty feet high with sniper towers on each corner and in the center of each wall. It looked like a Supermax prison. Powerful spotlights illuminated the exterior. It was not even noon, but the spotlights allowed visibility through the blowing sand.

As their vehicle approached the twenty foot high, solid steel gate, the gate began to move to the right and recede into the perimeter wall. Once it had maneuvered sufficiently to allow the Yukon to enter, the vehicle proceeded to the interior.

The high walls cut the wind draft down considerably. The building appeared to be a cross between a military fortress and the Palace of Versailles. There were fountains, statues, beautifully manicured foliage, and lush, green grass. There were also strategically placed missile and machine gun turrets that were able to pop up out of the ground to handle an insurgent air attack or any aggressor that may make it over the walls.

The beauty of this venue would convince the novice visitor that they had been magically transported to another place and time. The 3-story building sat on 10 acres and contained 65,000 square feet of living space. It included six suites, three kitchens, swimming pool, shooting range, movie theater, hair salon, medical and hospital facilities, bowling alley, gymnasium, tennis court, heliport, and a fast food restaurant, just for the occupants, called Diego's. None of the facilities were exposed to the outside elements. Motion detectors and surveillance cameras covered every inch of the interior and exterior of the property.

The Yukon drove to the side of the building and entered what appeared to be a single-stall, stand-alone garage. After the vehicle entered the small building, the garage door closed behind it. The vehicle entered an elevator and began to descend to the parking garage, located 1-story below the main level.

When the elevator reached the garage level, the Yukon proceeded into the 60-car parking lot. It was complete with two service bays on the western side of the parking facility. The elevators were located at the far end of the garage from where they entered. They drove toward the elevators and passed an eclectic variety of cars, including a Rolls-Royce Phantom Drophead Coupe, a Bentley Continental GT Convertible, a Ferrari F-12 Berlinetta, a Lamborghini Aventador Roadster, and various other high-profile vehicles. All were late models and all rarely driven. The most interesting vehicle was an Icon Thriftmaster. This vehicle looked like a 1947 Chevrolet 3100 pickup truck, but was designed for that look with a 440 horsepower engine and the ability to reach a top speed of 185 miles per hour. It had a price tag of $245 thousand.

The Yukon parked a short distance from the elevator and all three men exited the vehicle and proceeded to it. The thinner man with the moustache pushed the call button and an elevator arrived immediately. They stepped in and one of the men produced a key that was placed into the elevator's call pad and turned. He then pushed the 'LL' button for 'Lower Level.'

The interior of the elevator was spotless and had a flowery smell that was masking an antiseptic odor.

Above the elevator's interior call buttons was a small flat screen monitor, which provided news headlines and the weather in various Mexican cities. Intermittent with this information would be a black screen that had the same words fly out at the viewer while majestic music played. The words were '¡*Bienvenido al Palacio de Barranca!*' (Welcome to the Palace of Barranca!).

This was not Javier's first visit. He was familiar with the ostentatious nature of his boss, Diego Barranca.

CHAPTER 5

Roger Legion moved at a swift clip from the conference room to Department 63 followed by Larry. He held the door open and Larry entered with Roger close behind.

Judge Daniel Jeckson was on the bench and a jury was seated. An opening statement had just commenced in a case where the plaintiff had contracted silicosis, a lung disease caused by long term exposure to silica dust. The defendants were various entities involved with the sand-blasting business or sand-blasting apparatus.

Judge Jeckson was 67 years old, 5 feet 10 inches, and 240 pounds. He had white, thinning hair, white moustache and drooping jowls. He spent most of his thirty-eight years in the legal profession as a defense attorney before switching to plaintiff work.

Larry stood in the center aisle and looked at Roger wondering what he wanted him to do. Larry pointed to several empty seats in the gallery portion of the courtroom. Roger had no concern about whatever was going on in the courtroom. He was focused on the task at hand.

He walked around Larry and as he passed him, he told him in a hushed voice, "Don't sit down."

In every courtroom, there is a wall approximately three feet high that separates the courtroom from the gallery where the public is allowed to view the proceedings. There is one swinging door, known as the courtroom gate that allows ingress and egress to the courtroom.

Roger Legion positioned himself at the courtroom gate and stared at the Judge with his arms crossed. After a moment, the bailiff and the entire jury turned their eyes toward Legion. It was then that he was seen by the Judge. The Judge's face displayed concern.

"Excuse me, Mr. Semblon," the Judge interrupted the plaintiff attorney and turned to the jury. "Ladies and gentlemen of the jury, we're going to take a fifteen minute recess."

As the Judge spoke, Roger entered the courtroom area and walked toward the door that was the entrance to the Judge's chambers. Normally, the bailiff would have stopped anyone proceeding toward the bench to inquire about the nature of their business. Legion did not stop.

"Bobby, how are ya?" Roger inquired to the burly, 230-pound bailiff.

"Good, Mr. Legion," the bailiff responded and they shared a quick handshake while Roger was still in motion.

Legion walked directly to the door, opened it, and walked through, as his gait remained constant. His semblance displayed aggravation and annoyance. He was followed by Larry and Judge Jeckson.

Once the Judge closed the door behind him, he began to speak.

"Roger," the Judge uttered and Legion turned to face him. "Are you going to pay the $3 thousand?"

"What did you say, Dan?" Legion was being intentionally disrespectful.

"Look, we can close this thing for another $3 thousand," the Judge told him. "That's an easy cost of defense decision. It's a no-brainer."

"I'll tell you what's a no-brainer, DAN. Keeping one of my guys prisoner until they come up with cash. Out on the street, that's a crime. And where's the plaintiff's attorney? If it's a settlement conference, he's supposed to be here."

"He gave me authority to settle," the Judge retorted and Legion spoke over him.

"Is that all you have to do for a settlement conference in your department, call it in? Next time, call him when the cops want to arrest you for being drunk in public and pissing on the side of a building."

"Roger, take it easy," the Judge said trying to assuage Roger's tirade.

As he spoke, the Judge's secretary, a slender woman in her mid-40s wearing a red and white striped dress, stood up and spoke.

"Would you like me to call someone?" she asked concerned over what Roger might do.

"Would you like her to call someone, Dan?" Legion inquired.

"No, Kathy, everything's fine," the Judge said putting the palm of his hand out toward her. "Roger, let's go in my office and talk."

Roger and Larry followed Judge Jeckson into his chambers. The room was large with one wall full of California Reporter books that appeared untouched. On one side of the room were windows that looked out onto Broadway. The other two walls were covered with family photographs and moments from the Judge's legal career.

As soon as the door was closed, Roger began to speak. All three men stood facing each other in the center of the room.

"To answer your initial question: we are not paying $3 thousand more. Get asshole to take $3 thousand less!"

"Roger, that plaintiff has some significant injuries."

"Are you deaf or do I stutter, Dan?"

"How am I going to do that?"

"Call that shithead right now and tell him that we are down here on an *ex parte* hearing. You are going to make a ruling from the bench on the indemnity agreement. You tell him that because his side drafted it, and it is so poorly drafted, that it was triggered when the claim was made. Tell him that if he doesn't settle, he owes me $126 thousand in attorney fees."

An *ex parte* hearing is generally a motion called before a judge without the other party present. The other party would have a chance to respond at a later time.

The Judge simply stared at Roger. His argument was cogent.

"You need a battery for your hearing aid or what?" Legion demanded.

"No," the Judge responded with a tone of surrender.

"What time should Larry come back to put it on the record?" Roger asked as his voice remained strident.

"Come back at 1:15," the Judge's voice remained docile.

Legion walked to the door, started to open it, and turned back to the Judge.

"I think your shoes go well with your black dress," Roger shared as a parting shot to further emasculate him. "And I think this secretary is cuter than the one you were tappin' before."

Legion proceeded out the door followed closely by Larry. Larry closed the door as he exited. They departed the courtroom and Roger did not speak again until they were on the escalators.

"Fat bastard looks like a walrus," he uttered.

Larry's head was spinning from the drama that had unfolded. He now understood Roger Legion's value to a client. It was immeasurable. Larry realized that Roger Legion was the standard that every lawyer, who strives to be great, should aspire to be.

CHAPTER 6

Javier Jimenez stepped off the elevator, accompanied by his two escorts, into the lower level of the Palace of Barranca. Immediately upon exiting the elevator, all three entered a room that was 12 feet by 12 feet, completely white, with two men standing facing them, dressed in a uniform of Dickies blue trousers and matching short sleeve shirts. Both men wore holsters with a semi-automatic sidearm and a walkie-talkie. Neither man appeared Mexican, but rather Aryan, with blond hair, blue eyes, tall and slender build, with a defined bone structure.

On the left side of the room was a counter that ran the entire length of the wall. The wall above the counter was filled with twelve video monitors displaying various scenes of the interior and exterior of the Palace. Each man was able to sit at a control station to monitor activity anywhere within the perimeter walls. They were also able to view the desert area outside the walls, including radar capability that allowed for a warning of any incoming aircraft within five miles of the compound.

"*Vacíe los bolsillos, por favor* (Empty your pockets, please)," said one of the uniformed men pointing to the counter. His Spanish definitely indicated that he was not native.

Javier removed his keys, change, and wallet, tossing them onto the counter. The same uniformed man then unlocked a door in the corner of the room at the end of the counter and from one of the keyboards, turned the lights on inside the area on the other side of the door.

"*Pasate para adentro pon los pies en donde se indica en el piso* (Step inside and put your feet where indicated on the floor), the same blond-haired man said. "*Luego ponga las manos sobre la cabeza* (Then raise your hands above your head).

Javier entered the full body scanner and followed directions. The interior millimeter wave scanner circled around him and a 360-degree x-ray image of Javier appeared on one of the monitors. It was quickly reviewed and then the uniformed man spoke into a microphone on the counter.

"*Cierra la boca y los ojos* (Close your mouth and eyes)."

Javier complied and a light mist of hydrogen peroxide sprayed his entire body. The purpose of this was an attempt to kill any germs that might have attached to him.

"*Puedes bajar las manos* (You can put your hands down)," the voice said and Javier once again complied.

A door on the opposite side from where Javier entered now opened and he entered the office of Diego Barranca. The room was 50 feet long and 50 feet wide with the walls and floor made of highly polished marble. On the ceiling was a gaudy fresco of Pancho Villa standing on top of Mexico with his large sombrero, long, black moustache, and two bandoliers filled with bullets, Villa was holding a rifle and saying, "*¡Viva Mexico!* (Long live Mexico!)." The walls were covered with autographed pictures of Mexican celebrities. The walls reminded a visitor of a pizzeria, instead of a drug lord.

Diego Barranca sat behind his desk reading the latest copy of the *Robb Report* magazine. This magazine, for the ultra-affluent, provided Diego with most of his impulse buying ideas.

Diego was 28 years old, 145 pounds, 5 feet 6 inches tall, with acne ravaged skin, and black hair combed back to create a pompadour style. The hair on the side of his head was close cropped. He visited the in-house hair salon weekly and was known for changing the style on a regular basis.

He wore a Ralph Lauren, long sleeve, buttoned, blue striped shirt. His pants were from a company called Kiton in Italy and his shoes were short cowboy boots, custom-made of calfskin in El Paso, Texas by a company called Lucchese.

Diego's desk was at the far end of the room. It was 12 feet long and 6 feet wide. This is where Diego was sitting as Javier entered the room. Diego continued to focus on the magazine until Javier spoke up.

"*Hola, Diego* (Hello, Diego.)," Javier told him.

"*Hola*," Diego answered continuing to look at the magazine. "Give me one second." After a moment, he looked up. "Javier, how are you?"

"*Muy bien* (Very good)," Javier responded.

"If you don't mind, I need to practice my English. More and more, as I speak to money people around the world, it is more important than Spanish. Also, I do not shake hands any longer, it spreads germs."

Diego was a neurotic mysophobiac. He feared germs and had an unhealthy fear of contamination. This was the reason for the hydrogen peroxide spray before entering the room and the constant smell throughout the premises of antiseptic cleaning agents.

"It is not a problem," Javier advised.

"Good," Diego said and leaned back in his chair. "Did you take care of that problem with the gangbangers?"

"It's taken care of," Javier answered.

"My father always said you have to set an example and then others will fall in line." As Diego spoke, Javier glanced over at a cabinet of machine guns, swords, and grenades. "You probably heard that a few months back the government down here authorized militias to take on the cartel violence. A group up in Badiraguato, in Sinaloa thought they were going to disrupt one of our supply lines."

"We found out who the two leaders were. We took those two and their families and we placed all their heads on stakes and put them at the entrance to their town. And guess what? No more trouble from the militia."

"Your father was always wise," Javier recalled. "He knew when to be cautious and he knew when to take action."

"How's your friend, Jimmy Flowers?"

"Good. As far as I know."

"No problems?"

"No."

"Let me ask you. How did you meet that guy?"

Javier leaned forward in his chair.

"Years ago, my family was working in the tuna industry. When things were slow, we would go down to one of the Mexican ports, pick-up some drugs and bring them to San Diego. The Coast Guard started clamping down on the tuna boats. In those days, Jimmy ran everything. He realized that only boats coming up from the south were being targeted as potential drug smugglers. He came up with the idea to take the boats on a long, circular path out into the ocean past L.A., if necessary, and come south. After that, the boats were never bothered."

"Is he still pushing prescription drugs?"

"In addition to a lot of other things. That's my under-standing."

"Javier," as he spoke, he picked up a letter opener that was in the shape of a small sword. In his left hand, he held the handle with his thumb and index finger. He pressed the point of the sword into the index finger of his right hand and rolled it back and forth. "You should know what's going on in your territory."

"I know what's going on in my territory," Javier's voice was deliberate.

"Good," Diego responded. "I like to hear it." He set the letter opener on the desk and placed his arms on the arms of his chair. "I've been presented with an opportunity that would give us access to high quality prescription drugs."

"You want me to flip them quick to Jimmy?"

"No."

"What do you want?" Javier quizzed.

"In the ideal world, I would want him dead. But that may be seen as a bit of an overreaction. No, I think Jimmy needs some protection or maybe even a tax. In exchange for a modest percentage of his drug operation."

"Diego, he operates in a very limited territory and we have never had a situation where our interests conflicted. His whole system is sophisticated and high tech. And we benefit from information he shares with us. I say, let him keep his territory."

"His territory? HIS TERRITORY?" Diego's volume and temper flared and he returned the chair to its upright position. "You forget your history, Javier. All the land in the southwest United States belonged to Mexico and those imperialist dogs took it from us. And we let them. So, now we can cut their grass, clean their houses, and pick their vegetables. All while they spit on us. Jimmy Flowers operates there because we allow it. Now, he's going to pay for the privilege. Tell him I want a meeting. Here. Within the next couple of days."

"I'll talk to him tomorrow."

Diego stood from his chair.

"Good," he responded and paused for a moment. "Let me show you something," Diego told him as he walked around to the front of the desk. He held his left arm out and slightly pulled back his sleeve. "You know what this is?"

"A watch?" Javier guessed at the obvious answer.

"No. It is a Patek Philippe timepiece. It's got a thing in there called a tourbillon. The movement of the watch takes gravity into account. It cost me $395 thousand. What kind of watch you got?"

"Timex," Javier answered.

"You think they're the same – your watch and mine?"

"They both tell time – no?"

"So, is the slave the same as the owner? They're both men. They sleep at night, they eat, they want a woman every once in a while. But if you think they are the same, then your vision is clouded. That, my friend, is dangerous."

Javier ruminated. "My vision is not clouded," he asserted.

"Good. Now, go tell Jimmy Flowers what I want and make him understand. *¿Entendido, esé?* (Understood?)"

"*Si* (Yes)."

Diego's father, Hector, had died one year earlier and Javier feared Diego's rise to power. In San Diego, everyone was making money, but Diego would not leave it alone. Like a spoiled child, he would not rest until he got his way.

CHAPTER 7

Both Roger Legion and Larry Larkin did not utter a word to each other as they sauntered back from the courthouse to the America's Finest City Building. Once they were in the elevator, destined for the 24th floor, Larry decided to break the silence. Both men were stoic, looking forward, watching the floor numbers increase.

"I'm sorry about the tie," Larry told him, attempting to be genuine with his apology.

Roger turned his head to look at him and wanted to be genuine in his response.

"There's a John Wayne movie, called *She Wore a Yellow Ribbon*. In it, John Wayne says, 'Never apologize, it's a sign of weakness.' It's a good movie. You should watch it."

Legion resumed his stoic position. Larry stared at him for a quick moment. He thought Legion was crazy. A madman out of touch with reality.

"Listen, Roger. I've got a lead on some new business."

As he finished his sentence, the elevator doors opened to the 24th floor. They both stepped off, but Roger stopped to hear Larry's pitch.

"It's a healthcare company, called Realizar Health in Orange County. I'm told their billings to outside law firms last year were in the mid six-figures. They want to talk to us."

"Who's their insurance company?" Legion inquired.

"They have a self-insured retention of $100 thousand. They have excess insurance and catastrophic coverage above that."

A self-insured retention means that Realizar Health would be responsible for the first $100 thousand of any claim.

"Who are they sending?" Legion wondered.

"Their risk manager. A guy named Jim Roth. He's the guy who makes decisions on defense counsel. He's out of Irvine."

"How soon are they ready to talk?"

"Whenever you give the word."

"All right," Roger responded. Let's pick a date at the end of the week. Check them for conflicts. See what you can find out about these guys and the guy they're sending. We don't want to waste our time if they're deadbeats. Let me know what you find out before they show up."

"All right," Larry said as he departed from Legion to proceed down the right side or eastern hallway. Roger's office was in the far corner of the western hallway. As he headed toward it, he could see one of the attorneys, John Hamishaw, sticking his head in to see if Roger was in his office.

John Hamishaw was 5 feet 11 inches tall, 175 pounds, in good shape, due to the genes of his parents, not through any exercise regimen. He had brown hair that was always perfectly combed and all of his suits came from Legion's personal tailor. He wore glasses that were semi-rimless with a tortoise shell color. They made him look like an academic. He had been at Legion and Associates for seven years and had four children, all below the age of nine.

John waited for Roger to reach him before he began to speak.

"My *Valiant* case," John uttered with a touch of sarcasm.

"Cy the Guy?" Legion retorted with a smile.

"That's the one. The people from Scripticon want to come in and see us."

"Any problems?" Legion's serious countenance returned.

"They're bent out of shape over a discovery request for forensic testing on their system. I told them I could move for a protective order."

Legion ruminated for a moment.

"No. Don't do that. Let's get them in here and see what the problem is. When do they want to do it?"

"As soon as you can."

"Set it up for this week," Roger instructed.

"Done," John uttered and immediately commenced an about-face back to his office.

Legion slowly sauntered into his office and took in the breathtaking view of the ocean as he had done so many times before. As he gazed at the Pacific Ocean, his cell phone reverberated. He removed it from his inside coat pocket and looked at the Caller ID. The call was from his wife, Valerie.

CHAPTER 8

Rays of light pierced through the closed shutters in Nina's bedroom. She lived on the fifth floor of the Algonquin Apartments located on Sixth Avenue near Laurel Street. The entrance to Balboa Park, home of museums and the San Diego Zoo were within walking distance.

It was nearing six o'clock in the morning and this Tuesday was about to begin. There was a man in bed with her, and she wished, like she had done so often, that she had magical powers like Samantha in *Bewitched*. Powers that would allow her to make him disappear forever and allow her to be fully dressed with a twitch of her nose.

Nina's luck with gentlemen was somewhat non-existent. She was a pleaser and always found a way to please a man, but never found a man willing to please her. She had recently received a wedding proposal from a man who wanted to change her fortune. That man was not lying next to her in the bed.

She hoisted her naked body to a sitting position and the bed sheet glided off her petite frame. She reached for her bathrobe on a nearby chair and donned it while looking forward to a shower.

Her male companion rolled over to look at her and gave her a light tap on her butt cheek.

"Good morning, sunshine," he declared with a slight yawn and a stretch.

Nina looked forward, appearing as if she might throw up. Her China doll complexion was not as bright, but she wore no make-up. Her face wore an expression of melancholy that would overcome any artificial enhancement.

"I can't do this," she said, not turning her head to look at him.

"What?" he asked.

"This," she said waving her hand back and forth toward him like she was swatting a fly.

"It's just friends with benefits," he conveyed. "I see you at work all day long and every time I pass by, I think, I gotta have her."

"You're married. You have kids. I have a fiancé!"

"Oh, yeah? When are you gonna tell the old man, Legion, about the fiancé? Why is it such a big secret?" he queried.

"Because," she brooded and paused for a moment, "what if he won't allow both of us to work there?" Neither one of us want to quit."

"He's a gasbag. He believes his own bullshit, which makes him dangerous. He's a relic that should be put in an old folk's home, so he can retell his stories to a bunch of dementia patients over and over again."

She was sickened by the fact that he had no respect for the man who paid his salary and allowed his children to attend private school.

"We're done," she told him with rigid finality and stood from the bed.

"Nina," he called for her attention. "It's over when I say it's over. I'm a lawyer at Legion and Associates. You're what they call the 'hired help.' I pull the cart and you ride on the cart. I bring in the cash and you're an expense. Hopefully, you've figured out by now that Legion and Associates is an old boy's club and women serve no purpose except to serve lawyers. They are expendable. So, if you want to cause trouble, let's see who loses their job."

Nina walked into her bathroom and slammed the door closed. She was afraid of what Legion might say. Because she was afraid of Legion.

CHAPTER 9

A 2008, white Toyota Highlander pulled up to the curb, less than one block from the Bagheria Bedda Restaurant on India Street in the Little Italy section of San Diego. Javier Jimenez emerged from the vehicle and walked to the sidewalk. He glanced back at his vehicle and saw that one of his bumper stickers was starting to peel off. He tried to re-stick it without success.

The vehicle had two bumper stickers on the rear bumper. One simply said '*El Tri*,' the nickname of the Mexican national football team. This was the sticker that was peeling from the bumper and numerous attempts to re-stick it had failed. The other bumper sticker read 'Soccer Kicks Grass.'

It was 8:05 am and the restaurant did not open until 11:30 am. Javier knocked at the glass door, and shortly thereafter, the locking bolt turned and the door was pulled open to allow Javier to enter.

The man who answered the door weighed approximately 280 pounds, was 28 years old, and built like a pro football player. His head was shaved and he wore thick glasses. His black t-shirt tightly outlined his biceps and chest. His name was Donnino.

"Come on in, Javier. Jimmy's in the back."

"How you doin', Don?" Javier asked him.

"Good," he answered and followed him to the back of the restaurant.

The Bagheria Bedda had aged plank floors. Black and white checkerboard tablecloths covered the circular tables. Scenes from Sicily decorated the walls and a bar ran the entire length of the back of the restaurant.

Behind the bar stood an obese man, in his early 60s, bald, with three days of beard growth. He wore a blue windbreaker that was zipped up.

As Javier and Donnino approached the bar, Donnino reached out to the man behind the bar. The man handed Donnino an electronic metal detecting wand, like those used by TSA officials.

"You got a piece?" he asked Javier.

"Donnino, no," came a voice from the corner of the room near the kitchen entrance.

Jimmy Flowers had given a command. Whenever a command was given, it was followed to the letter. Deviation would never be considered.

Jimmy Flowers was in his early sixties, 6 feet tall, barrel-chested with an imposing frame. He had gray/silver hair and a goatee.

Donnino returned the wand to the man behind the bar. Jimmy greeted Javier with a handshake.

"Javier, my friend," Jimmy's voice was ebullient. "What can I get you to drink?"

"Nothing," Javier responded with a smile. "I come as a messenger at the behest of Diego."

"When does he have time to run anything? I thought all he does is look on the internet, read catalogs, and spend money all day?"

"Jimmy, if you knew some of the things this guy does, it would make you sick to your stomach," Javier cautioned. "He doesn't understand business. That makes him dangerous."

"What does he want?" Jimmy asked in a tone that had a disgusted tinge.

"He wants to talk. He wants you to come to his place."

"What's he want to talk about?"

Javier stumbled to respond. "He wants a piece of your business."

Jimmy smiled and slightly chuckled. "I guess he's a tough guy."

"When he was a teenager, he put so much of that snow up his nose, they called him 'Empty Eyes' because there was no soul in there."

"You got his number? Let's call him now. I'll give him my answer," Jimmy's voice was definitive.

"Jimmy, he'll put a bullet in me," Javier's voice advocated concern.

"Let's call him. We'll make plans. I won't give him an answer."

Javier lifted his cell phone from his breast pocket and selected a number from the directory of the phone. Before he dialed the last number, he looked up at Jimmy.

"After every phone call with him, I gotta get a new phone." He then pressed the last number. Javier held the phone to his head, but Jimmy could still hear the rings. The phone was finally answered.

"*Es Javier. Tres, dos, siete, nueve, ocho.* (It's Javier. Three-two-seven-nine-eight.)"

"*Verificación?* (Verification?)"

Then Javier spoke in German. *"Arbeit wird uns frei machen.* (Work will set us free.)"

"Verifica. Selecciona el idioma. (Verified. Select language.)"

"English," Javier told the voice. Let me talk to Diego. I'm here with Jimmy Flowers."

Javier looked at the phone and pressed the speaker button. He set the phone on the closest circular table between Jimmy and himself.

"Jimmy, are you there?" Diego's voice beamed with enthusiasm.

"Diego, how are you?" Jimmy asked.

"I'm good, Jimmy. How's your family?"

"They're good. Javier tells me you want to talk."

"I do. Can you come and see me?"

"No," Jimmy's answer was definite. "You're the one that wants to talk, you come see me."

"Jimmy, I can't set foot in the United States. Too much trouble."

"I'll guarantee your safety," Jimmy offered. "Here and back."

"I know your word, Jimmy, but, no. I'll send somebody."

"Can't Javier do it?"

"No. I want to send someone from over here. Javier will work out the details with you," Diego's voice became dismissive.

"Diego, let's get a few things straight. If your man has a weapon on him, he's not coming back. If he has a phone, we're gonna keep it. If we see any guys who are – sketchy – around, he's not coming back. Don't be pissed off about it, because you would do the same thing if I sent a guy down there. *Comprende?* (Understand?)"

"*Ho capito.* (I understand.)" Diego answered him in Italian. "Stay healthy, my friend." Those were Diego's last words before ending the call.

Jimmy Flowers had seen this threat on the horizon for some time. Diego only understood violence. Jimmy also understood violence, but he also knew that all any cartel really cared about was cash flow.

CHAPTER 10

Roger Legion continued his gaze out onto the ocean as he answered his cell phone.

"Hi, Val-e," Roger answered in an ebullient tone, one not generally associated with him.

"Roger, I just got off the phone with Peter and I had to call you," her eager and brisk tempo telegraphed to him that it was some kind of good news.

Roger and Valerie Legion had been married for forty-one years. They met at the University of California in San Diego when Roger mistakenly went to a French literature class that she was attending and she gave him directions to the class that he should have been attending. He continued to attend her class until she noticed him, and they were a couple ever since.

Valerie was a chemistry major and received a Bachelor of Science degree in Chemistry with a 4.0 grade point average. On a lark, she took the Medical College Admission Test and applied to only one medical school, Harvard University. She was accepted, but wanted to help Roger achieve his dream of becoming a lawyer. She worked at a pharmacy while he was in the Marines and at California Western School of Law.

On the day Roger graduated from law school, he had a job lined up with the San Diego City Attorney's Office. The day before he started that job was the last day his wife ever worked outside of the home again.

Valerie was 5 feet 2 inches tall, 105 pounds, only two pounds more than the day they were married. She was a devout Catholic and loved to be with dogs. The Legions had two dogs. A West Highland Terrier named Daisy and a Bichon Frise named Susie. Valerie volunteered several days a week at a "no kill" state-of-the-art animal shelter in Carlsbad. The largest single philanthropic contributor to that animal shelter was the Valerie and Roger Legion Foundation.

Valerie and Roger had three children: two girls and a boy. The oldest girl, Deborah, was a licensed attorney and her sister, Sarah, was a licensed pharmacist. Both girls were stay-at-home moms and each had two small children.

The Legion's son was named Peter, after the great apostle from the Bible. Peter was a vascular surgeon at Johns Hopkins Hospital in Baltimore. He was married with a toddler and a newborn.

"Peter wants to have the baby baptized at St. Elizabeth Seton."

St. Elizabeth Seton Catholic Church was located in Carlsbad, California and was the church that Roger and Valerie attended.

"That's great news. I really wasn't looking forward to a trip to Baltimore," Roger confessed. "How soon?"

"As soon as I can get a date from the church. Can we treat them with plane tickets?" The enthusiasm of her voice did not waiver.

"Sure."

"Should I try to do it online?"

"No," Roger replied in a pensive tone. "Call that girl we used before in the village. The Rancho Santa Fe village. What was her name?" A moment passed. "Rebecca."

"First class?" Valerie wondered.

"Absolutely. And tell her to make the flights as direct as possible."

"Roger, they're gonna need four seats. They gotta bring their dog."

"Val-e, you know me, buy the first class seat for the dog first."

"Okay. That's wonderful. Do you think we can have an afternoon party?"

"Sure," Roger's answer was mild and low-key.

"Who should we invite?"

"Invite your friends from church."

"Okay, I'll start a list. We can go over it when you come home. You think the girls and their families can come over and stay while Peter's here?"

"I don't care as long as it doesn't end up with raised voices and people wanting to kill each other. I don't do well in that environment," Legion's voice tinged with sarcasm.

The Legion's lived in a 12,000 square foot house in Rancho Santa Fe, the most affluent community in San Diego County. The house was situated on four acres and had six bedroom suites, a swimming pool, tennis court, and a playground. There was also a guest house that was used by a Mexican family. The wife, Lupe, cleaned the Legion's home and the husband took care of the grounds.

"It will be so exciting to have all our babies back together under the same roof. You and I will take the grandbabies and the kids can do whatever they want," Valerie gushed.

"You're the Mama-bird. It's your show." Roger enjoyed her excitement. "Tell Lupe, we're gonna need her for some overtime."

"Okay, honey, I'll see you later. Sorry I took up so much of your time."

"You can call me anytime, hun bun." She knew Roger had a smile on his face.

"Okay, bye Rodge," she told him and ended the call.

Roger walked back to the doorway and glanced down the western hallway and then the northern hallway. He realized it was time to transform back from happy family man, Dr. Jekyll, into successful lawyer, Mr. Hyde.

CHAPTER 11

The City of Oceanside is a coastal city located just south of the Marine Corps Base Camp Pendleton. It is the third largest city in San Diego County. It has a six-mile long stretch of beach and it has a reputation for affordable housing, with a great influx of military personnel from the Base.

In some instances, with affordability brings undesirables.

Arthur Clexx and Lisa Natasi lived in a second floor studio apartment on Ditmar Street, just seven blocks from the ocean. It was small and cramped, a pastiche of modern below-the-poverty-line living. They had a Murphy bed and Artie, as Lisa called him, always left it opened. Nothing hung on the walls and anything else in the apartment was either a gift, from a Goodwill Store, or stolen: the result of a 'five-finger' discount.

Artie Clexx was 46 years old, 5 feet 10 inches tall, 160 pounds, with a six-inch scar that ran from his left eye down to his chin. His face was pocked from severe childhood acne and he enjoyed sharing cigarettes with Lisa. His hair was white and thinning, but his moustache still retained a semblance of blond. At one point, Artie had a five hundred dollar a day drug habit. He had been out of prison for a little over a year after serving eight years for armed robbery and second degree murder in the High Desert State Prison in Susanville, California.

Lisa Natasi was 47 years old, 5 feet 3 inches tall, barely 100 pounds. She was definitely too thin for her frame. She had brown hair, with occasional gray roots and she wore her hair in a beehive style, where she took her long hair and piled it into a conical shape, pointing slightly backwards. She once had the beauty of a goddess: breathtaking and alluring. She was talented with make-up and gave off a youthful, party-girl appearance. When her marriage began to crumble four years earlier, she turned to methamphetamines to ease the pain. Drugs began to deconstruct her and the damage became irreversible. Her 5-year-old only child, Christopher, was taken away and she devoted every waking moment of her life to finding a way to get him back.

Artie and Lisa met at a Narcotics Anonymous meeting. Both were required to go as part of a court-ordered sentence. They both believed it was a waste of time, but it allowed them to be together and enable each other. They combined forces more out of necessity than infatuation. Neither could afford to pay rent of $450 a month.

At 3:50 pm, Artie had just finished the last beer from the refrigerator and the television was blaring. He lay down on the bed and let out a mighty yawn, just as he heard the key turning in the apartment door's lock. The door opened and Lisa stepped in, wearing a red and black shirt from a drugstore called Prescription Script, and glared at him.

"I thought you were workin' today?" she uttered as if on the verge of collapse. She looked harried and tired.

"I'm waiting for Tizoe to get back from Yuma," he responded while still watching the television.

"Why does he have to bring the stuff to Yuma?" she asked while closing the door and setting down her purse.

"Because the cops got eyes on the pipe recycling places around here. The guy in Yuma doesn't ask any questions."

"So, I guess that means you're not gonna get paid until Tizoe gets back from Yuma?"

"Yeah, but he should be back either late today or tomorrow."

"Did you go see your parole officer?" Lisa now stood with her arms crossed.

"Yeah, stupid bastard asks how it's coming lookin' for work? Who the hell would hire an ex-con? I wouldn't. Then he wants to tell me about a job on a farm, were I could bale hay and shovel shit. I only have to drive sixty miles to get there," Artie retorted with annoyance.

"Just tell him what he wants to hear," Lisa advised.

"I did. How was your day?"

"Sucked. You know, down at the drugstore, I'm the one in charge of make-up. This woman comes up to my counter with her toilet paper, those wipes with the alcohol on 'em, some shit for hemorrhoids and wants to pay for 'em at my register. Hey, my counter's for make-up, not for your asshole shit. That place used to be a good place to work, but no more. I'm counting the days until I can tell'em to shove it." Her rant ran out of steam. "What are ya watching?"

"It's a *Cops* marathon. This is the third one. There's five more to go," Artie declared as he continued to gaze at the television.

As they spoke, the station had a news break at the top of every hour. The following short new story caught Artie's attention:

Caltrans announced today that they had completed their retrofit project on the Coronado Bay Bridge and all damage caused by a terrorist attack that occurred 18 months ago has been corrected. The terrorist, Remy Kalm, was believed killed in the incident, but his body has never been recovered. The attempt to blow up the bridge was foiled by a local attorney, Roger Legion.

"Speak of the devil," Artie declared with a deliberate, articulate, and pensive tone. He turned to Lisa. "He's the son-of-a-bitch," referring to Legion, "that robbed me of my lottery payday. That's what else I did today. Collected more recon on that big score I'm gonna take down. We're gonna do it together, right?"

Lisa shrugged her shoulders and started biting on one of her thumbnails.

"Is it big money?" she wondered. "We gonna get my son back?"

"Baby, with this score, no more boostin' copper pipe. We're one and done. Then we'll go get your son." He then stopped and stared at Lisa. "Are you A-boot?" Artie inquired. "Your high beams are on."

The term 'A-boot' is slang for being under the influence of drugs. The term 'high beams' indicated that her eyes were open wide, generally associated with taking crack.

"No!" She was indignant in her response. "Unlike you, I have a real job."

"Ya holdin'? That spike is really callin' my name."

Artie wondered if she was in possession of any drugs and he would like to use a hypodermic needle to inject them intravenously.

"Nothin'," she answered. "I got some tex-mex."

Lisa indicated that she had some marijuana.

"That stuff you have is all seeds. Oh, man, now I gotta go on a tweak mission."

A tweak mission was a search to find crack.

"Wait a minute," Lisa declared. She entered the bathroom and quickly returned. "Ta-Da!" She held up an eighty milligram tablet of OxyContin.

"All right," Artie announced with a victory smile. "Get the mortar and pestle, our favorite spoon, and the hype-stick."

These were the tools a junkie would use to create a liquid form of the drug. The hype-stick was a hypodermic needle.

"Are you nuts?" Lisa shockingly told him. "I've gotta work. I can't have track marks."

"All right," he replied in disgust. "Let's split it. I'll shoot mine. You can wash yours down with some Jack."

The Jack he was referring to was Jack Daniels whiskey.

Artie began his industrious effort for an intravenous hit of OxyContin and Lisa began to imagine how she would spend the booty from Artie's score.

CHAPTER 12

As a Gulfstream G150 aircraft slowly taxied to a stop at the private terminal of the McClellan-Palomar Airport in Carlsbad, California, Donnino and Anthony Rotto stepped out of a 2010 white Escalade, waiting for the plane's lone passenger. Anthony was 38 years old, 210 pounds, bald with brown hair. He wore a black t-shirt with a sport coat and blue jeans.

When the airplane stopped, the hatch door opened and a stairway was wheeled out to the plane. As soon as the stairway was in place, Donnino and Anthony boarded the plane.

Inside sat a young man, 28 years old, 160 pounds, clean-shaven, with black hair. He wore a black suit, white shirt, with a red tie.

"*¿Hablas Inglés?* (Do you speak English?)" Donnino asked.

"Yes," the man answered.

"Stand up," Donnino requested as Anthony just looked on with a rather menacing visage. The man stood and faced Donnino. "Put your arms out to your sides."

The man complied and Donnino stretched out his arm to Anthony and snapped his fingers. From behind his back, Anthony produced a metal-detecting wand, the same one that was used by

Donnino at the Bagheria Bedda. Donnino passed the wand over the front, sides, and back of the man. He then patted him down.

"Let's go," he told him and the man exited the plane with Donnino and Anthony close behind.

Donnino drove and the man sat in the passenger seat with Anthony seated behind him. Not a word was spoken as all three men looked straight ahead. They drove westbound on Palomar Airport Road and turned northbound onto Interstate 5.

After a minute, the man asked, "Are we going to Oceanside?"

"Maybe," Anthony told him.

From Interstate 5, they took Highway 78 east and exited at Rancho Santa Fe Drive, approximately sixteen miles from their starting point. They headed north to South Santa Fe Avenue and pulled into the parking lot of what appeared to be a small, desolated strip shopping center. It contained no more than five stores and three of them were vacant. Of the remaining two, one was a Vietnamese grocery store and the other was a smog testing shop. The smog testing shop was their destination.

In California, all cars over five years old are required to have a biennial smog check to make sure that the vehicle is not emitting excess pollutants. Smog shops are licensed by the State of California and generally, only provide this service.

The Escalade pulled around to the back of the building and parked against the structure near the only open overhead door.

"Let's go," Donnino announced and all three men exited the vehicle.

They walked inside the shop where the floor and walls were an aged battleship gray color. When you entered the bay, there was a large fan that could blow any smog or odors out of the building. There was also a dynamometer, a revolving device built into the floor that would allow the service technicians to accelerate the revolutions per minute of the engine without the vehicle moving. A computer monitor on a wheeled platform allowed transmission of results directly to the Department of Motor Vehicles' headquarters in Sacramento, California.

There was an area in the garage with seats for customers to sit in while the testing was being performed on their vehicles. Also, there was a counter used by patrons to fill out paperwork. It all appeared dusty. There was a Buddha statue on the counter and sticks of unlit incense sat in front of the statue.

The front area of the shop, near the road, was a glass wall with a glass door and there was only one other door in the garage bay. As the three men entered, Jimmy Flowers emerged through that doorway.

"He speaks English," Donnino advised Jimmy.

"What's your name?" Jimmy inquired.

"Jose."

"Let's go talk, Jose," Jimmy informed him and pointed to the door through which Jimmy just entered. Jose led the way, followed by the three men.

They entered a small room that was as dusty as the garage with furniture dating back to the 1950s. There was a circular table and five chairs that surrounded it. There were posters on the wall with Vietnamese words on them. The proprietor of the shop, a man named Ro, walked out of the office. He was 45 years old, 5 feet 5 inches tall, weighed 135 pounds, with black hair and dressed in green coveralls.

"Jimmy," Ro said in broken English, "I'm going to pick up some parts. Just pull the overhead door down when you're done."

"Thanks, Ro," Jimmy told him and complimented it with a handshake.

"Anytime, Jimmy," Ro stated as he swiftly moved through the room and out the door to the garage.

"Have a seat, Jose," Jimmy told Jose and he immediately sat down. Jimmy, Donnino, and Anthony remained standing.

"Who sent you?" Jimmy asked with a forceful tone.

"Diego Barranca."

Jimmy walked over to another table that was against the wall and picked up a green telephone and a speaker box that was attached to it. He set the items in front of Jose.

"Get him on the phone," Jimmy demanded. "It's a secure line."

Jimmy pushed a button on the speaker box and a dial tone could be heard. Jose pushed the necessary buttons and waited for an answer.

"*Es Jose. Cuatro, ocho, dos, nueve, siete.* (It's Jose. Four-eight-two-nine-seven.)"

"*Verificación?* (Verification?)"

Then Jose spoke in German. "*Mehr sein als scheinen.* (Be more than you appear to be.)"

"*Verifica. Selecciona el idioma.* (Verified. Select language.)"

"English," Jose told the voice. "Get Diego."

A moment passed. Then Diego's voice filled the air.

"Jimmy," Diego's voice was effusive, "I'm glad Jose made it. How's the weather there?"

"What do you want, Diego?" Jimmy asked as more of a demand than a question.

"Jimmy, I've been concerned about you. You know we've had some problems lately with these gangbanger animals and biker gangs. They want a piece of everybody's business, including yours. I'd like to offer you some protection."

"Aren't those guys out in places like Lakeside and El Cajon?"

"It's only a matter of time before they come knocking on your door."

"What would it cost me for this protection?"

"Thirty percent of your operation. That's a bargain." Diego's voice would not hide his attempt to mask his slyness.

"Diego, here's my answer: No. I'm not afraid of them or you."

"Jimmy, this is a young man's game. You should think about enjoying your family, while you still have a family to enjoy."

"Now, you gonna threaten me and my family? I would have more respect for you if you told me you were gonna tax me. You forget that when your father was targeted by the DEA and the FBI, I was the guy who made the witnesses disappear, I got the indictments dropped."

"Good for you. That was then, this is now. If it makes you feel better, call it a tax. But I want thirty percent. You either give it to me, or I'll come and take it."

"Diego, I don't trust you. You're a junkie and I don't do business with junkies."

"That's all you do business with, old man. Poison is poison. I don't deceive myself."

"Here's a bit of business advice: run your idea by the Gringo, so he can tell you 'no'."

"He doesn't tell me how to run my empire," Diego's voice continued to raise as the conversation progressed.

"Are you deaf and dim-witted?" Jimmy demanded a response. "The Gringo is your money man. The way I hear - all you do is waste money, you're nothing but a little bitch."

"FU. . ." Diego started to scream an expletive and Jimmy disconnected the call. He then turned to Jose.

"It was nice to meet you, Jose. Time to go," Jimmy advised and pointed to the door out to the garage.

Jose sauntered out to the garage followed by Donnino, Anthony, and Jimmy. They all walked directly to the overhead door and Jose was approximately six feet ahead of Donnino.

As soon as Jose took a second step out of the garage, like a clap of thunder, the sound of a rifle was heard and Jose was dropped by a bullet that went right through his skull. His body slammed to the ground in front of the Escalade.

Donnino and Anthony both pulled out semi-automatic handguns and Donnino turned back to Jimmy.

"Go back in the office!" Donnino commanded and Anthony proceeded to see if they could get a visual on the shooter.

Jimmy entered the office and the telephone that was just used to speak with Diego was ringing. Jimmy picked up the receiver.

"I thought you were going to guarantee my safety?" Diego spoke in an eerily calm manner. "Maybe you and your family are not protected as good as you think?"

"I don't fear someone who has the diminished capacity of a 5-year-old child."

"Stay healthy, Jimmy," Diego cautioned and the phone call was disconnected. Jimmy walked back out into the garage.

"Donnino," Jimmy signaled him to come closer. "Call Javier and tell him what happened. Then call Savie at the harbor. See if he's got any boats up here in Oceanside. Otherwise, we'll bring this package down there.

Savie was an old friend of Jimmy's, who engaged in some fishing and cargo delivery. He also specialized in body disposal.

Jimmy then turned to Anthony.

"Anthony, tell the head guys to keep their eyes open. Diego wants to play rough. Let's play rough."

CHAPTER 13

For some reason, Thursday at Legion & Associates was always busy. Most of the attorneys were out of the office, but the telephones continued to ring with disproportionate constancy. Nina, the receptionist, was a professional at the task and she handled it like a four-star virtuoso. The occasional visitor was a welcomed relief.

When the doors of the elevator opened on the 24th floor, Nina was focused on transferring a call to the Accounting Department on the 23rd floor. She did a double take as if the man in front of her had appeared out of thin air. His apparel included a tailored Brooks Brothers suit and a wide smile.

"May I help you?" Nina inquired.

"I'm here to see Larry Larkin. I have an appointment," he answered in a congenial voice.

"Can I get your name?"

"Jim Roth from Realizar Healthcare."

Nina pushed a button on her telephone panel and waited for a response.

"Mr. Larkin," Nina said, "Jim Roth from Realizar Healthcare is here to see you." Then, after a moment, she again spoke into the phone, "I will."

"You can go right into this conference room," Nina advised, pointing in its direction. "Mr. Larkin is on his way."

Jim Roth was 54 years old, 5 feet 9 inches tall, with a slender build, and black hair. His clothing and grooming defined affluence, but he appeared approachable and you knew that you could be friends with this guy. Even though he had the look of a collegiate intellectual, he had the smile of a car salesman.

Larry Larkin moved expeditiously out of his office, but instantly returned and removed his suit coat from a hanger on the back of his door. He again speedily moved toward Roger Legion's office.

Roger was in his office reviewing complaints from new files that were received at the law firm that day. Roger assigned all the files in the office to the attorney he felt was best equipped to handle that particular file, including himself. He also handled the initial answer to all of the complaints. Larry's knock interrupted his focus.

"The guy from Realizar Healthcare is here," Larry advised.

"Com'on in," Roger told Larry and motioned for him to come closer.

Larry walked in holding his suit coat and stood in front of Roger's desk.

"Yeah?" Larry wondered what Roger wanted.

"What did you find out about these guys and this guy in particular?"

"Their website is pretty vanilla. They primarily focus on women's healthcare issues. It looks like they run Urgent Care operations. This guy, his name is Jim Roth. He's a lawyer, but not admitted to the California Bar. I couldn't find anything else out on the guy."

Roger rose from his chair and locked eyes with Larry.

"Put your suit coat on," Roger demanded and Larry complied immediately. His voice still echoed his disgust over Larry's loose tie earlier in the week. "Let's go."

Roger followed Larry out of his office and down the hallway. Larry believed this was going to be his golden opportunity to make rain.

CHAPTER 14

Diego Barranca sat in the underground office of his Palace and perused the photos of the latest copy of _Playboy_ magazine. He looked up for a moment and thought it was too quiet. He pushed a button on his telephone keypad.

"_¡Sí, Señor,_" a voice answered.

"In English!" Diego demanded.

"Yes, Sir."

"Play some music," Diego requested. "I'm in the mood for some _Banda el Recodo._"

Banda el Recodo was a renowned band throughout Mexico, famous for playing Banda music. This type of music was an imitation of military bands and sounds similar to polka music. It was believed that military leaders during the Mexican Revolution, like Pancho Villa, played this type of music after a victory to promote their power. This type of music is particularly popular in Northern Mexico, especially the state of Sinaloa.

As the music filled the air, so did the sound of the phone on Diego's desk. Only internal phones were allowed access to call in to him. Otherwise, outside calls to him required a complicated verification system that changed daily. The Caller ID indicated that the call was coming from his *centinelas* or sentries. These were his guards that were allowed closest access to him.

"Yes," he answered.

"Serge Stiroy is here to see you," replied the non-accented voice.

"Send him in. He does not need to be fumigated," Diego advised.

Part of the wall on the left side of Diego's office rolled back and he could see the glass of the full body scanner. The glass door of the scanner opened and out stepped a gentleman followed by one of Diego's Aryan-looking security men, dressed in a blue uniform with a holstered semi-automatic weapon.

Serge Stiroy was in his mid-50s, 230 pounds, with broad shoulders, and curly, thinning salt and pepper hair. He wore aviator-style glasses, a yellow, golf shirt, and khaki slacks, with a New York Mets baseball hat. He also carried a briefcase.

Serge was a finance analyst and currency evaluator for the Barranca Drug Cartel. He specialized in piping money to offshore accounts through different countries and laundering it back for corporate use in the United States.

As soon as Serge entered the room, the security man began to speak.

"Mr. Barranca, this man has a weapon in his briefcase. It appears to be a handgun."

Diego shot Serge a quick glance.

"You don't plan on shooting me today, do you Serge?"

"Not today," Serge answered nonchalantly and shook his head.

"It's all right," Diego told the guard and the guard returned to the outer evaluation area.

Serge plopped himself down in one of the chairs in front of Diego's desk. He was relieved to be off his feet.

"What can I get you to drink?" Diego asked and leaned back in his chair.

"Diet Coke," Serge answered and then sneezed. The thought of germs filling the air sent a chill down Diego's spine. He pushed a button on his telephone.

"¡*Coca de Dieta, ahora!* (Diet Coke, now!)" Diego barked into the phone.

"My allergies are actin' up. I don't know why they would bother me in the desert?" Serge wondered and blew his nose into a handkerchief.

"You should not have a problem here. The Palace is climate-controlled. Always the same temperature, the air is filtered, and constantly cleaned."

Serge acknowledged his comment.

"Where did you find Hans and Fritz out there?" Serge inquired referring to the Aryan-looking security guards.

"First impressions are very important. When someone comes to the Palace, I don't want them to think they are in the parking lot of a Home Depot. I want them to think they are entering a place of power, discipline, and strength."

Then there was a knock at a door to the right of Diego. He placed his thumb on a biometric pad on his desk and the door lock clicked. An older, Mexican gentlemen entered, dressed in a butler's tuxedo with white gloves carrying a silver tray with a can of Diet Coke and a glass of ice. Diego looked at the butler and pointed to Serge. The butler walked over to him.

"May I pour it for you, sir?" he asked.

"Please," Serge responded.

The butler poured the soda into the glass and left the glass and the can on a small table that was situated between the two chairs in front of Diego's desk. The butler hastened his retreat and Serge took a large sip of his refreshment.

"How's our mutual friend?" Diego queried.

"The Gringo sends his regards. So, what's going on that requires you and I to have an audience?"

"Jimmy Flowers," Diego uttered his name in disgust.

"What about him?" Serge speculated.

"He disrespected me. I want him dead."

"How did he disrespect you?" Serge was interested in the answer.

"He called me a junkie."

Serge stared at him for a moment.

"Now, Diego, I don't mean any disrespect, but it was my understanding that you have had substance abuse problems in the past?"

"Forget the past. I want that old bastard dead! And you tell the Gringo the way he understands. You and him are the same: Jew, right? You get rid of Jimmy Flowers, we take over his business. Our income stream will increase 30 to 40 percent. I know he understands that."

Serge was perturbed at Diego's anti-Semitic remark.

"The Gringo's got alotta history with Jimmy Flowers. He's helped us out on more than one occasion."

"Remind the Gringo who keeps the supply lines open in Sinaloa, Durango and Chihuahua. The Golden Triangle. I'm the guy who keeps the money coming in by the truckload. He should think about keeping me happy."

"Look at your Palace," Serge reminded him. "I know of no other drug lord who lives in a place like this. I don't know many people who run a country and live in a place like this." Diego and Serge stared at each other for a moment. "I'll tell him what you want and I'll let you know what he says."

Serge knew what the Gringo was going to say, but he did not want to be in the same room as Diego, when Diego heard it.

CHAPTER 15

Larry Larkin entered the large conference room followed closely by Roger Legion. Jim Roth's eyes were transfixed on the Pacific Ocean and its image of endless water.

"Jim, good to see you," Larry told him, breaking his gaze. They met for a handshake and a wide grin.

"Larry, how are you doing?" Jim asked.

"I'm fine. This is Roger Legion," Larry conveyed.

"The famous Roger Legion," Jim declared and they met each other with a strong handshake.

"I don't know about famous," Roger answered with a smile. "It's nice to meet you, Jim."

"Let's sit down," Larry suggested. "Do you want anything to drink?"

"No, thank you. The young lady already offered me a beverage."

"Let's have a seat," Larry proposed.

Legion sat at the head of the table, near the door that they entered. Jim Roth sat on the window side of the table and Larry sat across from him.

"The view here is incredible. I could stare at it all day," Jim asserted, then changed the subject. "You guys keeping busy?"

"All the time," Roger answered, again displaying a smile.

"Well, maybe I can keep you a little busier," Jim told them. "Realizar Healthcare is a chain of 18 healthcare units located throughout Southern and Central California. We are primarily focused on women's healthcare issues."

"Can you share with us the type of lawsuits that you generally deal with?" Larry inquired.

"Sure. We have everything from basic general liability matters, like a slip and fall inside the building or in the parking lot, to our liability as it relates to medical malpractice."

"Are the healthcare professionals, employees or independent contractors?" Roger wondered.

"They're all employees, so we're on the hook for any malpractice."

"What's the volume of claims that you see in a typical year?" Larry relished the answer.

"I don't know if there is such a thing as a typical year, but my strategy is to get attorneys involved almost immediately, so there's no down time if a lawsuit comes through the door. I don't have the exact number, but I can tell you that we paid out in excess of $650 thousand in legal fees and costs in the last calendar year."

Larry's smile mimicked a Cheshire cat.

"How do you handle settlement authority?" Larry's questions came quickly.

"To be honest, our goal here is not so much to save money as to develop a uniform strategy throughout the company as to the manner in which claims are handled. I believe that if there is one nexus from which decisions are made, then we will achieve that objective. I believe we can start by giving Mr. Legion $100 thousand worth of authority for each claim and then we can see if you need more. Anything above that, you get it from me with a phone call."

Larry just nodded as Jim spoke, awaiting his chance to handle the next question.

"How do you handle billing? Our billing." Larry continued his direct examination.

"Once again, our goal is to streamline the process. My suggestion, and I have received authority to proceed with this, is to issue you a check for $1 million to handle your legal fees and any costs associated with the claims. At the end of the year, if there is any money left over, your firm will get to keep it as a bonus. If the billings or costs exceed $1 million, you simply bill us as you would any other client."

Larry looked at Jim and smiled, then looked at Roger.

"What do ya think?"

Roger was introspective as he gazed at Jim like he was searching for the right question at a deposition. Then he found it.

"Let me ask you something, Jim. Would you define for me the term, 'women's healthcare issues'?"

"Sure. Realizar Healthcare provides niche services which are primarily focused on female reproduction."

"So, would you call them 'abortion clinics'?" Roger's delivery stilled the air in the room.

"Roger, 'abortion clinics' is one of those annoying buzzwords that politicians like to bandy about, like 'Pro-choice' and 'Pro-life.' I hope that it doesn't impact your decision."

"In all honesty, it does," Roger said as he leaned toward Jim.

"Wait a minute, Roger." Larry moved into his version of rescue mode and wanted to once again point out the highlights of

Jim's program. Roger raised his hand in the direction of Larry's face and shut him down.

"Jim, I appreciate that you came in here and pitched us your business. Usually, it's the other way around. But, I don't want to get involved with what you're selling. It is too much of a hot button issue and when it goes to trial, I end up becoming the face of it. I don't want that type of publicity, nor do I want a target on my back. With what you're offering, you can get anybody to take this work."

"But, we want you, Mr. Legion," Jim was succinct.

"A million dollars is tempting, but," Roger acknowledged and Jim spoke up.

"What about $2 million?"

Roger stared at him in a dismissive fashion and stood from his seat.

"We're done here," Roger announced. "If you need your parking validated, Nina will take care of it for you. It was nice to meet you, Jim."

Jim stood from his seat. He was trying to analyze Roger Legion. Jim's serious visage suddenly regained its wide smile.

"If you change your mind, call me," Jim graciously conveyed.

"I'll call ya, Jim," Larry added and both he and Roger watched Jim Roth exit the room and go directly to the elevator doors.

He pushed the call button and an elevator arrived almost immediately. As Jim was about to enter, he turned back and looked at Roger Legion's outline through the fancy alabaster glass.

CHAPTER 16

Larry Larkin stayed seated as Roger Legion stood and watched Jim Roth exit the room.

"Do you know how hard it is to get a guy like that, the trigger man in an organization, the guy who can make a decision on defense counsel right now, the guy who can change your destiny and that of this whole law firm, in a room to talk business?" Larry asked. As he spoke, his cadence sped up and his volume, along with his anger, continued to increase.

"Think about it, Larry. What that guy was offering was a sweetheart deal that's too good to be true." Legion plunged his right index finger into the table. "Have you ever heard of a legal billing system that has no oversight? Every client we deal with is looking for ways to cut their legal bills. These guys are just gonna let us go wild? It doesn't make sense."

"Roger," Larry said as he rose to his feet to stare Legion directly in the eye, "we deal with insurance companies that are tighter than a duck's ass. The reason for our existence is because plaintiffs are so greedy and insurance companies are so cheap. Realizar is self-insured. Maybe they're on a learning curve or maybe they've been burned in the past. I don't know and I don't give a shit. I say let's take the deal while it's out there. Because we are gonna be kicking ourselves in the ass when we find out who gets this sweet plum."

"Larry, take my word for it, there is something dirty about it. The cases aren't just hot, they're nuclear."

"Bullshit! And so what, anyway? When did you ever back down from a fight?" The veins on the side of Larry's head were throbbing and Roger remained remarkably cool.

"Larry you are the type of guy who is always focused on what is right in front of him. You never look past it. You never look at the horizon. The horizon determines whether you're gonna land safely or crash."

Larry responded instantaneously without giving any thought to Roger's comment.

"You're afraid," Larry was going to try a Roger Legion mind trick on him. "Is that it? Or, is it because it deals with abortions? Do you suddenly have scruples? All the bullshit you spew around here about slaying an adversary, but now it depends on who you're defending? I did this for this firm, for you, and for me. But if YOU AREN'T MICRO-MANAGING EVERY LITTLE BULLSHIT THING AROUND HERE, YOU WANT NO PART OF IT!"

As Larry uttered his last sentence Roger's temper flared and they both started to top the volume of the other.

"WHY DON'T YOU GO OUT AND START YOUR OWN LAW FIRM AND YOU CAN HANDLE THIS GUY'S CASES!"

Both men just locked eyes for a moment in a deadly stare.

"Because for some reason," Larry said with measured, angry, articulation, "they want a narcissistic, egotistical sociopath, who would kill a guy because his shirt collar is unbuttoned."

Legion thought for a moment about what Larry had said.

"If you had ever displayed that degree of passion in the courtroom, this guy would have been here today begging *you* to take his work."

Legion turned and exited the room. Larry sat down again in his chair, staring forward thinking about what Legion said and if there was any way to salvage a deal with Realizar Healthcare.

CHAPTER 17

ST. ALBANS, VERMONT

The City of Saint Albans, Vermont is the county seat of Franklin County. Located in the northeastern corner of the state, it is the home to approximately seven thousand people and is situated on 15.5 square miles of land. The northernmost engagement of the Civil War, the St. Albans Raid, took place there on October 19, 1864. It is the home of the annual Vermont Maple Festival and is known as the 'Maple Syrup Capital of the World.'

It is a non-descript place whose urban landscape fits perfectly into a Norman Rockwell painting. Its bucolic setting and quiet lifestyle provides an idyllic home for anonymity.

It was just before noon. Hershel Gordon sat in a booth across from Serge Stiroy in the Green Mountain Café on South Main Street perusing the menu for the lunch choice of the day.

Hershel was 59 years old, balding, heavyset, with black hair being overtaken by gray. Sitting in the booth was a snug fit for him, but he enjoyed the food too much to complain. Hershel worked on Wall Street for twenty years before becoming involved with a friend of his father, who had a problem involving the laundering of drug money. Hershel had connections in the Cayman Islands,

Switzerland, and South Africa to assist in resolving that type of inconvenience.

Hershel was the architect of the Cartel System in Mexico. He was the man referred to as "the Gringo." He controlled the movement of money and also made legitimate investments through a closed corporation of thirty ultra-affluent individuals. Everyone who owned shares in the corporation was either a billionaire or became a billionaire through Hershel's investment acumen.

This "golden touch" provided Hershel with, perhaps, the most powerful position within the cartel. The drug lords were allowed to run their operations as they saw fit, but without any excessive violence in the United States. The main goal was always to keep the cash floodgates open. Any excessive violence that may trickle into the United States required an okay from Hershel, so that it would not affect the value of the stock.

When Serge spoke with Diego Barranca, Diego told him that he wanted permission to kill Jimmy Flowers because Jimmy had disrespected him. In reality, Diego's excessive lifestyle was eroding profits and he sought to make that up by seizing a portion of Jimmy Flower's drug business.

A waitress appeared at the table, dressed in jeans and a paisley t-shirt with a small, order pad.

"Are you guys ready or do you need another minute?"

Hershel smiled at her and set the menu down. Serge also set his menu down.

"I'll have a maple burger and can I have my French fries without salt?"

"Sure," she replied as she wrote. "Is medium okay?"

"Yes. Can I also get an ice tea?"

"Got it." She turned to Serge. "What would you like, sir?"

"I'll have a Caesar salad with chicken and an ice tea."

"Very good," she told them, picked up the menus, and walked back to the kitchen.

Hershel looked at Serge and his smile dissipated.

"What does Diego want?" he demanded with a perturbed grimace.

"He wants Jimmy Flowers dead."

Serge delivered the line with deadpanned eloquence.

"Are you kidding? Why?" Hershel was flabbergasted by the notion.

"He says Jimmy disrespected him."

"What did he call him an asshole or a retard?" Hershel wondered. "If he did, Diego should thank Jimmy for the compliment."

"Diego says he called him a junkie."

"Big deal. His father told me once, he put so much cola up his nose, he burned out his mucus membrane. That's why he gets colds all the time. He walked around so stoned, they called him 'empty eyes.' And his stupid father always covered for him." He then added rhetorically, "He's sick, he's got a cold." Hershel's voice echoed disgust.

"He also says the revenue stream would increase considerably with that person out of the way."

"Listen carefully, Serge." Hershel made sure his eyes were locked on Serge. "Because I'm only gonna say it once: I don't want Jimmy Flowers touched. The Barranca Cartel has been so successful for so long because we follow the Jimmy Flowers rule book. He doesn't have to help us out, but he does. And I'm grateful for it."

"I understand," Serge conceded. "It may cause some bad blood with Diego."

"The problem with Diego is Diego. His father should have given him a beating instead of a Ferrari. Now he thinks he has the keys to the toy store. You tell him 'the Gringo' says 'No.' Make him understand, otherwise, I'm concerned about your ability to communicate. Tell him I don't believe in confrontation, I believe in elimination. Understood?"

The waitress returned with two ice teas and set one in front of Hershel and Serge. Serge did not look forward to his telephone conversation with Diego, but he did not care because he was only the messenger.

CHAPTER 18

At 8:20 am, Artie Clexx sat in his red, 1978 Ford Econoline van focused on cars coming into the parking lot at Saint Elizabeth Seton Catholic Church in Carlsbad. He backed the van into a non-conspicuous location that was in the shade of a tree.

Artie wore jeans and a wool shirt with a worn, green t-shirt under it. The neck on the t-shirt was frayed and holes could be seen where the collar was separating from the shirt. He also wore a John Deere baseball hat. In his mouth was a toothpick that went up and down as if moving to the beat of music where none played. In his right hand, he held a Bic lighter that he constantly ignited and then turned off.

Then she arrived. Valerie Legion drove a new, lunar blue metallic, Mercedes-Benz S550 into the parking lot and parked against a sidewalk that led to a staircase. Roger was not fond of a Mercedes S550, but that is what she wanted.

The church staircase that she ascended, ushered visitors to a piazza, situated directly in front of the church.

Mrs. Legion wore a dress, shoes, and purse, all by Michael Kors. The dress was belted and was an indigo, blossom print. Her shoes were Winston Flat strappy sandals and her purse was a black,

Jet Set tote. Her clothing only served to enhance her beauty and refinement.

When Artie looked at her, the eloquence of her clothing did not impress him. All he saw was a dollar sign.

For the past four days, he surveilled Valerie Legion. Her daily itinerary consisted of attending daily mass, which commenced at 8:30 am and concluded at approximately 9:10 am. On one day, she attended the Women's Christian Fellowship meeting, which caused her to stay at church until 12:30 pm.

On the other days, she went from church to the K. & T.R. Animal Shelter located on Faraday Avenue in Carlsbad. The initials stood for 'Kisses & Tummy Rubs' and it was a state-of-the-art animal shelter and hospital. The facility claimed to have no fleas within it as all dogs were thoroughly cleaned before entering. There was no charge to people who could not afford the service. The only caveat was that an owner would allow their dog to be neutered or spayed if it was not already done. Also, it was an 'absolute' no-kill shelter.

Valerie Legion would take various dogs, waiting for adoption, for a walk. She would walk around the facility and make sure that all the caged animals had some degree of exercise.

Inside the facility, there were couches, similar to those found in the lobby at Legion and Associates, and mattresses for the dogs to rest on after their brisk constitutional.

Artie went into the K. & T.R. Animal Shelter one afternoon when he knew she would not be there. Inside, he saw a life-size portrait of Valerie Legion and a plaque thanking her and Roger Legion for making a dream come true. The goal of the shelter was to make sure no dog in San Diego County went without food, medical attention, or lived in fear.

The cleanliness of the facility only served to remind Artie of the squalor in which he lived. His visit only served to amp up his anger and his goal of forcing Roger Legion to "make things right."

CHAPTER 19

On a desert road shortly after 2:00 pm, off Highway 37, also known as the Caborca-Puerto Peñasco Highway, a Sonora, Mexico State Police car responded to a report of a suspicious vehicle parked along the roadside. The police car was a black and white, late model Dodge Charger with the words "POLICIA ESTATAL" (State Police) on the white doors. The car was manned by two officers and pulled up behind the suspicious vehicle.

The lone vehicle sitting in the 105-degree heat was a 2008 Toyota Highlander. It sat like a lonely sentinel on the side of the road amidst drifts of sand forming around the tires.

As the police car pulled up, they could see the windows of the Highlander were rolled down. The officer in the passenger seat called the California license plate into the dispatch station to determine if the car was stolen or if there were any outstanding warrants associated with it. There were none.

The officers stepped out of their car, and drew their service weapons, with the doors left open to use as shields, if necessary. The officer who drove spoke up.

"*¡En el carro, déjeme ver sus manos!*" (In the car, let me see your hands!)

The only reply came from the wind swirling the sand.

Both officers slowly walked around the doors to their vehicle and approached the Highlander, keeping their Smith & Wesson .45 caliber handguns aimed at the vehicle and ready to fire. As they proceeded closer to the vehicle, the officer on the passenger side called out to his partner.

"En la puerta hay sangre." (On the door, there's blood.)

Running down the center of the front passenger door was a narrow line of dried blood that had trickled from the open window. Both officers slowly proceeded closer until they could view the contents of the interior.

Inside sat four bullet-riddled bodies that were all decapitated. From their clothing, they appeared to be two men and two women. The first officer was mesmerized by the violent scene and spoke with a voice just loud enough to overcome the wind.

"Mejor llamamos la policía federal. Esto es el trabajo de los cárteles." (We better call the Federal police. This is the work of the cartels.)

"¡Mira!" (Look!), the other officer yelled out and pointed. Down the road, approximately twenty-five feet, were four iron stakes rising six feet from the ground and a head sat on each one.

There was Javier Jimenez, his wife, Corrina, his son, Eduardo, and his daughter-in-law, Rosalita. Pinned to Javier's cheek was his tongue, which was slit up the center roughly two inches.

On the rear bumper of the Highlander, the wind finally blew the '*El Tri*' bumper sticker from the car and into the wind.

CHAPTER 20

John Hamishaw finished scanning a deposition transcript of a member of the Medical Board of California, in preparation for a client meeting that Roger would also attend. The client was Scripticon, a company that provided equipment hardware and management system programming software for the electronic prescribing of medication.

He started to fiddle with the silver cufflink on his left shirtsleeve. John noted the time was 9:55 am and at that moment, the phone on his desk rang.

"Yes," he answered, not planning on taking any calls in light of his meeting.

"Attorney Weston Avery is here to see you for your ten o'clock appointment," responded Nina, the receptionist.

"Please show him into the large conference room and I'll be right there."

He stood from the desk, grabbed the most current volume of the file that was the purpose of the meeting and began a trek to Roger's office while putting on his suit coat. Roger was standing in his doorway as John approached.

"You ready?" Legion asked.

"Yeah," he replied, while straightening the fit of his coat. "Let's go."

They walked down the western hallway at a brisk gait and John entered the conference room followed by Roger. There were two men there, looking out the window, transfixed on the Pacific Ocean.

"Hello, Wes," John said in a pumped-up, buoyant voice. It broke Wes' hypnotic gaze.

"John, good to see you," Wes advised and met him with a vice-grip handshake.

Wes was 48 years old, 5 feet 10 inches tall, 195 pounds. His hair was a silver-gray. Twenty years earlier, he could have been a male model because everything about him was appearance. He wore a black, pinstriped suit and a red tie with a white shirt.

"This is Roger Legion," John informed him. Wes shared a handshake and a smile with Roger.

"Nice to meet you, Wes," Roger informed him.

Then Wes turned to his companion.

"This is," he hesitated for a moment wondering how he should introduce him, "Vincent Fiorito, he is one of our major shareholders."

Both John and Roger then shook hands with Jimmy Flowers.

Jimmy wore a solid, black suit, white shirt, and a black tie. It was the same outfit that he normally wore to funerals.

"Let's sit," John suggested and everyone followed his directive. "Would anyone like something to drink?"

"I'm fine," Wes replied.

"So am I," Jimmy added.

"Perhaps we could begin with a quick summary of where we are in the case," Wes suggested.

"Absolutely," John announced. "As you know, the plaintiff, is a gentleman named Cyrus Valiant, he is a lawyer and former medical doctor. He never practiced medicine, but he lost his license about a year ago, after he was charged with writing excessive prescriptions for controlled substances. He claims that the accusations are false and that the indication of excessive prescribing of medications is the result of an accounting and/or computer error within the electronic prescribing system, which is the electronic generation, transmission, and filling of a medical prescription, utilized by various pharmacies. He is suing for all kinds of emotional distress damages. The bottom line is that he wants his medical license back."

"Mr. Legion," Jimmy spoke up, "have you ever dealt with this individual?"

"I have. I have had two trials with Cy 'the Guy' Valiant. In both instances, I obtained a defense verdict. Cy likes to tell anyone who will listen that he is a doctor and a lawyer. He thinks it gives him some special credibility. He will mention it at every opportunity. His real name is Adolph Verbinski. As you have probably noticed, he loves the media and the spotlight."

"He appears to be somewhat of a bloviator," Jimmy added.

"I think bullshitter is a better term," Legion augmented Jimmy's comment. "This guy's got an office in an old strip mall in Chula Vista and he drives an Isuzu pickup truck."

"Not anymore," Wes uttered. "It appears that his fortunes have changed. Our information is that he's driving a new Bentley."

Roger was somewhat taken aback by the comment. He could not picture it in his mind.

"What is the status of the litigation?" Roger posed his inquiry to John.

"Discovery cut-off is coming up. Valiant wants his expert to perform onsite forensic testing of the system hardware and software. We objected to the request as being vague, ambiguous, and overbroad. Perhaps, we could move for a protective order."

"No," Legion said decisively. "I don't like that. All a protective order does is bring attention to something that we don't want to give attention to. That's what we want to avoid."

"Has there been any discussion regarding settlement?" Wes inquired.

"The plaintiff is absolutely against it," John answered. "He wants to go to trial."

"So do we," Legion declared conclusively.

Jimmy Flowers then spoke up.

"What bothers me is that word 'forensic' in the discovery request."

"Let me ask you something," Legion spoke directing his question to Wes and Jimmy. "Is the system audited by the state?"

"Every year," Wes answered.

"All right," Legion pensively responded and pivoted to John. "Get a copy of the State audits for the pertinent years. Find out who the person most knowledgeable for the prescribing system is in Sacramento and let's notice his deposition."

Jimmy Flowers then interjected a request.

"Do you mind if I speak to Mr. Legion alone?" As he spoke, he looked at John.

"No problem," John advised and stood from the chair. "Call me if you need me," he told Legion and exited the room.

Jimmy then looked at Wes as if he was expecting something from him.

"Do you mind," Jimmy asked Roger, "if Mr. Avery waits in your reception area?"

"No," Roger answered. "If you would like anything to drink, just tell the girl, she'll get it for you."

Wes appeared slightly disheartened as he rose from his chair and exited through the door at the far end of the conference room.

Jimmy Flowers was about to share some interesting information with Roger Legion.

CHAPTER 21

Diego slammed the telephone receiver so powerfully into its cradle that it took a slight bounce and fell to the floor.

"JEW BASTARD!" his incensed voice spewed with vociferous ire. He then slammed his fist down into the desk. "Do you believe the nerve of that son-of-a-motherless-whore, Gringo, to tell me how to run my operation? I'm the one with a target on my back, while that *la grasa de cerdo* (the fat pig) lives in the middle of nowhere off the sweat of my labor. You know I can go talk to my people in Ecuador, Columbia, Venezuela and they will okay a bullet in that Jew's ass today. And I will tell them how things are done, not the other way around, like this bullshit. I tell you this: On the souls of my dead mother and father, I will kill Jimmy Flowers."

Diego's visitor remained stoic, not wishing to add any gasoline to the fire. Diego stared forward without focus, attempting to ponder his options.

"How we doing on those other things?" Diego wondered.

Before he received an answer, his telephone rang.

"Hold it," he said to his visitor, then picked up his phone receiver, "What?" he demanded with disdain.

"The new arrivals are here," answered a voice. "Do you want them sent to Dr. Hurado?"

"No. I want to inspect them first. I'll be there in a few minutes," Diego advised and hung up the phone. He re-directed his question to his visitor. "So, what's going on with these other things?"

Diego's visitor was Jim Roth, the risk manager from Realizar Healthcare that met with Roger Legion and Larry Larkin the day before in Legion's office. Realizar Healthcare was indirectly owned by the Barranca Drug Cartel. On this day, he wore a blue, button shirt, without a tie, blue pants, and a brown sport coat.

"I met with the attorney, Legion," Jim answered with strategic focus. "He's an interesting guy. He's good, and he knows it. He said 'no.'"

"No?" Diego was flabbergasted. "How much did you offer?"

"Two million."

"And he said, 'No'? What about our man on the inside?" Diego spoke quickly and wanted quick answers.

"He said he would work on him. He thought once Legion thought about it, he wouldn't pass it up."

"I'm done asking the Gringo for anything. This lawyer either comes along with us or he's a dead man," Diego advised conclusively. "And what about the other one?"

"I should receive a status report on that shortly," Jim responded with a resolute tenor.

Diego wheeled his chair back and stood up.

"Come with me, I want to show you something."

Jim rose from his chair and Diego placed his thumb into the biometric pad on his desk. The door to Diego's right made a 'click' sound and Jim followed Diego out into the hallway.

The men set out on a trek that maneuvered through three different hallways, each requiring Diego's thumb on a biometric pad to allow entrance to the next hallway. The final door they went through was an entrance to a large darkened room that echoed like an auditorium. At one end of the room was a stage that was brightly lit by spotlights.

Jim absorbed the size of the room and wondered about the purpose of its utility. Diego's smile boasted pride.

"ISA!" Diego bellowed like a triumphant conquistador.

Through one of the doors near the stage emerged a well-dressed woman, 58 years old, beautifully coifed hair, and every detail of her existence seemed to have attention. Her name was Isa Cabrera. She was a Cuban National, who came to the United States with her family when Bautista was deposed. Years later, her husband had problems with the United States Government, so she moved on because she had no interest in going to prison.

Her official title at the Palace was Etiquette Administrator. She spoke many languages, and also had the ability to read and write them. Isa was proficient in communicating in the sixty-two indigenous languages still spoken in Mexico and the one hundred dialects that are spoken in various parts of the country. Diego would call on her occasionally for translation assistance.

"Diego," Isa responded, being genuinely pleased to see him. "It's good to see you."

"Isa, this is a friend and visitor, Jim Roth."

"Nice to meet you," Jim responded to his introduction.

"It is my pleasure," Isa acknowledged.

"What do you have for me today?" Diego asked.

Isa turned back toward the stage and, with a raised voice, called out, "*Sácalos!*" (Bring them out!)

Then, four naked women were paraded out onto the stage for Diego's perusal. All four women were slender, shapely, and none were taller than Diego. All four were afraid, trembling, and holding their arms crossed against their breasts.

"Where are they from?" Diego asked Isa.

"Guadalajara, Zacatecas, Tampico, and Real de Catorce."

Isa shared with Diego the locations from which these girls were abducted. Diego would send men on specific missions to find women. He did not want any that lived close to the Palace, but he did want a specific age and body shape.

"We get them ready for my harem," Diego told Jim and then began a slow walk in front of the stage. His gaze had a sliminess that could easily induce vomiting. When he reached the last girl, he turned to Isa.

"Tell this one," he said pointing to the fourth girl, "to wash her make-up. She looks like a *el gitano* (gypsy)."

Diego never spoke directly to any of the women that were brought in. He walked around to the end of the stage and stepped up onto it. He again spoke to Isa.

"Tell them to put their arms down."

"*Baja los brazos ahora!*" (Put your arms down, now!) Isa barked and they all complied.

Then Diego walked up to the first girl, grabbed one of her breasts, and squeezed it. He then went to the next girl and did it again. When he did it to the third girl, he turned to Isa.

"Ask this one if she has children."

"*¿Tiene usted hijos?*" (Do you have children?)

"*Si,*" (Yes) the girl responded.

"They are going to miss you," Diego pronounced, not directing the comment to her.

When Diego grabbed the breast of the fourth girl, she slapped him in the face. He shook it off and smiled. He then caught the attention of two Palace guards standing by the door. He waived them over.

"Take her," he told them referring to the girl who slapped him. They each took one of her arms and dragged her off the stage as she kicked and screamed. He then turned to Isa.

"Miss Isa, take them to Dr. Hurado and once they get a clean bill of health, work your magic to make them my courtesans."

Isa ushered the remaining three girls off the stage and Diego returned to speak with Jim.

"We send them to a doctor for a complete physical and blood test. As long as they have no sickness, Isa will turn them into fine ladies of the Palace, available to me whenever I desire."

"What happens to that girl who slapped you?" Jim wondered.

"For the next couple of hours," Diego explained nonchalantly, "the palace guards will have some fun with her. They will torture her, gang rape her, sodomize her, and oral," he paused, "something, I can't think of the word. Then they take her out in the desert, a couple of miles from here, where we keep a backhoe. They'll dig a hole, put a bullet in her head, and bury her. Then, she never existed."

What Diego did not share was that the same fate awaited any girl who became pregnant.

Jim was repulsed, but remained calm.

"How many girls do you have here?" Jim queried.

"Ten to fifteen. It depends. Let's go."

Jim quickly glanced back at the stage trying to comprehend the savage brutality of Diego Barranca.

CHAPTER 22

After Wes Avery, the general counsel for Scripticon, exited the large conference room at Legion and Associates, Jimmy Flowers turned to Roger Legion to make a comment.

"He's not as good as he thinks he is."

"I believe that statement could be said about any lawyer," Legion responded.

"May I call you Roger?" Jimmy inquired.

"Of course," Legion retorted immediately.

"You can call me Jimmy. Some people call me Jimmy Flowers. Have you heard that name before?"

"It's not ringing a bell.

"Mr. Avery mentioned that I was a major shareholder in Scripticon. That's not quite correct. I am the only shareholder. Removed a few times through shell corporations, but it's only me."

Legion nodded his head in acknowledgement.

"I assume," Jimmy continued, "that anything said here is protected by the attorney-client privilege?"

"Yes, it is," Legion answered.

"I've been involved in organized crime operations in San Diego for nearly forty years. By far, the largest source of my income is derived from the sale of prescription drugs. The only territories that I service are in affluent parts of town like Rancho Santa Fe, La Jolla, Del Mar, and Coronado. I am not involved with street drugs like cocaine, heroin, and methamphetamines."

"Years ago I realized that the most vulnerable part of a drug sale is the point of sale. The moment when the cash is traded for the product. Police set up sting operations or they know where the crack houses are located. So, I determined that the best place for the point of sale for a drug transaction to take place is in a drug store. A place where it is not out of the ordinary and probable cause should be minimal."

"I view healthcare in this country to be similar to Prohibition in the 1920s. It presents an opportunity for enterprising people to become very rich. Seven years ago, I purchased Scripticon, so the framework was already in place."

"You're not going to tell me that 'Cy the Guy' is right about his accusations," Legion's voice echoed concern.

"Not exactly," Jimmy calmly shared. "Let me explain the process."

Roger's curiosity was more than piqued.

"We have a team of individuals, many of whom are licensed medical professionals, in addition to attorneys, certified public accountants, and a variety of other licensed professionals. They are vetted and scrutinized more closely than a Supreme Court justice. Those people are referred to as 'prescribers' and they have the ability to upload or update prescription information through a verification process on the Scripticon system."

"Normally, the next stage in the process would be to send the prescription to a 'transaction hub.' Before these," Jimmy searched for a word, "'unique' prescriptions reach a transaction hub, they are intercepted and matched up with a legitimate doctor's DEA number, oftentimes one that is friendly to us, and the number of pills never exceed a 30-day supply. The use of any particular doctor is never abused. We know the amounts where the Medical Board would become suspicious. The system will also create an electronic medical record for the individual ordering the drug. So, in the electronic world, everything looks fine."

"What happens if a pharmacist wants to call the doctor with a question?" Legion inquired.

"They won't. We only use independent pharmacies. Not the chains. They'll see a code on the electronic prescription, which essentially means no questions asked. The system is loaded with fail-safe measures to avoid detection. We have had the state audit us for the past five years and never had a problem."

"I think chain pharmacies have gotten too big in the past few years."

"It allows the little guy to stay in the game."

"Now," Roger wanted to re-focus, "let's get back to the problem at hand. Was 'Cy the Guy' one of your prescribers?"

"No," Jimmy retorted decisively. "On the street, they would call him a 'candyman' because he just wrote a lot of prescriptions to make money on the side. My concern is what his expert may or may not be able to do. The program which undertakes all this surreptitious activity is called an Analog Brogue. If you hear that term, we need to go to battle stations. The local cartel and I are having some *relationship* difficulties right now. I'm sure they would love to see me and my organization go down in flames."

"Analog Brogue. All right. I appreciate your confidence in sharing the factual situation with me," Roger advised.

"Roger, you seem like a very pragmatic man and I have all the faith in the world in you. But I must tell you that one of the options I would seriously consider is to settle the matter *out-of court*."

Roger knew that Jimmy meant having Cy 'the Guy' killed.

"I am not going to say 'no' to that, but it would bring a lot of light on a case that we are trying to keep under the radar. I'm sure that once I get him into court, I can mop the floor with him."

"I look forward to it," Jimmy voiced with a smile. "If you need me, call Wes," he said pointing out to the lobby. "I'm not big on the telephone. You can always stop by my restaurant."

"Where's that?"

"The Bagheria Bedda in Little Italy."

"I've been there before. It's excellent."

"Come in for dinner sometime. Bring your wife."

Both Roger and Jimmy stood from their chairs and Roger held a door open for Jimmy.

"Nina," Roger called out to get her attention. "Would you please call Mr. Hamishaw and let him know the Scripticon people are ready to leave?"

Roger shook hands with Jimmy and Wes Avery and engaged in small talk with both men until John Hamishaw arrived. There was something about Jimmy Flowers that Roger admired. The same could be said for Jimmy regarding Roger Legion.

CHAPTER 23

Roger entered his office and picked up the receiver of the telephone on his desk before sitting down. He glanced through the directory on the phone and pushed one button. On the second ring, it was answered.

"This is Glenn."

Glenn Edgarian was Roger Legion's go-to private investigator. His exceptional investigative skill, coupled with his alluring charm, made him a weapon to find out information that any other investigator would tell you is not accessible. He seemed to know everyone. When you hired Glenn, you hired access. Glenn always provided Roger with Cadillac service and always wanted to provide that bit of information, beyond the assignment, that would make Roger Legion's star shine.

"Glenn, Roger Legion, how are ya?"

"Good, Roger, how are you?

"I'm doing well. You keeping busy?"

"Always trying. Alotta deadbeat debtors these days."

"You got time for me?" Roger asked.

"Always." Glenn was quick with his response. "Do you want me to come over or can you tell me over the phone?"

"You know Cy Valiant?" Roger looked out the window as he spoke.

"Cy 'the Guy.' King of the bullshitters. The other day I saw him doing a press conference on the steps of the court house. Nobody was there and his secretary and paralegal are asking him prepared questions. If you ask the guy, 'How do you get to the ocean?' the first thing he wants to tell you is that he's a doctor. The guy's a total whack job."

"I'm glad you know him," Roger acknowledged. "I've got a case where he's the plaintiff."

"The one dealing with the prescriptions?" Glenn wondered.

"That's it. Have you done any work for us on it?"

"No. Larry," Glenn hesitated for a quick moment, "Larry Larkin asked me if I had anything going on it."

Roger paused for a moment as he pondered Larry's interest in the case. Larry Larkin and John Hamishaw worked together on various cases, but this was not one of them, as far as Roger knew.

"I want a financial background check on Cy Valiant. The guy never had two nickels to rub together and now I hear he's driving a Bentley. He won't talk settlement, he wants to go to trial. That's not the Cy that I knew."

"It will be done. Any restrictions or budget constraints?" Glenn asked.

"Do the necessary. But," again Roger paused, "don't tell anybody over here about this assignment."

"You got it my friend. I can probably start on it tomorrow. Should have it done in a day or two."

"All right. Sounds good. Thanks, Glenn. Take it easy."

"Thanks, Roger. I'll be in touch."

With that, the conversation ended. Roger remained intrigued about Larry's interest in the file. He walked out the door of his office and thought he would ask Larry about his sudden interest in the case.

Legion walked down the northern hallway and then down the eastern hallway. He found Larry Larkin speaking with John Hamishaw in John's office. Roger entered the office and the conversation stopped. John Hamishaw was the first to speak.

"Hey Roger, good meeting today," John's comment echoed success.

"I think it went well," Roger told them as he stared at Larry searching for introspection. "Have you been doing any work on the *Valiant* case?" He posed his inquiry to Larry.

"I was a little slow," Larry said, remaining matter-of-fact, "so I did some research on the forensic testing discovery issue."

"Let the paralegals and the law clerks do the research," Legion told Larry. "Understand, John?"

John nodded in agreement.

"If you get slow, come and see me," Legion instructed.

"All right," Larry responded nonchalantly.

"How was your conversation with Jimmy Flowers?"

Roger did not react to John's knowledge of Jimmy Flowers' street name, but it was like a bomb going off in Legion's brain. Jimmy Flowers was introduced in the meeting as Vincent Fiorito. Legion wanted to know how John knew that name, but did not want to pursue it in front of Larry.

"It was good," Roger remarked. "Nothing substantive, though."

"Why did he want to talk to you in private?" John eagerly wondered.

"I don't know," Legion responded. "You should ask him."

Roger turned to leave and then turned back to John.

"Be sure to send me the date and time for the 'meet and confer' meeting on the *Valiant* case."

"I'll do it right now," John uttered, but his visage seem to indicate that he knew Legion was being deceptive.

Legion walked back to his office and before he reached the doorway, his office phone was ringing. He sped up his pace and answered it.

"Yes," he responded through the speaker phone to Nina.

"Cyrus Valiant is on line 5."

Roger thought for a moment that this call would be interesting.

"Put him through," and the phone once again rang.

"This is Roger Legion."

"Roger, this is Cy Valiant."

His voice was slow and his words were slurred.

"Hello, Cy," Roger calmly uttered.

"I…wanna…make…sure," Cy related with pregnant pauses.

"Cy, are you all right?" Roger knew he was either drunk or high.

"Yeah, I gotta…I gotta cold." Again silence.

"Why did you call me, Cy?" Roger articulated.

"I want to make sure that you are gonna be the guy at the 'meet and confer' meeting. I know nobody at your place can take a piss unless you give the okay."

"I will be there," Roger confirmed.

"And no bullshit with State Audit Reports. That's not good enough."

Cy's slurred delivery telegraphed to Roger that someone was sharing information.

"We'll talk about it at the meeting. You better sober up, Cy," Legion uttered and ended the call.

Legion moved to his chair and sat down gazing at the Pacific Ocean. Roger Legion had a problem. And he needed to find a solution.

CHAPTER 24

Artie Clexx and Lisa Natasi sat in a booth at Angelo's Restaurant in Oceanside waiting for the number of their afternoon lunch order to be called. Angelo's had a reputation for good fast food and a lot of it. Despite its name, the restaurant did not serve Italian food. It served basic burgers and fries, Mexican, and Greek food. The interior of the restaurant was reminiscent of a 1960s fast food eatery in both décor and age. There were four Angelo's Restaurants in San Diego County and they were all located on the same street: Highway 101, parallel to the ocean. Three of the four restaurants were in Oceanside and this particular one was immediately north of the Carlsbad/Oceanside border.

Artie wore the same clothes he wore all week, down to the John Deere ball cap. Lisa wore a pair of Merona skinny denim jeans and a blue Merona petite short-sleeve lace top. Merona is a brand sold at Target stores and Lisa's slender figure wore them well.

She took a mirror out of her purse and continued her attempts to make sure her hair was as perfect as possible and also to put some final dabs of make-up in place. Artie stared at her and wondered what she was doing.

"Listen," he said gently pushing her hand and the mirror down to the table.

"What?" she answered with mild irritation.

"I'm ready to go."

"Where? The food hasn't come yet," Lisa pronounced with obvious subtlety.

"I'm not talkin' about here. I'm talkin' about my score. What days do you have off next week?"

"I don't know. They post the schedule today."

"All right. As soon as I see your schedule, I'll figure the timeline out. We're gonna grab her in the church parking lot. We'll bring her to that empty parts warehouse off Mission Ave. near the Oceanside Airport."

"Why there?" Lisa wondered and her face indicated that the place had somewhat of a slime factor.

"Tizoe's the security guard they got watching the place. We can get in and out of there, hide the van, no questions asked."

Artie's faith in the crime was evident.

"You got an escape plan and how we're gonna get the money all figured out?"

"Lisa, it's beautiful. We set different pick-up places all over the county. We tell him we want the cash in chunks, say a million at a time. If we see a cop or somebody gets pinched, our new friend is dead. We do it over and over, except for the last chunk of cash. That would be the pick-up where they would be waiting to grab us. So, we don't want the last chunk. We set it up, but you and I are out of town while they wait for us to come pick it up. We'll call a third party to let them know where she is."

"You know," Lisa announced after she heard his plan for the ransom, "that sounds pretty good. You really think we're gonna get millions?"

"I told ya: this job is one and done. I wouldn't take a chance unless it was worth my while. So, the take down is gonna be serious. And you know, I'm not going back to the slammer. Tizoe's gonna get us the weapons we need."

As Artie finished his sentence, the number for their food order was called over a loudspeaker. Artie got up from the booth to retrieve the food. All Lisa would think about from this point forward was how her life was about to change.

CHAPTER 25

As Friday evening settled in, Nina stood in her kitchen as the sound and scent of Orville Redenbacher microwave popcorn filled the air. Nina wore a Nautica, light blue, short sleeve pajama top and matching bottoms. From one of her cupboards, she pulled out a bowl that was her specific popcorn bowl. When the microwave turned off, she waited for the popping to stop. She then removed the bag, opened it slightly to let the steam out, and after a moment, opened it the rest of the way and poured it into the bowl.

She then obtained a wine glass from a different cabinet and an open bottle of Sutter Home White Zinfandel from the refrigerator. She poured a glass of the wine and returned the bottle to the icebox.

Nina then moved her base of operations from the kitchen to the couch in front of her 32-inch flat screen television.

On the couch was a paper bag that contained two magazines that she purchased on the way home from the Barnes & Noble in the Hazard Center Shopping Center in the Mission Valley section of San Diego. She placed the bag on her lap and reached for the television remote control.

Nina reviewed her list of programs on her digital video recorder (DVR) and started to play the oldest of five episodes of *Say Yes to the Dress*.

The music from the TV show's introduction filled the air and Nina slid the two magazines from the bag. One was called *Premier Bride* and the other was called *Brides*.

Nina began to multi-task on the one topic that she dreamed about her entire life.

CHAPTER 26

Deep within the Palace of Barranca, Jim Roth sat in Diego Barranca's office, awaiting Diego's arrival. Diego still required Jim to be fumigated, but he relaxed the search requirements to allow him quick entry.

Jim was dressed in his usual business casual attire, and stood from the chair to admire a cabinet that Diego had on the wall. The contents were surrounded by thick glass and Diego's biometric thumbprint was required for access to the contents.

In the cabinet was a gun rack, complete with McMillan CS5 rifle, which is a .308 caliber concealable subsonic suppressed sniper rifle and Sidewinder Venom, 12-gauge shotgun with a 10-round rotary magazine. There was also a 9mm Uzi submachine gun and a black AK-47 submachine gun. Also, within the cabinet, were at least ten clips for each gun and assorted grenades.

Jim also noticed, in the corner of the room, near the door for entrance into the Palace, two swords, approximately thirty inches long. Both were in a sheath with a handle guard and the blades had a slight curve.

Jim heard Diego yelling at someone outside the door and he returned to his seat. Diego entered and stopped to look at him with a broad smile.

"It is good to see you my friend," Diego told him as he moved quickly to his chair.

"It is good to see you," Jim replied.

"How are things in San Diego?"

"If you want to ask me about the weather, it's perfect."

Diego's gaze became more primal.

"Every day that I know that soul-less animal, Jimmy Flowers, is still drawing breath, I get sick to my stomach."

Jim interlaced his fingers and placed them in his lap with his elbows on the arms of the chair.

"Well, let's talk about that, then. In regard to Realizar Health, I talked to the guy who works for Legion. He tells me Legion is not interested and it's a dead issue."

"How much did that guy at Legion want?" Diego inquired.

"He wanted a million dollars, but we didn't front any of it, because I feared this current scenario. He also wanted his wife and his kids taken out."

"What are they teaching in law school these days?" Diego asked rhetorically.

"Bloodthirsty 101," Jim replied with a slight smile.

"If this guy is no help to us, then he is a liability. Do you have any more use for him?" Diego wanted to know.

"He's able to provide us with inside information on Legion's strategy for our other situation."

"When it's over, he goes too. Don't pay him anything. Just string him along."

"Understood," Jim replied.

Diego stared at him thinking about his next move.

"What about this other thing with the lawyer who's a doctor?" Diego inquired.

"Cy the Guy? I saw him over the weekend. He's a train wreck. When I saw him, he was holed up in a high-end hotel with three hookers going through coke like it was sugar in a coffee shop."

Diego gnawed on his tongue in disgust.

"How much is that guy into us for?" Diego wanted to know.

"At least one and a half million, plus the kilo of coke we gave him, which he's been going through at a high rate of speed."

"How is this guy going to be the lawyer in his case? I've never met the guy and I can't stand him."

"I don't know. But there's a problem there."

"All right," Diego shook his head as an idea was percolating. "I'm going to send this 'Cy the Guy,' a little reminder to help him re-focus. Nothing major, but sufficient."

"We can always bring in a lawyer to represent him," Jim advocated.

"All right. If we need it."

Diego pivoted to his desktop phone lifted the receiver and pressed two numbers. He waited for an answer.

"Send in Miguel Acacia."

Diego placed the receiver back in its cradle and turned his gaze to Jim.

"Jim, I have to tell you that I am disappointed with these developments. These things are the result of trying to be civil. In this line of work, that's impossible."

Just then, a knock at the door interrupted Diego. He clicked the door open using his thumb pad and Miguel Acacia entered. He was 32 years old, 5 feet 9 inches tall, with black hair combed to the side and skin that appeared tough and weathered. He wore a black, paramilitary outfit, complete with an empty sidearm holster. He stood at attention at the end of Diego's desk.

Diego looked at him and back to Jim.

"He is the best of my *Sicarios*." Diego advised.

Sicarios were hitmen within the cartel responsible for assassinations, and assistance with any other criminal activity carried out by the cartel, including kidnapping, extortion, and theft. They also had the primary responsibility of defending the Palace. Diego also used them as a separate line of personal defense for himself.

Diego returned his gaze to Miguel.

"I've got an itch I want to scratch," Diego told him. "Get a team together. It's a lawyer in San Diego, named Legion. He's on the 24th floor of the America's Finest City Building."

"Just him?" Miguel asked with a thick accent.

"You know what I think," Diego responded. "If you are going to kill a snake, you should also make sure that you destroy the nest." A moment passed. "You understand what I want?"

Miguel nodded in acknowledgement.

"Diego," Jim Roth interjected, "let's think about this for a minute."

"No," Diego said with finality. "Now, we do it my way."

Part 2

CHAPTER 27

At the Price Chopper grocery store, located at 170 Swanton Road in St. Albans, Vermont, Herschel Gordon, the man also known as 'the Gringo,' was performing his weekly shopping routine. It consisted of picking up a list of needed items and items on sale. One of his weekly chores was to peruse the Price Chopper weekly flyer and he and his wife planned their meals around the sale items.

Herschel was in the pasta aisle attempting to sort out the different types of Barilla pasta available. Price Chopper had a ten for $10 sale and they had a wide selection of various sundries for that price, including Barilla pasta.

As he reviewed a box of penne pasta and ziti for the best freshness date, he heard a familiar voice.

"Herschel."

He diverted his glance away from the macaroni to see Serge Stiroy standing at the end of his cart. He placed the two boxes into his cart while tallying how many more boxes were needed to add up to ten. Then, he addressed Serge.

"What's going on?" Herschel asked.

Serge looked around to make sure there was no one within earshot.

"It's Diego" Serge advised. "He's ordered a hit on Jimmy Flowers' lawyer. But not just the lawyer, the entire law firm."

"What the hell is wrong with him?" Herschel responded in disgust. "He doesn't think that'll be loud?"

"I don't know what he thinks. But it sounds like he's starting to go off the reservation."

"When is this happening?"

"They're mounting up for it now."

Herschel's mind raced for an option.

"Tell Jimmy Flowers and tell the lawyer. Now."

"All right," Serge answered, nodding in agreement.

"Go!" Herschel commanded and Serge did an about-face to swiftly exit the store.

Herschel returned to selecting four more boxes of pasta before turning his attention to locating the 8-ounce cans of Hunts tomato sauce with no salt added. These were also on sale at the price of ten for $10.

Meanwhile, Serge sat in his car, pressing numbers on his cell phone, racing to communicate with a gangster and a lawyer.

CHAPTER 28

Serge Stiroy sat in his rented Chevrolet Malibu while making phone calls in the parking lot of the St. Albans, Vermont Price Chopper grocery store. After sharing the news of Diego's planned massacre of Legion and Associates with Jimmy Flowers' people, he contacted his inside man at the phone company to retrieve Roger Legion's cell phone number.

In less than three minutes, Serge had the number and dialed. Serge knew the approximate time for the killing spree, so he would be able to provide a fairly accurate time of arrival for the assassins. Legion's cell phone was answered on the third ring.

"Hello," Legion's baritone voice announced.

"Mr. Legion," Serge declared. "In two minutes, a helicopter will land on the top of your building. The men inside that helicopter are coming to slaughter you and everyone in your law firm. Guide your actions accordingly."

"Who is this?" Legion asked and Serge disconnected the call.

Back at his office, Roger Legion stood in shock and dread as he saw a helicopter, capable of holding up to eight men, approaching from the south.

Legion darted out of his office like a looter trying to evade police with his sole focus on setting off the fire alarm to evacuate the building. The alarm was located near the elevators between the men's and women's rest rooms.

As he moved at a brisk clip, he saw a man that he did not recognize, waiting to speak to him. He was 32 years old, 6 feet 2 inches tall, 190 pounds, dressed in a Tom Ford Charcoal Suit, with black, Salvatore Farragamo shoes, white shirt, and a yellow tie with a black diamond pattern. He wore wire rim glasses and his black, nicely-trimmed hair was parted on the side. From his stylish look, his profession could have been anything from a college professor to a magazine model. He started to speak when Legion was within ten feet of him.

"Mr. Legion." Roger slowed down, but wanted to continue. The man held out his open palm to stop him. "My name is Rolf Adler. Jimmy Flowers sent me to help you with your situation."

Roger was relieved, but extremely concerned.

"The phone call said they were gonna be here in two minutes," Legion advised.

"They're not even on the roof yet," Rolf told him.

"Let me pull the fire alarm to evacuate the building," Legion uttered.

"No. I'm here with a team of men. I am going to send one of my men down a couple of floors to start a fire. Nothing major. Just enough to keep the firemen busy. I am going to give you a list of things I want you to do.

"First," Rolf said, "I want you to call whoever is in charge of the floor below. Tell them it's an emergency and they have to evacuate now. It's 3:30, so tell them they can all go home for the day."

Legion nodded in agreement as Rolf continued.

"Then, I want you to go to the offices on this floor and tell everybody it is an emergency and they have to get out now. Make sure they understand that they can't come back up here."

"All right," Legion acknowledged.

"If any of your people come up here, while we're still here, we're going to have a problem."

"I'll make sure it doesn't happen," Legion assured him.

"Where's this person?" Rolf inquired, pointing to Nina's empty chair.

On the countertop, in front of where she sat, was a folded cardboard placeholder that said, 'Be Right Back!'

"She's probably in the ladies room," Legion said.

"Go get her first. After you make a sweep of the floor, we'll talk again."

Legion moved rapidly, at an agile pace, and he could see through the frosted glass that the conference room was filled with at least ten men standing inside. There was no time to wonder as to their involvement.

Rolf reached behind the collar of his shirt and pulled up a corded earpiece that he affixed to his left ear.

Legion rushed to the ladies room door and entered. Nina stood in front of the mirror with a lip brush and provided a slight touch-up.

"Nina," he told her without pause, "everyone's going home early, but we have to leave now."

She was slightly startled by his presence, but immediately complied. Legion rapidly moved from office-to-office barking an order for movement NOW! No one asked why. Everyone that he spoke to adhered to his demand. He also found time to call Louise, his secretary, on the 23rd floor to begin evacuation procedures. Legion then returned to speak with Rolf.

"I counted eight, plus the girl," Rolf asserted.

"So did I," Legion concurred.

"Good. At the other end of the hall, there's a freight elevator. Can I get the key?"

Legion reached into his pocket and gave him a small keychain.

"I'll leave them on your desk when we're done. Where's the maintenance room?"

"Right next to the freight elevator."

"Okay. We're gonna clean-up when we're done. We only clean organic materials. If any glass gets broken or a copy machine gets hit, I can't do anything about that."

"No problem. I'll stay and help you," Legion conveyed with fearless bravado.

"No," Rolf was succinct and definite. "This is what I do. You wanna help me, just make sure nobody comes back up here."

"All right," Legion conceded.

"One final thing: when you go downstairs, I want you to take a picture of yourself. Either with other people or a selfie. I will call you later and tell you why I need that picture."

"Thanks," Roger sincerely uttered.

Rolf held out his hand and smiled. They shared a strong handshake.

"Let's get you a ride." He then opened the door to the conference room to speak to another young man sitting at the table in front of a laptop computer.

"Get a car for a nonstop to the lobby," Rolf told the man sitting at the table.

Three keys on the laptop keyboard were hit and the elevator doors opened. Roger Legion entered and he looked out at Rolf who smiled at him as the doors closed.

Roger admired Rolf's calmness and focus in the heat of crisis. Legion knew firsthand the value of those traits.

Rolf entered the conference room and the twelve men inside looked to him.

"Let's go to work," he directed.

As he spoke, a helicopter was about to land on the roof of the America's Finest City Building.

CHAPTER 29

As the Bell 429 Global Ranger helicopter lowered to touch down on the helipad of the America's Finest City Building, Rolf Adler and his men made plans for the assassin team's arrival. Rolf had twelve men with him, all dressed in finely tailored suits, clean-shaven, and they all wore a corded earpiece for communication.

"Billy, do we have control of the environment?" Rolf asked the man sitting at the laptop.

"Waiting on the electrical," he answered. "We got it now."

"Give us an arctic blast and lower the shades," Rolf directed.

From the laptop, Billy was able to control the air conditioning on the floor and lowered it to 60 degrees, the lowest possible setting. The 24th floor also had a shade system recessed into the ceiling, wherein a shade made of heavy duty vinyl polymer rolled down a track and then sealed to create complete darkness if desired. The system had been created for home theaters and was useful in commercial buildings for various presentations.

"Shades are lowered," Billy told him.

"Lock them in place," Rolf conveyed.

He then placed two hard case suitcases on the table that were brought in by one of the other men. They were both black with an aluminum alloy frame around the exterior for reinforcement.

The first one was 2 feet wide and 3 feet long. It contained twelve handguns (2 layers of six guns) with molded foam around each gun.

The second suitcase was the same type of suitcase, but was one foot wide and eighteen inches long. Within this suitcase, there were twelve pairs of glasses. Each had a yellow tint lens and they were larger to allow you to place them over your personal glasses.

"Gentlemen," Rolf spoke as he looked around the room, "fill your hand and let's bring things into focus. Then take your positions."

The gun that each man grabbed was a modified Smith & Wesson model 39 semi-automatic pistol. This gun was calibered at 9mm and had a silencer or suppressor on the end of it to mitigate any noise from firing. In addition, it had a slide lock mechanism to further cancel noise from the bullet. When used with subsonic ammunition, the noise from firing is tremendously reduced.

Normally, when a semi-automatic gun is fired, the top of the gun or slide retracts from the power of the bullet to strip off another round for firing. This gun will not do that when it is equipped with a silencer.

This type of gun was originally developed by the U.S. Navy for Navy Seals during the Vietnam War to deal with dogs that were used as alarms to warn Vietnamese soldiers about approaching enemies. The gun is referred to as a Hush Puppy. It is primarily used for clandestine operations.

The glasses utilize thermal vision technology, which detects the temperature difference between background and foreground objects. The glasses pick up thermal radiation and do not need a source of illumination. Also built into the glasses is facial recognition software, like a digital camera, but the eyes of the individual can be distinguished as the glasses shade them differently.

Miguel Acacia, Diego Barranca's top hitman, sat next to the pilot and before he or any of his men exited the helicopter, he put his palms out to the pilot, showing all ten fingers, and shook them. This indicated that he planned to be back in ten minutes.

Six men exited the helicopter, led by Miguel. They were dressed in black, paramilitary gear, and each wore a balaclava to cover their face. Only their eyes were visible. They each had a semi-automatic holstered sidearm and a Sig Sauer .40 caliber MPX submachine gun. This gun was short, with a tactical look and could fire ammunition at a rate of 850 rounds per minute.

The men accessed the building through the only roof entrance and swiftly moved down floor after floor until they were just outside the door to the 24th floor. Miguel waited to make sure all the men were ready before they entered the 24th floor.

There was an eerie calm that bothered none of the assassins because they really did not know what to expect when you entered a law firm. They stood for a moment in front of the elevators looking at Nina's reception area. All the doors on the floor were closed. Then Miguel started giving directions.

He pointed to one man and wanted him to go to the far corner of the eastern hallway. He pointed to another man to stay at this end of the eastern hallway, where they stood. He then directed a third to stay at this end of the western hallway. Thereafter, Miguel proceeded cautiously down the western hallway toward Legion's office with the remaining two men.

Billy, Rolf's man at the laptop computer, was watching all of their actions. When they reached Legion's door, their plan was for one of them to turn the handle and open it quickly. Miguel would barge in and start blasting. The third man would be a back-up to Miguel, if necessary.

Miguel raised three fingers on his left hand as he was going to count down for his compatriot to rush the door open. Miguel went to two fingers and as he went to one finger, Billy shut the lights on the entire floor. Pitch, black darkness enveloped it. As he did it, the fire alarm went off. This was unplanned and caused by one of Legion's people pulling the alarm on a lower floor with the belief that it would assist in the evacuation.

The initial noises on the 24th floor were various quick, sharp puffs and one 3-shot burst from a submachine gun. Rolf's men were waiting in the various offices, library, kitchen, and maintenance closet. When the lights went out, they had one second to spring from their covert locations and take a shot.

In the confusion, Miguel could be heard running down the western hallway toward the elevators in total darkness. Rolf was now in the reception area and from his line of site, he could see the thermal image of Miguel, created by the difference in the cold, ambient air and Miguel's warm body.

Rolf's glasses locked on Miguel's face and two small, target-type circles covered his eyes. In one motion, Rolf leveled his gun and pulled the trigger. It was as if he needed no time to sight the gun.

The bullet struck Miguel in his left eye and went deep into his brain. The bullet transferred its energy to Miguel's head, took him off his feet, and straight to the floor. Then Rolf spoke to Billy through his earpiece.

"Let there be light."

The lights came on as the alarm continued to blare.

"All targets acquired?" Rolf asked, speaking to his men through their radio.

He then received a chorus of 'affirmative' and 'roger.'

"Get them on their backs and get the weapons," Rolf told the men. "Tommy, get the body bags. Scott, Greg, let's go get the helicopter. Scott, grab the persuader."

All of Miguel's men were shot in the eye. The purpose of this was to minimize blood splatter and instant incapacitation. The persuader that Rolf referenced was a Resistance Rocket Propelled Grenade Launcher or Resistance RPG. It has a range of 200 feet and fires laser-guided rockets. It is handheld and primarily used to take down helicopter gunships.

Rolf and his two men rode the freight elevator to the roof. Rolf exited the elevator and walked to the driver side of the helicopter. The helicopter had significantly powered down, but your voice had to be extremely loud for any communication.

Rolf did not appear to be a threat and the pilot opened a small window next to him to hear what he was going to say.

"HOW MUCH LONGER ARE YOU GOING TO BE HERE?" Rolf screamed.

The pilot held up five fingers and mouthed the words '5 minutes.'

Rolf nodded in agreement and pointed to the other side of the helipad. One of Rolf's men was holding the Resistance RPG aimed at the pilot while the other man held his 9mm Glock 17 pistol at him.

Rolf gave his men the thumbs up and went back inside to complete his work on the 24th floor.

CHAPTER 30

On the 18th floor, in a luxury suite of the Marriot Marquis Hotel, located within walking distance of the San Diego Convention Center, Cy 'the Guy' Valiant and two girls from a company called S-Court Services spent the last 24 hours in a hedonistic bacchanal.

Cy Valiant was 49 years old, 5 feet 8 inches tall, and weighed 320 pounds. He had thinning blond hair, an enormous gut, and if he walked a few feet, he thought he ran a mile. He had a double chin and red cheeks brought on by high blood pressure.

Cy promised the girls thirty-five hundred dollars each. They were willing to engage in any type of sexual adventure that Cy could envision. He also allowed them to order room service and they were allowed to take anything they wanted from the mini-bar. Cy also provided the cocaine for their partying.

Cy was married with three children and his wife thought he was out of town on business. He told the people in his office not to bother him unless "somebody dies."

It was nearly 11:00 am. He and the two escorts were naked in bed and Cy was still in somewhat of a drug-induced haze. His need to urinate became overpowering and he pushed one of the girls, so she would get up and allow him egress off the bed.

The window shades in the bedroom were closed, but rays of light pierced through, giving Cy some indication that it was no longer nighttime.

While he sat on the toilet relieving himself, there was a knock at the door. He finished and took a hotel bathrobe from the back of the bathroom door and put it on. It barely wrapped his rotund girth and he loosely tied a small portion of the belt.

"Who is it?" he called out as he walked to the door.

"Room service," a voice answered.

Cy did not recall ordering room service lately, but one of the girls may have done so. He unlocked the door and opened it. As the door was opening, a man stepped in from the hallway and punched Cy in the face with his right fist. The blow sent Cy down on his back like a thrown bag of concrete.

The assailant's fist contained brass knuckles and the wallop cut the left side of Cy's face from the corner of his nose to the corner of his mouth.

The man who hit Cy was 28 years old, 5 feet 11 inches tall, totally bald, and 220 pounds of muscle. Near one of his eyes was a tattoo of a tear.

Another man came in wearing a blue windbreaker, 5 feet 9 inches tall, 180 pounds, with long hair, combed back. He had a moustache and an unlit cigarette in his mouth.

After the second man entered, the door closed behind him. The first man stood over Cy and pulled out a semi-automatic Ruger SR 45 handgun and aimed it at Cy's face. This was a .45 caliber gun that was made of alloy steel. The man pulled the hammer back on the gun ready to fire.

One of the naked girls appeared in the bedroom doorway and stepped back, shocked by the events that were occurring.

"Hit the road, girls," the first man told them. "NOW!"

He then turned his attention to Cy.

"Where's the credit card that Jim Roth gave you?"

The blood from Cy's facial cut was beginning to pool on the left side of his head near his ear. He acted like he was going to try to get up.

"Stay down, fat boy!" the first man told him and pushed Cy's shoulder back to the ground with the barrel of the gun. "The next time you're gonna go off the balcony. Tell us where it is?"

"On the couch over there," Cy advised turning his head slightly to the left. "It's in my wallet, in the inside breast pocket."

The first man turned to his accomplice and told him, "Go get it."

The accomplice complied and the two girls appeared from the bedroom disheveled, but ready to leave.

"Get out!" the first man demanded. His voice was deliberate and succinct. Both girls hustled out the door.

The first man once again refocused on Cy.

"Where's the blow?"

He wanted to know where Cy was keeping his cocaine.

"Bathroom."

"Got it," the second man called out as he rummaged Cy's wallet. "Hey, there must be three thousand bucks here."

"Grab it. Then go in the bathroom and get the blow."

"That's my money," Cy asserted.

"Call a cop," the first man declared. "Once you get sober, call Roth. If you pull this kind of shit again, I'm gonna have to come back and visit ya. And next time, I won't be as nice."

The second man emerged from the bathroom with a Ziploc gallon size bag that was half-filled with cocaine. The first man took a step back from Cy and lowered the hammer on his handgun. He holstered his gun behind him and both men left the suite.

The pain in Cy's face was excruciating. He wondered if the previous events really happened, but he knew the nightmare had just begun.

CHAPTER 31

As the afternoon sun continued to wane, Artie Clexx lay on his Murphy bed in his Ditmar Street apartment in Oceanside thinking about the details of his plan. His fingers were interlaced behind his head, like a perpetrator waiting to be handcuffed, and he stared at the ceiling watching the movements of a small spider. If Lisa saw it, she would want it killed, but it didn't bother Artie.

The air in the apartment was heavy and warm from the greenhouse effect of the afternoon sun. An old, oscillating fan moved the warm air back and forth, but gave no relief from the heat. An occasional breeze blew in the window and it reminded Artie of a first sip from a bottle of Coca-Cola.

Artie's cell phone began to play the theme song from *The A-Team* television show, which he used as a ringtone. The Caller ID indicated it was from his friend, Tizoe, his partner in the criminal activity of stealing copper pipe for sale to salvage yards.

"Tizoe, what are ya doin'?"

"Come out front," he responded.

Artie rose from the bed and casually left the apartment. He sauntered down the hallway and out the front door. There, parked in front of the building, was Tizoe leaning against his red, 1995 Ford

F-150 pickup truck. Tizoe was 31 years old, 5 feet 10 inches tall, with an African-American gangbanger look. He wore a doo rag on his head, sunglasses, and five days of beard growth. He also wore a white, muscle t-shirt and black jeans. He was on parole after serving three years in prison for grand theft auto.

As Artie approached him, Tizoe smiled and took out a cigarette.

"I got the stuff you wanted," Tizoe advised and lit the cigarette.

"You got one for me?" Artie inquired, pointing to the cigarette.

Tizoe retrieved the pack and Artie took one. Artie had his own lighter and made sure the cigarette was lit before continuing the conversation.

"Let's see the stuff," Artie told him.

Tizoe jumped into the bed of the truck and unlocked a large toolbox, made of diamond plate sheet metal that ran the width of the truck. Artie also jumped up onto the bed of the truck to watch Tizoe's activity.

The first item he removed was wrapped in a kitchen towel and could be held in one hand. He gave it to Artie. Artie made sure no one was in the general vicinity, then peeled the cloth back to review the contents.

Within the cloth was a Rexio, 6-shot, .38 Special revolver. The gun had a blue finish and a 1.7-inch barrel.

"What's this?" Artie answered with a tinge of disdain.

"What you wanted," Tizoe told him.

"What kinda gun is this?"

"It's a Rexio."

"A Rexio? I never heard of that before."

"It's from Argentina."

"Is it a real gun?"

Tizoe eyed him with a smirk.

"How about I put a bullet in your ass and you tell me. You don't want it, give it back to me."

"No, I'll take it," Artie declared. "What else you got for me?"

Tizoe then removed the top layer of tools, which sat on their own shelf, for access to larger tools situated below them. Wrapped in a larger cloth was some type of rifle or shotgun. Artie knelt down next to Tizoe for a closer look. Tizoe uncovered the weapon.

"Remington 870," Tizoe nonchalantly spoke, "12-gauge, Marine Magnum. Nickel-plated. Water won't bother it. A little over three feet long, 13-inch barrel, easy to maneuver."

"How many shells does it hold?"

"Six. There's five in there."

"All right. I don't plan on killin' anybody," Artie told him.

"That's how every one-eight-seven starts out," Tizoe shared his pearl of wisdom.

A '187' is the California criminal code section referencing homicide.

"Thanks, man," Artie said and jumped out of the truck. He walked over to his van, opened the sliding side-door, and placed the weapons within it. Artie's van had no windows in it except for the driver's window, passenger's window, and the windshield.

Artie returned to Tizoe's truck.

"Here," Tizoe tossed a small object to Artie that he caught with one hand. "A speed loader for the revolver. That's all I got."

The speed loader would allow Artie to quickly reload six bullets into the gun once the original six were fired.

"I'll replace whatever ammo I use," Artie advised. "You working security every day this week?"

"For the next ten days at least."

"It's gonna happen before the end of the week," Artie proudly proclaimed. "I'll let you know."

"You wanna go for a beer?" Tizoe asked.

"Can you spot me? I'm tapped on funds. Lisa gets paid today, so I can pay you back when she comes home."

"Let's go around the corner," and with that, the weapons for Artie's score were now in place.

CHAPTER 32

At the Palace of Barranca, Diego Barranca and Jim Roth were enjoying some afternoon target practice at the on-site shooting range. Both men wore safety glasses and before entering an area comprised of six shooting lanes, Diego and Jim entered a room, whose door resembled a bank vault door.

"This is where we keep the Palace weapons," Diego advised. The room was meticulously clean and there was not a weapon in site. Diego touched one part of the wall and a non-descript biometric pad for his entire hand, began to move the walls. There was now a room on each side of them that flooded with light as the walls moved.

In one room, was a ten thousand square foot area of weapons. There were row after row of tactical submachine guns, shotguns, sniper rifles, and pistols. At one end of the room, there was a trailer, from a tractor trailer, loaded with ammunition.

"Over five thousand weapons. Enough to equip an army. In the caged room," Diego pointed to a smaller room in a far corner with walls of heavy chain link, "is the explosives. If it's out there," he pointed toward the desert, "then it's in here." He allowed Jim a moment to take it all in. "If anybody wants to try to kill me, I say, 'try.' I got scud missiles out there, they can't even get close."

Jim surveyed the room and simply stated, "Very nice, Diego."

"Let me show you something," he told Jim as he walked over to a row of non-military weapons and picked up a shotgun off the rack. "Look at this," he said as he handed the gun over to Jim. "You know what that is?"

"It looks like a very nice shotgun."

"It's a Holland and Holland. Called a Royal over-and-under. Twenty gauge. The stock is made of walnut. You see my initials there?" Diego pointed to golden letters D and B engraved in the side of the gun within an exquisite, detailed pattern in the metal. "It's gold inlay. This gun cost me $127 thousand."

"You are a man of fine taste, Diego."

Jim's comment brought a smile to his face.

"Let's shoot it," Diego announced.

As they proceeded to the area where the shooting range was located, one of Diego's servants advanced toward them at a brisk clip.

"Excuse me, sir," the servant called out. "You have a high priority e-mail from Miguel Acacia that just arrived."

Miguel Acacia was Diego's best hitman who led a team of six men to the offices of Legion and Associates in a failed attempt to kill Roger Legion and his entire law firm.

"I'll take it in my office," he advised and handed him the shotgun.

Both Diego and Jim moved at a speedy gait down several hallways back to Diego's office. When they arrived at the office, Diego pulled up his e-mails and on the wall behind him was a 52-

inch video monitor that would allow Jim, from his seat in front of the desk to also see the e-mail.

They waited for a moment as the e-mail loaded and when it finished, there was a simple line on the e-mail that said:

CLICK HERE FOR SLIDESHOW

Diego clicked it and a series of photos appeared for ten seconds each before they seemed to dissolve. The first five photos were the faces of the five members of the hit squad, each shown with one of their eyes blown out. The sixth photo was of Miguel Acacia, also with his left eye missing. The seventh photo was a picture of six body bags loaded into their helicopter. The eighth photo showed the helicopter in flames heading into the Pacific Ocean. The final photo was of Roger Legion, smiling with other people in front of the America's Finest City Building.

Rolf Adler, the man sent by Jimmy Flowers to assist Roger on the day of the assassination attempt, asked Roger to obtain a photo of himself that day. The purpose was to inform Diego that his men had failed.

After Roger's picture dissolved, Diego continued to stare at the blank screen. Jim wondered what sort of primordial reaction Diego may have to these events.

Diego looked down from the screen and began to rub his forehead. He then looked up and locked eyes with Jim. In a calm, calculated voice, he uttered three words.

"Call the Christophers."

CHAPTER 33

UTICA, NEW YORK

Utica, New York was once a city that dreamed of becoming a metropolis. Located along the Erie Canal, the city was ideal for industrial development. During the late 1800s, local textile mills became a magnet for employment and growth in the city. By the middle of the next century, all the textile mills moved south, and nothing replaced them except urban decay.

Utica was also the victim of political corruption that commenced in the 1940s when the political scene began to be controlled by the Italian community and it reached its zenith in 1957, when *Look* magazine dubbed it "Sin City" for its extensive political corruption and extensive organized crime influence.

Since the mid-1950s, population continued to dwindle, going from a high of approximately 101,000 in 1950 to approx.-imately 62,000 in 2012.

The only event that slightly stemmed the tide of population loss was the infusion of immigrants from Bosnia attempting to escape their war-torn nation. Utica welcomed the immigrants and earned the title of "Second Chance City."

As with any immigrant population, there are always those members that want the easy life quick and they try to find it through a criminal enterprise.

The Christophers were a team of three brothers who were mercenaries or "mercs." The primary service they provided, for which they had obtained worldwide notoriety in the criminal world, was assassination.

The leader of the group was Marc Christopher. The given name of his family was DeCristoforo, before it was Americanized. He was taken from a life of juvenile delinquency and brought to Parma, Italy, where he was taught old-school methods of murder at the hands of a grand master in the art of the kill named Fiero DeMasi. Marc handled all the logistics for the team. He planned the hits and his brothers helped him carry them out.

The middle brother, John, earned a Bachelor of Science degree in both electrical engineering and computer science from Rensselaer Polytechnic Institute in Troy, New York. John handled all the technical aspects of an operation.

The youngest brother was Tom. Their parents were both dead shortly after his birth, so both Marc and John were protective of him. Marc had him learn all aspects of weaponry. Weapons were his responsibility for a job.

At approximately 8:40 am on this Wednesday morning, Marc Christopher emerged from Our Lady of Lourdes Catholic Church in Utica, New York, located on Genesee Street, with a smile on his face after thanking the priest for a fine homily.

Marc was 35 years old, 6 feet tall, 185 pounds, with blue eyes and close-cropped black hair. He wore a Canali suit made of lightweight wool that was dusty gray with delicate pinstripes. His shirt was light blue in color and his tie was a muted red and made of fine, Italian silk. He wore Santoni boots, which were made from the buttocks of a horse and required six months to cure the leather for essential suppleness.

Marc's friendly smile gave off a look of innocence and he attended mass daily regardless of what city he was in.

In front of the Church was a half circle driveway for drop-off and pick-up of congregants. Waiting for Marc, in a late model Buick LaCrosse was his brother, John. John was 33 years old, 5 feet 10 inches tall, 170 pounds, with brown eyes, and a salt and pepper goatee. His hair was recently shaved off and light stubble covered the top of his head. John wore jeans and a black hooded sweatshirt that read "Utica Club" on it.

Once Marc was in the car, it took off north on Genesee Street and the conversation began.

"Where's Tom?" Marc asked.

"He's on top of the building. We got everything up there. Nobody bothered us. He's all set."

"No problem with neighborhood people?"

"It's all moolies over there. They're not up yet."

John was indicating that the neighborhood, where their work was to take place, was primarily African-American.

"Did you check the communication stuff and all the frequencies?"

"Tom and I did a sound check on everything."

"Is this the car I'm gonna drive?"

"Here's the keys," John told him and handed him a duplicate set of the keys.

"What does he have in the trunk for me?"

"An M-4. It's got one clip in it, 30 rounds. I also brought a barrel clip, if you want 150 rounds."

The weapon John referred to was a Colt M-4 carbine, assault rifle. This submachine gun is primarily used by U.S. military forces and fires a 5.56 caliber cartridge. The rate of fire for this gun varies from 700 to 950 bullets per minute.

"Where's the tablet?" Marc asked referring to a computer tablet.

"It's in the back seat."

"Is your vehicle in place?" Marc wondered.

"Yeah. It's on the street behind the building. I can watch that activity without the need for cameras. When you're done, come and pick me up."

"Where are you gonna park this car?"

"Up the street, a block or two."

"Just make sure it doesn't get towed."

"How long are you going to be in there?" John wondered.

"Just a few minutes."

"Do you think we shoulda waited till they moved this guy?"

"No," Marc answered, slightly aggravated with the question. "They could arraign him right in the courthouse next door. Plus, if they move him, they'll have extra security and a decoy. The timetable is too tight for anything else. My way is the only way."

John drove north on Genesee Street and took a left hand turn onto Lafayette Street. He maneuvered several one-way streets and slowly passed in front of the Utica Police Station to the south and the Utica Memorial Auditorium to the north.

The Utica Police Station was Marc's destination. John stopped the car in front of the front doors to the building. Marc placed an earpiece in his ear that appeared to be an earbud for a cell phone. In reality, it was a transmission device for walkie-talkie communication.

"Tom, you ready?"

"All set," he answered.

Marc nodded to John and stepped out of the vehicle with the computer tablet. From the car, he walked directly to the front doors of the police station.

CHAPTER 34

Roger Legion was proceeding with his day as if nothing unusual had happened the day before. The only sign of anything unusual were three bullet holes in the northern hallway ceiling. These were caused by a 3-shot submachine gun burst by one of Miguel Acacia's men before he was put down.

Roger was reviewing pre-bills, which are essentially the law firm's billings prior to a final draft that goes to the insurance company. For the most part, the lawyers were conscious of what was required and what they could and could not get away with in the billing arena. Roger always reviewed them because he wanted no surprises after the fact.

Before he finished the first sheet of the first bill, his office phone came to life.

"Yes," he inquired.

"Cyrus Valiant is on line 2," Nina responded.

"Put him through," Roger told her and leaned back in his chair. The phone rang again and he pushed a button to answer it.

"Hello, Cy," Roger uttered in a much less strident voice than he would prefer.

"Listen, Roger, I wanted to do our 'meet and confer' telephonically. I had a little accident; I fell at the house. I had to get stitches, so I'm all black and blue."

"That's too bad, Cy," Roger mentioned as he looked at his electronic calendar. "We were scheduled to do it at 2:30. Do you want to do it now?"

"Might as well get it over with," Cy's voice echoed stern indignation.

"Let me get John in here," Roger advised and placed Cy's call on hold. Roger dialed John Hamishaw's office, but there was no answer. He then called Nina.

"Yes, Mr. Legion."

"Is Mr. Hamishaw here?"

"I think he's in with Mr. Larkin."

Her comment caused Roger to pause.

"Please find him and tell him to come to my office immediately. Thank you."

Roger looked at the phone and in particular, the blinking light on the line being held by Cy the Guy. He wondered if Cy really was involved in an accident and, if so, what the real story was.

John Hamishaw ran to Legion's office, just as Roger would expect.

"What's going on?" John quizzed and walked directly to one of Roger's chairs.

"Cy Valiant's on the phone. He wants to do the 'meet and confer' telephonically – now."

"All right," John replied in a tone of surrender. "Do we need the file?"

"I don't." Roger's voice was definite. His steel-blue eyes penetrated John to the point where it was making him uncomfortable.

"Let's go," John pressed with a smile, looking at the phone, unable to lock eyes with Roger.

Roger pushed a blinking button on his phone.

"Cy, John's here now," Roger directed.

"Hi, John," Cy said.

"Hello, Cy."

"Roger, the bottom line here is that I am not going to accept state audits in place of forensic testing on Scripticon's computer system."

"Let me ask you this, Cy:" Roger prepared to pose his inquiry, "How do you know that we are going to provide you with state audits in response to your discovery demand?"

"I thought you said something about it," Cy sheepishly answered.

"I did not. So, I would like an answer to my question: How do you know that we are going to provide you with state audits in response to your discovery demand?"

Roger looked at John waiting to hear Cy's answer.

"Look, it makes logical sense. You think that because it comes from the state, it has some type of persuasive value. It does not."

"Like having a medical degree that's never used. But, apparently, going through the motions gives you the voice of God."

Roger's words stopped Cy in his tracks.

"Hey, Roger, that's a low blow. I got you guys on the ropes and that's why you're attacking me."

"Cy, I'm pointing out a fact. Have you even received our supplemental response to your discovery request?"

"I think I saw it."

John Hamishaw shook his head giving a negative response.

"No, you haven't, because we haven't sent it. Now, why don't you wait for the response, and if you don't like it, we can go through this exercise again." Roger's voice telegraphed that his interest in dealing with Cy 'the Guy' was waning.

"If you try to answer my discovery demand with state audits, I am going to bring a Motion to Compel and request sanctions against you for deliberately and intentionally failing to answer."

"Cy, I hate to tell you, but you don't know what you're talking about."

John then decided to speak up.

"Wait, wait, wait," John interjected, trying to bring the rhetoric down to a visceral level. "Why don't I see if I can get a copy of the source code. Would that do the trick, Cy?"

A source code is a collection of computer instructions that can be interpreted using human readable text.

Roger looked at John as if John had lost his mind.

"Maybe it will," Cy suggested, "but I have to see it first."

"NO!" Roger's voice echoed in the room like a lion's roar.

"First of all, he never asked for it," Roger's voice was fast and final. "And second, this lawsuit deals with alleged accounting inaccuracies caused by human error. We're not going to blow it up to put the operating system on trial."

"Oh, now you're a computer expert! I'm going to hold a press conference and . . ."

"We're done here," Roger cut him off and disconnected the call. His hardened gaze turned to John.

"What is wrong with you?" Roger demanded an answer.

"I was trying to come up with a solution that everybody could live with," John implicitly pleaded.

"Bullshit! That's malpractice. You can lose your license for that kinda shit."

"Listen, Larry suggested it. I just thought it was a good suggestion."

"Oh, Larry suggested it," Roger mimicked him, not being surprised at all. "Is he running this file or are you?"

John stood and looked at Legion. He wanted to display total disgust with him, but he feared his reaction.

"I'm running it now," Roger proclaimed. "This is what I'm telling you to do. Go down to the courthouse *ex parte* and get a gag order for this case. Talk to Marty Hannah to get a copy of an order. Don't come back without it." Roger's words were final. But he added one more comment. "John, negligence is one thing; sabotage is another."

An *ex parte* hearing allows one side in a litigated case to obtain immediate relief without the other party present. The other party would have a chance to respond at a later time.

Marty Hannah was another attorney at the firm who specialized in writing for both common and unique situations.

"Roger, you are over-reacting," John spoke in a slow, calm, deliberate voice.

"Where were you yesterday afternoon?"

Roger's change of subject caught John off guard.

"I was," he thought for moment, "here."

"No, you weren't. We all went home early yesterday. You weren't here."

As Roger finished his sentence, the phone rang. While he continued to gaze at John, he pushed the intercom button.

"Yes," he spoke, not breaking his gaze.

"Glenn Edgarian is on line 4," Nina advised.

"Put him through," Roger told her. Then, he simply said to John, "Go."

Roger watched John Hamishaw exit the room and he knew that he had a problem.

CHAPTER 35

The Utica Police Department Headquarters, located on Oriskany Street West, was a relic in the city that had stood the test of time. Built nearly eighty years earlier, its basic brick and concrete construction, gave it the appearance of a small English castle or turn of the century prison that was built throughout the eastern United States during that time period.

Connected to the police department was a City Courthouse, primarily used for misdemeanor and non-felony types of criminal cases.

Across the street from the police station was the Utica Memorial Auditorium. Built in 1959, this was a large, circular, multi-use arena, built primarily for sporting events and concerts. In 1977, a portion of the movie, *Slapshot*, with Paul Newman, was filmed there. It was one of the first arenas in the country built without an obstructed view.

Surrounding both the police station and the auditorium were parking lots to handle activity at both locations.

Marc Christopher entered the police headquarters through the front doors and surveyed the reception area. It appeared to be from the 1950s with weathered oak decorum and thick glass on the windows. An oak counter that was approximately 4 feet high with glass above that sat along the right wall when you entered. Opposite that was a large corkboard containing both FBI and local "most wanted" criminals. Other than those items, the reception area was barren.

The sergeant-on-duty was Addie Pane. She was 48 years old and a 24-year veteran of the force. She had a slight frame and was a veteran of martial arts. Those who knew her would tell you that she could take a 250 pound man down to the floor before he knew what had hit him.

Marc approached the counter, standing behind one other gentleman. As he stood there, he listened to the conversation between Addie and two other officers.

"Hey, Hanley," Addie spoke up to get his attention. "You're a good Irish boy, right?"

Brian Hanley was a red-headed officer, still in his probationary period. He was slender with freckles.

"That's what me mother tells me," he answered her in a forced Irish brogue.

"Me and Zenzillo have a bet. We want you to settle it," she told him looking back to Officer Zenzillo, who nodded in agreement.

Guillermo or "Bill" Zenzillo was seated at a desk, reviewing the text of 9-1-1 calls as they came in. He was part of the Support Division and was able to re-direct police assets where needed. He was 245 pounds with white hair.

"Who's got the best cannoli? The Florentine or Caruso's?" Addie posed her inquiry to Hanley then crossed her arms awaiting an answer.

Hanley looked at her with slight concern and then glanced to Zenzillo.

"I think they're both good. I like 'em both."

"Congratulations," Addie replied with a smile. "That's the right answer. See, if you got that wrong, we'd have to take you out back and shoot ya. Anybody who can't answer that question, doesn't belong in this town or this department."

As Addie finished her speech, she noticed Marc at the window. His sophisticated clothing made him stand out from the usual clientele the officers were used to seeing.

"Can I help you?" Addie asked.

"I'm here to see Viktor Paravac. I'm with the public defender's office. I'm his lawyer."

Addie had a look of confusion on her face. She then went to a computer screen and quickly perused the e-mail captions that were received that morning.

"Well," Addie conveyed, "you know he's in protective custody. We're supposed to be given 24-hour notice for any visits."

"I believe my office did give it. I'm sorry if there has been a miscommunication." Marc's alluring charm made Addie want to help him.

"Let me call your office, just to make sure. May I get your name?"

"Daniel Winters. Do you need the number?"

"No. I've got it," she told him.

Next to her telephone was a list of frequently called numbers and she dialed the phone number for the Oneida County Public Defender's Office.

Inside a twelve-foot long Penske rental box truck, John Christopher sat at a card table with two laptop computers and a joystick. He also had two cellular telephones on the table.

When Addie started to hear the ringtone on her phone, one of John's cell phones began to ring. John had hacked the Public Defender's phone system and forwarded their calls to his phone.

"Public Defender's Office," John answered.

"Reggie O'Meara, please."

"Reggie's not in, may I help you?"

"This is Sergeant Addie Pane of the UPD. Do you know if you may have sent someone for an interview with a Viktor Paravac? He's high priority and we have him in protective custody."

"Yeah, we sent Danny Winters. He's helping us with overflow. Is there a problem?"

"No. We just didn't have a record of it."

"Really? I'm positive one of the secretaries called over there for it yesterday."

"No problem," Addie answered. "We got it under control."

She ended the call and looked to Marc. She pointed to a corner of the room where an unmanned metal detector, similar to one found in an airport was located.

"Hanley, can you check him through the detector and I'll bring the prisoner to an attorney conference room."

Addie disappeared through a door and Hanley walked over to the machine.

"Please remove any metal. Put it in the bin."

Marc placed some coins, his wallet, cell phone, and an ear bud, which appeared to be used for the phone into a small, plastic dish. He handed his computer tablet to the officer.

"Do I need to take off my belt?" Marc wondered.

"Nah, I'll pass the wand over it."

Hanley passed the metal-detecting wand over Marc's belt buckle. Marc then walked through the metal detector and a slight beep went off.

"You're okay," Hanley told him and allowed him to pick up his belongings. "She'll be out to get you shortly."

"Hey," Marc wanted to get his attention before he returned to the counter, "Is there a men's room around here?"

"Down the hall on the right."

"Thanks."

Marc moved quickly to the men's rest room and entered one of the stalls. The computer tablet that he brought with him was approximately one-quarter of an inch thick. He slid the back panel and in the battery compartment, held within a formed shape was a push knife or fist knife.

A push knife is a short-bladed dagger with a "T" handle, which is designed to be grasped with the blade protruding between a person's second and third finger. The blade on this push knife was 3.25 inches long and serrated on one side.

Marc removed the knife from its stored position and lightly touched the blade to feel a film of moisture on it. He then smelled it. It was the smell he sought. The smell of garlic.

CHAPTER 36

Roger Legion's anger continued to percolate. He never feared an adversary because he was always able to assess their ability, then implement the necessary tactics to defeat it. Now, he may be the victim of an enemy from within. A student from the school of Roger Legion.

He picked up the phone receiver and pushed a button on the phone.

"Glenn, talk to me," Roger's voice was pumped and enthusiastic.

"I've got intel for you," Glenn Edgarian, Roger's premier private investigator, replied. "Do you want me to come over or do it over the phone?"

"Are you available for lunch?" Roger inquired.

"Yeah."

"What's that place, we went to before, up by you?"

"*El Callejon.*"

"Is it the Encinitas Boulevard exit?"

"Yeah. It's right near the corner of Encinitas Boulevard and the 101," Glenn told him.

The Mexican restaurant was located on Highway 101, a major thoroughfare that ran along a large portion of the coast in California.

"All right. How's 12:30?" Roger asked.

"I'll see you then," Glenn advised.

"Take care," Roger told him and ended the call.

Roger's interaction with John Hamishaw still troubled him. He stood from his chair and marched out of his office, first heading down the northern hallway, then to the eastern hallway. The first thing he saw was John Hamishaw departing Larry Larkin's office.

John saw Roger and began the conversation before Roger was even close to him.

"I'm waiting for the 23rd floor to get me the pleadings. They just have to put the heading on it. Marty also gave me some points and authorities."

John was referring to the documents required for his attempt to obtain a gag order on Cy 'the Guy' Valiant.

"You won't need a points and authority. Save it for the hearing." Roger's voice was petulant.

A 'points and authority' memo generally provides the court with case law that supports the position taken in favor of the motion.

"Listen," John advised in an austere tone. "You asked me where I was yesterday. I was with Larry. We were having drinks."

"Where?" Roger quizzed.

"Roger," John was becoming bolder, "I'll tell ya, but I really don't think it's any of your business."

"If you were on the clock for this place, then it's my business." Roger's voice was strident and definite.

"Hennessey's, down on Fourth," John replied in disgust and made a hasty retreat away from Legion directly to the elevator.

Roger then looked inside Larry Larkin's office and knew that Larry had overheard the entire conversation.

"You need anything?" Larry wondered.

Roger shook his head in a negative manner as Larry walked over to him, all while Roger's eyes were locked on him.

"I spoke to Jim Roth," Larry told him enthusiastically, "and they're still interested. He's going to send me a summary of all the claims they had for the past calendar year. This way we can see the type of claims they're dealing with."

Roger knew that Realizar Health, through their representative, Jim Roth, had some ulterior motive and he wanted to find out what it was.

"See if he'll go $10 million on the attorney fees. If he says 'yes,' let's have another meeting."

Larry was slightly nonplussed by his comment, but now there was hope to wrangle a huge account.

"Hey, the most they can say is 'no.' Right?"

Roger broke his gaze and returned to his office. Before he sat down, he retrieved the business card of Wesley Avery, the general counsel for Scripticon, who met with Roger and John Hamishaw, along with Jimmy Flowers. Wes' phone number was written on the back of the card.

Roger dialed the cell number and Wes answered the phone.

"Hello."

"Wes, it's Roger Legion. How are you?"

"Good, Roger. How you doing?"

"I'm fine. I just have a couple of quick questions. Has anyone made any inquiries to you regarding the source code for your operation?"

"No. In fact, I know nothing about that. Anything regarding the source code would have to come directly from Mr. Fiorito," Wes told him.

"My concern is that someone may call saying they are from my firm. Any requests should come directly from me," Roger informed him.

"Mr. Fiorito would prefer that," Wes revealed.

"I've got another question: when I was with Mr. Fiorito, he said he had a street name of "Jimmy Flowers." Have you ever shared that name with anybody?"

Roger awaited the answer.

"Roger, I am strictly prohibited from sharing that information with anyone. I would be fired if I told that to anyone."

"I just want to know if you told it to anyone over here, at my place?"

"No." Wes' answer was definite.

"All right. Thanks a lot, Wes. If you need anything, call me."

With that, Roger ended the call. He now knew that John Hamishaw lied to him. There was a cancer growing at Legion and Associates and Roger Legion needed to surgically remove it. It was a betrayal that would not be tolerated. He needed a little more information before the snare could be fully baited.

CHAPTER 37

Sergeant Addie Pane escorted Marc Christopher to an attorney conference room located on the first floor near the back of the building. The room reflected the age of the building. The walls were yellow from paint and time. The floor was concrete and painted gray. In the center of the room was a stainless steel table bolted to the floor. On two sides of the table were round stools, like those in a soda fountain shop, also bolted to the floor.

Seated at the table was Viktor Paravac. He was 34 years old, 5 feet 9 inches tall, and weighed 160 pounds. He had black, bushy hair, significant facial hair, and a scar that ran along the right side of his nose.

Viktor had been arrested during a prostitution sweep at a party in a rather upscale home on Proctor Boulevard, one of Utica's more affluent neighborhoods. Viktor was supposed to be providing protection to the girls, but he was caught indulging in some pleasures with them.

Viktor worked for a man named Demir Mirko, who was another Bosnian national and also ran a methamphetamine ring. Viktor could also directly link Demir to a series of murders carried out by Demir. As soon as Viktor was arrested, the Oneida County

District Attorney began discussing a plea deal. When Viktor was initially jailed, an attempt was made on his life in the jail cafeteria. After that, he was deemed "high priority" and placed in protective custody at the police headquarters until the legal maneuvering involving Demir was concluded.

While Viktor sat at the table, with his left hand in a handcuff and the other end of the handcuffs connected to a steel ring soldered to the table, he continually tapped his fingers on the table in a nervous fashion, as he stared with a blank, vacant look.

"I need your cell phone," the Sergeant told Marc. "You can pick it up on the way out. Just come and get one of us when you're done."

Marc smiled and handed Addie his cell phone. As she was leaving, Viktor spoke up and Addie glanced in his direction.

"Sergeant," he spoke with a thick, Bosnian accent. "You know what I hate about America? Everything."

Addie then turned to Marc.

"Have a good time," she advised and left the room.

Viktor looked at Marc up and down.

"Who you?" Again, Viktor's command of the English language was deficient.

Marc reached into his pocket and retrieved the ear bud that appeared to be for a cellular phone. In fact, it was used for closed frequency walkie-talkie communication with his brothers.

"John, I'm in," Marc uttered nonchalantly, then turned his attention to Viktor.

"*Dobro jutro*, (Good Morning)," Marc told him in Bosnian.

"*Govorite li bosanski?* (Do you speak Bosnian?)" Viktor asked in amazement.

"*Nema vatre bez dima,* (Everything happens for a reason,)" Marc relayed to him in a cold, calm voice.

Viktor started to become nervous.

"*Ne razumijem,* (I don't understand,)" Viktor pleaded.

As he uttered the sentence, two explosions were heard somewhere in the distance, outside of the building. John had blown two transformers that energized the power grid under the police station and covered an area of nine square blocks in the vicinity. The power and lights in the building went out and an emergency lighting system went on to provide direction for exiting the building.

As soon as the lights shut off, Marc took Viktor's right hand and pinned it down. In the same motion, he pulled the push knife from his belt, behind his back, and rammed it nearly two inches into Viktor's carotid artery and twisted it to give the wound at least a one inch circular opening. Marc could see from the faint hallway light that blood was gushing out of Viktor. As he was plunging the knife into Viktor, Viktor tried to scream, but one second after stabbing him in the neck, Marc pulled the knife out and slashed his throat to silence him.

Marc held his arm down for a few seconds as blood hemorrhaged from Viktor. He let go of it and looked at his clothes to make sure no blood was on them.

Marc did not worry whether or not Viktor was dead. One of the methods of death he was taught was to cover blades and bullets with garlic. If the wound did not kill the victim, they would eventually die from blood poisoning.

Marc then placed his thumb on Viktor's forehead and made the Sign of the Cross, saying, "Remember man that thou art dust and unto dust thou shall return."

As Viktor twitched, Marc spoke on the walkie-talkie.

"Tom, I'm done. Make it rain."

Tom was positioned on the roof of the Utica Memorial Auditorium, situated across the street from the police station. He spent a vast portion of the night before bringing weapons onto the roof of the auditorium using a scissor lift.

Tom was 29 years old, 5 feet 9 inches tall, 185 pounds, with long, blond hair, parted in the middle. He wore jeans, a black t-shirt, and a jean jacket. He had Marc's look of innocence, but not his charm.

Tom walked to the edge of the round building closest to the front doors of the police station, carrying an FGM-148 Javelin missile launcher. This is a man-made, disposable, anti-tank missile launcher. It looked like a green, 3-foot long, plastic tube with a sighting monitor.

He placed it on his shoulder, aimed it at the front doors of the police station, and fired. The missile ejected from its launcher and the tandem warhead sailed directly into the front doors of the building.

As the missile hit, it ripped open the front of the building. A fiery explosion enveloped it from the interior of the building to the street level. The station shook in the darkness and thoughts of a terrorist attack immediately filled the minds of all inside, except Marc Christopher.

Everything in the reception area, including the three police officers, were destroyed. The concussive force of the blast destroyed a portion of the floor of the second story, which was now open to the outside street. Anything that provided an ignition source was burning. The building looked like an Afghanistan war zone.

Marc exited the attorney conference room and made his way casually over the rubble and out of the building. In the distance, he could hear sirens, so he knew that either police or firemen were on their way. When he reached the street, he looked at the top of the Auditorium and Tom nodded to him. Now, if Tom would get off the roof of the Auditorium quickly, and get to Marc's car, they would be done.

Marc walked directly to the car that John had waiting for him and started it. In the car's rear-view mirror, he could see flames coming from the front of the building.

"John, what's goin' on?" Marc asked with urgency.

"They're calling back all units not at an active crime scene. Wait," John hesitated for a moment, "the call just went out to the Troopers."

Marc was concerned regarding the involvement of the New York State Troopers. He knew they had helicopters and this would give them air superiority over the Christophers.

"TOM, WE GOTTA GO NOW!" Marc blasted.

Tom had one more weapon to put in place. The weapon was an M134 Minigun. This was a six-barreled machine gun, with rotating barrels like a Gatling gun, and was powered by an electric motor. It fires 7.62mm ammunition through a rotary breech at a rate of 2,000 to 6,000 rounds per minute.

The 85-pound gun sat on a tripod and Tom wheeled it to the edge of the building and locked the wheels in place to minimize movement from vibration. He then turned on a GoPro camera that was mounted on a sighting system. Tom started the motor and prepared to dismount the roof.

John Christopher moved from the box of the truck and returned to the driver's seat. From his laptop computer, he was now able to control the Minigun. The GoPro camera allowed him to have the same line of site as the gun and a handmade swivel system allowed a 120-degree range from one side to the other for the gun to fire.

Police cars began to converge on the police station and they initially moved to create a perimeter. Tom sprinted to the scissor lift and started to descend, when a police car coming along the back side of the Auditorium on Whitesboro Street spotted Tom.

He ran across some grass to the sidewalk of Charles Street, which was on the east side of the Auditorium. He could see Marc's car straight ahead.

In front of Marc, at the next street crossing, police cars were stopped to direct traffic and were holding it for an approaching fire truck.

Marc saw the police car about to stop Tom. He popped open the trunk, moved quickly to get out of the car, and grabbed the M4 rifle that was in the trunk.

As he was moving, he called out to John, "Do it."

Marc heard one of the officers scream "Freeze" to Tom and Marc opened fire on the police car. At the same time, John brought the Minigun to life as it strafed the police cars and anything else on the road or sidewalk. Bullets mercilessly rained down on the building, cars, and people.

Marc's first shot took down one of the officers while the other ran behind the patrol car to take cover. At the same time, officers in front of Marc started firing at him, so he would alternate his firing at a 90-degree angle between the cars in front of his car and the car that had tried to stop Tom.

It was as if a war zone had erupted. A cacophony of deadly ammunition pulverized the air. Bullets were ricocheting and first responders were forced to pull back as holes were being blasted into their cars and windshields were shattering and popping along with glass from the buildings.

Tom finally reached Marc's car. Marc spoke as he continued to fire at the officers.

"TOM, THERE'S A GRENADE IN THE TRUNK OF THE CAR. LOB IT AT THESE CARS," Marc yelled over the deafening roar of bullets filling the air and pointed to the two police cars directly ahead of them, approximately 1.5 blocks.

Tom followed Marc's command and a frag grenade exploded just as it reached the cars. Three policemen ran for cover as one of the cars erupted into a fireball.

Marc and Tom alighted Marc's car and took off at high speed. Several blocks away, they met up with John and had a switch car waiting. Before leaving, they torched John's truck and Marc's car.

They left Utica, listening to the police communications and national radio coverage of their work event. Their destination was the Syracuse Airport.

CHAPTER 38

El Callejon Mexican Restaurant in Encinitas, California is situated on Highway 101, with the ocean within sight. It is located approximately twenty-five miles from downtown San Diego. It provides patio dining with good food that most consider both healthy and delicious.

The air around the restaurant was filled with mariachi music and the occasional sound of an Amtrak train and horn. The restaurant was located on the same block as a commuter train stop. When trains passed, their sound was so powerful, it would drown out all conversations and music.

Glenn Edgarian saw Roger Legion pull into the parking lot and he waited for him by the door. Glenn was 57 years old, 6 feet 2 inches tall, 205 pounds, with a lean, muscular build. He wore business casual attire and his hair was short, feathered back with just a tinge of gray. He had a warm, inviting smile and possessed a keen ability to extract information without threats or intimidation. Not that he would ever engage in that type of activity. In a crowd, he would be picked out as a protector, not a threat. He had proven his mettle many times before, particularly with assignments from Roger Legion.

"Glenn, how ya doin'?" Roger asked before he reached him. They met with a handshake.

"It's a little slow, but I'm paying the bills."

They walked into the patio area and walls were painted bright colors with images of Mexican life. Even the chairs were painted a variety of colors.

They selected a table that was under a partial awning to minimize the sun in their eyes as they spoke. They were greeted by a tall waiter, head shaved, and a moustache, so thick and bushy, you might think it was fake.

"*Hola* (Hello), Sebastián," Glenn smiled as he addressed the waiter.

"Just the two of you?" Sebastián inquired with a thick accent, not Mexican, but from Spain.

Both Glenn and Roger nodded their heads in acknowledgement.

"What would you like to drink?"

"Water with some lemon," Glenn advised.

"Same," Roger told him.

Sebastián moved away from them quickly to obtain other drink orders from other patrons.

"You come here often?" Roger wondered.

"All the time. It's close to my office. Food's good. And the prices are decent. So, what's been going on down at your place?" Glenn queried.

"It's been a wild week and I've got some big headaches."

"Well, let me give you a little back story on your friend, Cy the Guy."

Roger rested his forearms on the table and clasped his hands. His focus on Glenn was laser precise.

"You know his office is down in a shopping center in Chula Vista?" Glenn began. "I found out he was tappin' a young, Filipino girl from a nail salon down there and he knocks her up. He convinces her to get an abortion. They go to a couple of appointments and then the date is set. Cy takes her up there on the day the abortion is supposed to take place and she is never seen again. Cy told everybody that she was so upset about the abortion that she never went through with it and she went back to the Philippines."

"Do you know the name of the abortion clinic?" Roger wondered.

"Uh," Glenn had to think for a moment, "Realizar."

Roger found Glenn's answer to be more than a coincidence. Jim Roth, the risk manager of Realizar Healthcare was in his office the week before, nearly bribing him to take his work.

"What else?" Roger quizzed.

Before Glenn was able to respond, Sebastián returned with the drinks, a basket of tortilla chips, and salsa fresca.

"You guys ready?" Sebastián asked.

"Chicken tacos," Glenn responded with a smile and without thought."

"Make it two," Roger echoed.

Sebastián dashed to the kitchen and Glenn continued his oral report.

"Shortly after this girl disappears, Cy's got cash. I found out that his mortgage was paid off, directly to the mortgage company, by a bank in Antigua. I also find out he bought a Bentley, and the money for that came directly from a bank in Belize. Cy also likes hookers with big bolt-ons," as Glenn said the last word, he placed both of his hands in front of his chest like he was palming two basketballs. "I saw one of the transaction slips. He's using a credit card from Realizar Healthcare."

"Things are a lot clearer to me now," Roger said, still assessing the information.

"I've got some anecdotal information that Realizar Health is a front for the Barranca Drug Cartel down in Sonora. This is just conjecture, but Cy must have something they want. I think they killed the girl and now they're funding him. Does this fit in with the case you've got going with him?"

"Unfortunately," Roger pointed out.

"You need me to dig deeper?" Glenn questioned.

Roger was pensive and reflective.

"You know what I would like?" Roger conveyed. "You know Hennessey's, down on Fourth?"

"I know the bartender and everybody who works there."

Roger expected nothing less from Glenn Edgarian.

"John Hamishaw and Larry Larkin said they were having drinks there, yesterday afternoon, around 3:30. See if you can verify that. Also, see what you can find out about this guy named Jim Roth. He is supposed to be the risk manager at Realizar Health."

"R-o-t-h?"

"That's it."

"Any special instructions?"

"The usual. Only deal with me," Roger warned. "If any of the other attorneys call you regarding Cy 'the Guy,' let me know right away."

"Done," Glenn assured.

Sebastián reappeared at the table and set their meals before them.

CHAPTER 39

On this Thursday, Artie Clexx decided that he was ready. The only thing he needed were zip ties and his friend, Tizoe said that he would provide them. The plan was for Artie and Lisa to wait in the parking lot of St. Elizabeth Seton Church and grab Valerie Legion before the mass began. Then, they would take her to an abandoned parts warehouse, where Tizoe was the security guard.

Lisa Natasi sat in her bathroom weeping.

"What's wrong?" Artie asked wondering how this would impact the job.

"He won't let me talk to him," Lisa wailed through tears and tissues.

"Who?" Artie wondered.

"My ex-husband, Asshole! He won't let me talk to Chris."

Chris was her five-year-old son, who was taken away from her because of her illegal drug use. Her ex-husband relocated to North Carolina shortly after their divorce was finalized.

"Listen, we gotta focus. I told you, after this score, we will go and get your son. We will have the money to fight them in court. So, come on, we gotta go," Artie sternly advised and grabbed her by the arm to stand her up.

"Save a bullet for that ex-husband of mine," Lisa transformed into a bloodthirsty predator. "That's what I owe him."

Artie preferred Lisa in this mode as opposed to a weakened state.

"Okay, come on, let's go."

They moved swiftly to the van, got in, and put on their seat belts at the same time. Artie then slid the key into the ignition, turned it, and all he heard was a series of clicking sounds.

He tried it again. Then a third time. The battery was dead.

"GOD DAMN IT!" he proclaimed.

He began to rub his forehead pondering options, then surrendered to it.

"You got a cigarette?" he asked her.

Lisa began to retrieve one from her purse. Artie knew they would miss the window of opportunity to snatch Valerie Legion. The job would have to wait for another day.

CHAPTER 40

Diego Barranca continued to brood about the failed assassination attempt on Roger Legion. Jim Roth had flown in that morning from San Diego and Diego wanted to discuss their options regarding that matter.

"What do you hear from our friend, Cy?" Diego inquired with a sly smile.

"Looks like he has a new attitude and a face that's sliced open. Thirty-five stitches. But I think it had the desired result. He is now focused on the task at hand," Jim conveyed.

"I want tighter scrutiny over any money that goes his way. Understand?" Diego announced.

"Understood," Jim responded.

As Jim gave his answer, Diego's office phone rang. He answered it.

"Yes." A moment passed. "Show him in. He does not need to be fumigated," Diego expressed and returned the receiver to its cradle.

"Marc Christopher is here," Diego announced to Jim.

Both men looked forward to a conversation with him.

Marc entered the room with a smile and arms extended, overflowing with bravado. He wore a dark blue Berluti lamb's wool sport coat, mohair trousers, a purple cotton and silk shirt, silk tie, and leather boots.

"Diego," Marc exclaimed. "How's my favorite germaphobe?"

"Staying healthy." Diego eyed him up and down before he sat. "You look like you're doing well."

"Can't complain," Marc answered. Then he turned to Jim. "Jim, how are you?"

Jim and Marc exchanged a handshake.

"Can I get you something to drink?" Diego asked.

"I'm fine. Thanks."

"And your brothers?" Diego wondered.

"They're good. We're keeping busy."

"Based on what I see in the news and the papers, it looked like quite the event up there in Utica," Diego remarked.

"I don't know what you're talking about, Diego," he answered with a smile. "Now, what do you have that's so important?"

"I've got a lawyer that I want dead," Diego's voice became distinctive and genuine.

"What's his name?" Marc asked.

"Roger Legion. Downtown San Diego."

"Sounds pretty basic," Marc concluded.

"What will you charge?" Diego inquired.

"Why don't you send your own men?"

"I want to distance myself from it."

Diego did not want to tell Marc about the failed assassination attempt.

"So, what do you think? A hundred thousand dollars?" Diego queried.

"One hundred thousand dollars?" Marc said with amazement. "When was the last time you hired me? I won't get out of bed for that amount."

"So, how much then?" Diego wanted an answer.

"Diego," Marc uttered with a steely gaze. "Six men and a helicopter? That means your friend is being protected. By a professional. That hikes up the cost of doing business."

Diego was exasperated at Marc's knowledge of the prior events.

"How high?" Diego's annoyance was evident.

"Three million," Marc was succinct.

A pall blanketed the room.

"One bullet. Three million dollars? Did you get hit in the head up there in Utica?"

"No. I'm good at what I do. I know it and you know it. If you could get it done cheaper, I wouldn't be sitting here. So, if you don't like the price, get somebody else to do it. The reason you come to me is because you know I can get it done. How much did you lose just on the helicopter? I guarantee that the reason your guys failed is because of sloppy prep work. I'm sure when they walked into that trap, it was the first time they were ever there. And they did nothing to control the environment. You can never trust that the environment is going to match a drawing. You need boots on the ground."

Diego looked at Marc.

"All right," Diego conceded. "Fifty percent up front?"

"Diego, you got amnesia or Alzheimer's? You know how I work. It's one hundred percent up front."

Marc knew that Diego would attempt to shortchange him if he waited until completion of the job for half of the payment.

"All right. I'll get you cash."

"No, no, no." Marc was adamant. "Diego, you just keep on surprising me. How far do you think I'd get with $3 million in cash? I bet one of your guys would pop me before I got out of the garage. Wire it to my account in the Seychelles. As soon as I verify it's there, I'll go to work."

The Republic of Seychelles is a 155-island country located off the east coast of southeast Africa. It is known for its island beauty, but has also developed an attractiveness for criminals for its lack of an extradition treaty with the United States.

"It will be done," Diego apprised. "First thing in the morning."

"Good. I'd shake your hand, but I'm afraid you would have a stroke."

The comment brought a smile to Jim's face and Diego's.

"If you see Jimmy Flowers up there," Diego added, "feel free to put a bullet in his head. And I'll send you another three million."

Marc rubbed his chin for a moment.

"He's sort of 'high profile' in this neck a the woods," Marc observed. "Did you get the proper 'okays' on it?"

"If I did, he would be dead by now."

"You get the authorization, call me first. I'll cut you a break on the price."

"All right. You still going to church every day?" Diego wondered.

"Every day."

"I admire your discipline," Diego observed.

"It's got nothing to do with discipline," Marc's voice was strident. "I learned long ago that without religion, without the love of a superior being, then you are alone. And there is no worse way to die."

Diego nodded in acknowledgement, not agreeing fully with Marc's philosophy.

"Still," Diego added, "you are a man of discipline."

"When I was learning my craft, my *maestro*, Fiero DeMasi, would make all the students play a game of chess every night. You had to play until you won. This way you learn the value of strategy and varying it. Because if your opponent learned your strategy, you were destined to lose before the first move."

"What if it was a draw?" Diego wondered.

"You don't meet your objective. You play again. While I detested it at the time, the concept has served me well."

Marc stood from his chair.

"Can one of your guys take me back to the airport?" Marc asked.

"Of course," Diego told him. "One final thing: Whatever you do, I don't want it loud like Utica. I don't care how you do it, but not loud."

"Understood." Marc then turned to Jim Roth to share a handshake. Jim stood. "Jim, always a pleasure."

"Same here," Jim responded with a wide smile.

"Jim, make sure we have his account wiring instructions," Diego announced.

Diego was now confident that Jimmy Flowers would soon tremble at the sound of his name.

CHAPTER 41

Nina was in for the night and ready for bed by 7:30 pm. She plopped herself down on her living room couch and planned to channel surf to see if she could find anything interesting to watch. Nina wore a Lanz of Salzberg, blue, tyrolean striped, flannel nightgown. She passed on dinner this evening, but would consider a glass of wine before the end of the evening.

She picked up the remote control and pointed it at the television. It turned on and her cell phone rang. She muted the television and picked up the phone that was laying on an end table next to her. Nina was able to determine from the Caller ID that the call was from Diane Abrams.

Diane was Nina's best friend, who lost her leg in a car versus tractor trailer accident approximately two years earlier. Diane's husband was an attorney at Legion & Associates and he became involved with some drug dealers, who feared that he may testify against them if he was ever arrested. He was murdered in the parking garage at Legion and Associates approximately eighteen months earlier.

Diane's husband was abusive and she was in the process of divorcing him at the time of his death.

"Hey, girlfriend?" Nina asked.

"What up, my sister?" Dianne asked with a half-hearted attempt to sound ghetto.

"You gotta work on that, Dee. You sound about as urban as Donny Osmond," Nina proclaimed.

"Hey, don't talk bad about my boy, Donny."

"I know, he's off-limits. How was your day?"

"Just put the baby down, hopefully for the night. Went to the grocery store, today, and that was about it. What about you?"

"Same old thing."

"Did you see Mr. Wonderful?" Diane playfully inquired.

"No. He didn't come in at all today. I was a little worried. They didn't have him on the schedule to be out of the office. I called. I texted. He didn't respond at all."

"Does he have his kids this week?" Diane quizzed.

"He wasn't supposed to."

Nina's voice echoed sadness.

"Don't worry. He must be busy."

"I don't know," Nina wondered. "At work, he's real cold to me."

"I thought you said he's got to be like that so Mr. Legion doesn't suspect anything."

"Yeah, but you can still be nice about it," Nina conveyed her point.

"Listen, are you doing anything tomorrow night? It's the weekend. I'll get a babysitter. We'll go out to dinner and maybe a movie. What do you say?" Diane's voice was effused with energy.

"What are you on that makes you so happy?" Nina queried.

"Actually, I'm dead tired, but excited about doing something fun."

"Okay, if he doesn't call me, we're on." Nina promised.

The conversation between Nina and Diane would continue for another ninety minutes and dealt with a plethora of topics. As she spoke, all Nina could do was worry that her fiancé was slipping away from her.

CHAPTER 42

As dusk began to settle on the Palace of Barranca, Jim Roth knocked on the door of Diego's office. From inside the office, Diego was able to see who it was from a monitor in the hallway and placed his thumb on the biometric pad. Jim heard the click and entered. He stood at the end of Diego's desk.

"Diego," Jim advised, "I'm on my way back to San Diego. I wanted to let you know that your little excursion up to see Mr. Legion may not have been a total waste of time."

"How so?" Diego wondered.

"I received a call from one of his lawyers. Now, he wants to talk about the Realizar Health account. But he upped the price."

"How much?"

"Ten million."

Diego began to laugh.

"He must need a wheelbarrow to carry those balls of his."

"Do you want me to ignore him or talk to him?" Jim wanted to know.

Diego was slow to respond.

"Why don't you set up a meeting with him? Someplace away from his office. Talk to him, then put a bullet in his head. I'll give you the three million instead of the Christophers."

Jim just looked at him for a moment.

"Sounds tempting, but I don't like to get my hands dirty that way."

"We can make sure it's clean. That nobody is going to be looking for you," Diego assured him.

"It's not in my wheelhouse," Jim declared.

"Still," Diego slowly pronounced, "talk to Legion. Promise him the world. Take his temperature."

"It's done."

"Now," Diego said changing the subject, "I want you to help me with something before you leave."

Diego pressed several buttons on the keyboard of his computer. On a large 52-inch monitor behind him displayed a white room, with white carpet, a white leather couch, chairs, and ottoman. In the room were a dozen young women, in their early 20s of Mexican descent. All the women wore white bathrobes. They were unaware that they were being watched.

"This is my harem," Diego expressed pride.

"I want your opinion on which ones I should bed down tonight."

Jim did not want to be part of this exercise.

Diego dialed two numbers on his phone and pressed a button for the speakerphone.

"Good evening, Diego," came a voice over the phone.

The voice belonged to Isa Cabrera, the Palace Etiquette Administrator.

"Please have the girls line up for review," Diego told her.

A garbled voice could be heard over the phone line and all the girls lined up next to each other facing the camera.

"I like to admire them," Diego told Jim, "without being distracted by their physical features."

Diego pushed a button on his keyboard and zoomed in on the first girls face. He moved the camera from girl-to-girl as they displayed fake smiles and a distinguishable level of uncomfortableness.

"What do you think?" Diego asked Jim. "Which one would you take?"

"I think they're all nice."

"Ah, Jim. Always the politician." He pivoted back to the phone. "Isa, have them take off their robes."

Once again, the garbled voice was heard and all the women unloosened their robes and dropped them to the floor. All the girls were slender and shapely. Diego focused on their breasts and brought the camera in for a tight shot on them.

"I don't like the nipples too big," Diego asserted seriously.

Diego again refocused on the phone.

"Isa, have them turn around."

Isa once again barked an order and the girls turned around. Diego now focused on their buttocks, searching for any imperfections.

"I don't like the big – how do you say – caboose. They say the black people like that. I can't understand why anyone would want their woman to be a pig."

"Different strokes for different folks," Jim replied with a smile, trying to mask his repulsion of Diego.

"What does that mean?" Diego asked.

"Everybody likes something different."

Diego again turned back to the phone.

"Isa, have number two and number eight prepare. I don't want to smell anything other than soap and water. Be sure they're clean down below. I don't want my sheets soiled."

"It will be done, Diego."

"Where is the girl from last night?" Diego quizzed.

"Dr. Hurado is keeping her in the infirmary. Her jaw was broken and her cheekbone was cracked."

"It got a little rough. Tell the doctor not to spend any more time with her. I'll give her to the guards in the morning," Diego advised nonchalantly.

Jim knew that a torturous death sentence had just been placed on one of the young ladies after she suffered a beating at the hands of Diego.

"I've got to get going," Jim told Diego. "Call me if you need anything."

Jim left Diego's office, scarred by the savageness of Diego Barranca.

Part 3

CHAPTER 43

Marc Christopher rose early, just after dawn, and peered out onto the harbor from his eighth floor room at the Hilton San Diego Airport/Harbor Island Hotel. He looked beyond the yachts and lesser sea vessels to focus on the horizon and Roger Legion.

As he leaned against the balcony rail, wearing a t-shirt and boxer shorts, he played various scenarios in his mind to accomplish the death of Roger Legion.

Whenever the Christophers stayed at a hotel, they always had two adjoining that were connected by a common doorway. One room would always have two beds and the other would have a king size bed. Marc never wanted to wonder or worry about the location of his brothers. All three of the Christophers had their own family and children, but Marc wanted them to be constantly reminded that they are not on vacation. There was a job to be done.

Marc planned to attend church this morning at St. Agnes Catholic Church in Point Loma, located approximately seven miles away. He always looked forward to attending a new church and meeting a new priest.

"You got a plan?" John asked after walking in from the adjoining room that he shared with Tom.

Marc pushed off from the railing and walked back into the room.

"My *maestro* (teacher), Marc said ponderously, "the great Fiero DeMasi, would always say '*Sfruttare una debolezza.*"

"What's it mean?" John asked.

"Exploit a weakness," Marc conveyed. "That's what has to be done in this instance." He spoke not looking at John, but rather sharing a revelation. "That's what I need to find."

As he spoke, Tom emerged from the bedroom, looking disheveled, still in a drunken haze of sleep.

"Well, I hope you find it fast. If I can't enjoy this place, I'd rather get out of it," Tom told them.

"This job is making all three of us millionaires. So, we can invest some time," Marc reminded him as he walked toward him, finishing his sentence when he was within three feet of Tom. "We need to give our clients, like Diego, some good customer service."

"Jesus Christ, who gives a shit about some beaner dope peddler. You would do the world a favor if you put a bullet in him."

Just as Tom finished his sentence, Marc moved with a lightning motion, placing his right hand around Tom's throat and racing him back to slam his body into the wall while still holding his neck.

"I don't care what dispersions you wish to cast on others, but you will not use the name of my savior, the Lord Jesus Christ, in vain. You do it again and I'll crack your skull. Do you understand me?" Marc uttered his words coldly and with an underlying rage. His eyes were filled with danger and Tom feared his next move.

John knew better than to interfere.

"All right," Tom said sheepishly. "I'm sorry."

"Don't forget it," Marc advised and backed away, letting go of the grip on his neck.

"John," Marc quickly refocused, "were you able to check the infrastructure on the electronics in his building?"

"Fairly new," John replied. "It would take a day or two to hack it."

"Would you have to be on-site?"

"At least six to eight hours on-site. The rest I could do remotely."

"Did you talk to Toomey?"

Toomey was an old man, who lived in the Arizona desert, near Mesa, Arizona. He had a warehouse and was their connection in the southwest United States for any and all weapons, technology, and explosives.

"Yeah, I'll pick up a box truck today from a rental place," John told him, "and go to the freight hanger to pick-up our special stuff. It should be there by ten o'clock. Then, Tom and I will take a ride to Mesa. I figure I'll see what he's got, not unless you want something special."

"No, that's fine. I'll do some recon in and around the building. Did you get the guy's anchor info?"

John reached into his pocket and handed Marc a folded sheet of paper.

"It's all on there. He drives a black Caddie, the license plate is on there."

"How far away does he live?"

"About twenty-five miles to the north. A place called Rancho Santa Fe."

"I've heard of it," Marc advised. "Very high end." Marc glanced at his brothers. "Get ready and we'll go get somethin' to eat."

The genesis of the Christopher's plan to assassinate Roger Legion had begun.

CHAPTER 44

As Roger Legion reviewed e-mails, Larry Larkin swiftly entered his office after giving the door a quick rap. Roger swiveled his chair, leaned back, and lowered his reading glasses to the desk.

"Good news. I spoke with Jim Roth at Realizar and they are still interested," Larry's voice was energized.

"At $10 million?" Legion queried.

"I told them and he said he would work on it. But he wants to have another meeting."

"All right. Set it up. Later this week," Legion informed him. "Have you seen John Hamishaw?"

"I thought he had something going on at court this morning in the *Valiant* case. That discovery dispute."

The discovery dispute dealt with Cy 'the Guy's' request for an onsite forensic review of Jimmy Flowers' Scripticon hardware and software. Both Roger Legion and Jimmy Flowers were adamant that this type of testing would not take place.

"It's not on our calendar," Roger spoke quickly as he rose from his chair. "Why would he go there without me?"

Roger Legion's anger was beginning to boil.

"He can handle it," Larry uttered.

This was a situation that Roger feared.

"Do me a favor," Roger instructed Larry as he headed to the doorway. "See if you can get John on the phone. Tell him not to do anything until I get there. If you can't get him, call the clerk in the Discovery Referee's department and tell them I am on my way and to please wait."

With that, Roger Legion disappeared from the room like a cheetah chasing its prey.

CHAPTER 45

In the third floor men's room of the Hall of Justice, the downtown San Diego County courthouse, Cy 'the Guy' Valiant sat on a toilet in the handicap stall with his pants up, going over in his mind the points he would argue in favor of his position that his expert should be allowed to go forward with forensic testing on the Scripticon system.

As he sat there, he continued to sweat profusely and felt he needed a little 'something' to level himself out. He reached into the inside breast pocket of his Stafford black striped suit from J.C. Penney's Big & Tall department and retrieved a small, plastic bottle with a screw-on top, that was approximately two inches long and a quarter-inch wide.

He unscrewed the cap and attached to the inside of the top was a long, thin, small-scale spoon. He held the bottle on its side to fill the petite spoon with pure cocaine. This was Cy's personal stash that he would not share with anyone.

He snorted it in a flash, recapped the bottle, and made a few exaggerated breaths in. At the same time, he pulled on his nose and pulled his fingers back and forth under it to make sure that no powder may be visible.

Cy stood from the toilet, picked up his briefcase, and walked out stopping in front of the sink. His cherubic cheeks were bright red. He thought about throwing some water on his face, but reconsidered and simply exited the bathroom.

As Cy walked across the hallway to Department 64, he saw Roger Legion ascending the escalator to the third floor. He stopped to wait for Roger.

"I thought I saw your boy was here?" Cy quizzed.

"I was just running a little late," Legion told him and stared at his face for a second. Cy's face was blue, purple, and swollen along the line that was stitched from his interaction with brass knuckles. "We wanted to make sure it was covered."

They proceeded to the courtroom and Cy's mouth was on cruise control.

"Don't think you're gonna play any of those games where you own the judge and you can get him to bark on your command. If the Judge goes against me, I'll take it to the Court of Appeal. I don't care. So, you better tell your client, they better make with the goods, or I'm going to put their ass in a sling and I'm going to have your bar card."

Cy was threatening to have Roger Legion disbarred.

Roger was ignoring Cy, which only added to his vitriolic rant. John Hamishaw was seated in the courtroom gallery and Roger walked over to him and stood looking down.

"There's two ahead of us," John advised indicating that the Judge would take care of two other matters before their hearing.

Roger's steel-blue eyes pierced through John.

"You and I have to talk when this is over," Roger informed him, alluding to the hearing.

"And another thing," Cy came over from the plaintiff's table to continue his tirade, "Don't you start that bullshit about the State Audits. They're useless. Theh. . . ."

Cy's speech was cut off. He began trembling uncontrollably and with his left hand reached for the right lapel of his suit coat. He went down on one knee and immediately dropped to the floor like a discarded dumbbell.

"Call an ambulance!" Legion yelled out to the bailiff and vaulted over the short wall that separated the courtroom from the gallery. He went down on one knee as Cy continued to tremble. He loosened his tie and the top button of his shirt. Roger then took two fingers to feel a pulse on the side of his neck. "Com'on, Cy. Stay with us."

Roger was about to commence cardiopulmonary resuscitation when emergency medical technicians burst through the doors.

Legion stepped back from Cy and allowed the EMTs to take over. They placed Cy on a gurney and he continued his random twitches without consciousness.

The discovery hearing would not go forward on this day.

CHAPTER 46

At 8:23 am, Valerie Legion pulled into the upper parking lot at St. Elizabeth Seton Catholic Church in Carlsbad. She always parked her blue, Mercedes-Benz S550 in approximately the same location, near the entrance to the lot and against the sidewalk.

Valerie wore a Michael Kors, solid-trim, pleated, lace dress with Adriana sandals, and a large, Essex, Convertible Shoulder bag.

Two cars down from her, toward the church entrance, was Artie Clexx's red, 1978, Ford Econoline van. He stood adjacent to the open sliding-side door, waiting for Valerie to pass. As she did, he spoke up to grasp her attention.

"Excuse me," Artie uttered and Valerie looked in his direction, while slowing her gait. "My wife is not feeling well, could you help me?"

"What's wrong?" Valerie asked with concern as she approached him to look inside the van.

Lisa was on the floor of the van with her back to Artie and Valerie. Valerie lightly touched Lisa's shoulder.

"What's wrong, honey?" she asked.

In one swift, smooth movement, Lisa sat up and aimed the Rexio handgun, given to Artie by his friend Tizoe, directly at Valerie.

"I'm poor, Mrs. Legion," Lisa responded with a cold lack of sympathy.

"Get in, Mrs. Legion," Artie advised with scary serenity. "We don't want to hurt you."

Valerie looked at Artie and then back to the gun held by Lisa. She slowly moved into the van. Artie then began to look around to make sure no one was passing by.

"Put your hands behind your back," Artie told her. "Palm to palm."

He then slipped a zip tie over her hands and tightened it. Artie pushed off on the sliding side door and it closed. He proceeded to the driver's door.

In the parking lot, approximately one hundred feet away, were two sets of eyes that witnessed the events. It was Marc and Tom Christopher.

"Do you see what's going on?" Marc asked Tom as she first approached the open side door of the van.

"I see it, but what's going on?" Tom inquired.

"I think they're gonna take her," Marc buzzed in disbelief.

When Marc saw her go into the van and Artie shut the door, he knew his suspicion was correct. Marc and Tom looked at each other for a quick second.

"Do you want to stop them?" Tom queried.

"No," Marc's mind was deep in thought. Then, in a low tone he uttered, "Exploit a weakness."

"What?" Tom asked.

Marc opened his passenger door and set one foot out.

"Where are you going?" Tom wondered.

"To church," Marc replied. "Call John and tell him to pick me up in forty-five minutes. You follow them. Don't get too close. And don't get made. Wherever they go, just watch the place. Don't get out of the car."

"What if it's not what you think?" Tom asked.

"Walk by faith, Tom, not by sight."

Marc stepped out of the vehicle and adjusted his silk, yellow tie. He also wore a twill, white shirt and a black, Georgio Armani, cotton-blended suit. Tom wore the same jeans, a Pearl Jam t-shirt, and a jean jacket.

Marc started to cross the parking lot and watched Artie back out of his space.

CHAPTER 47

Not a word was spoken between Roger Legion and John Hamishaw until they reached the lobby of the America's Finest City Building and stood waiting for an elevator to arrive.

"I don't know what's bothering you now," John inquired, "but this routine is getting a little old."

Roger did not respond until they were both in the elevator with no other passengers. Then he set his laser gaze on John.

"How much are they paying you?" Legion queried.

"What?" John exclaimed as if shocked by the question.

"How did you know his name was Jimmy Flowers?"

"Roger, come on. You are grasping here. You lose control of something for one second, then you're in mega-paranoid mode."

"Well, if I was in court, in my own paranoid way, I would ask the judge to direct the witness to answer the question: How did you know – his name – was Jimmy Flowers?"

John just stared at him and thought about his next move.

"You should talk to Larry Larkin about this topic. He's positioning himself for a real sweet payday. He's gonna get a piece of the action of whatever your final number is for Realizar Health."

Roger wanted to refocus the conversation.

"What would have happened if I didn't show up today down at court?" Roger quizzed. "Cy would have gotten his discovery order and you would have said, 'There was nothing I could do.' Then, even if I fired you, you could still ask for your payday from your friends."

John's countenance feigned anger at the accusation.

"I'm outta here, Mr. Legion. You can take your job, and your warrior bullshit, your weaponize the facts, and everything else that makes you think you are such a powerful man in that deluded mind of yours and shove it up your ass."

"I would be careful, John," Roger warned. "If you've promised something to them, the way they sent men to kill me, they may send some men to kill you."

"Roger, it's my understanding that you're dead already."

John finished his sentence as the elevator doors opened. He bee-lined directly to his office. Roger contemplated his last sentence as he watched John walk away and disappear into his office.

Legion walked over to Nina and looked down at her from over her counter. She realized he was there immediately and looked up with a smile.

"I want to talk to you," he told her and pointed to the door of the large conference room.

Nina stood, keeping her wireless headset on and walked directly into the room followed by Legion. She feared that she might be in trouble. Neither one of them sat down.

"John Hamishaw just gave me his notice that he was quitting," Roger disclosed. "I don't want him to receive any more calls through the switchboard. If he gets a call, send it to me, just tell me it's for him."

"Okay," she acknowledged.

"Let me know if you see anything unusual with him," Roger requested. "That's it."

Nina did an about-face and returned to her desk. Roger picked up the receiver of the phone in the conference room and dialed Roy, the information technology person at the firm who worked on the 23rd floor."

"Roy, this is Mr. Legion."

"Hey, Mr. L, what can I do for ya?"

"Call our cellular phone company and have them shut off John Hamishaw's service immediately."

"I'll do it right now," Roy told him.

"Thank you," Roger acknowledged and ended the call.

He left the conference room and stopped at the office of one of the attorneys. The name was Ethan Paul. He was 34 years old, 6 feet 2 inches tall, 230 pounds, with black, wavy hair and thick, black, Wayfarer glasses. Roger always admired Ethan's imposing, intimidating look. When Roger reached his doorway, Ethan looked up and caught his eye.

"Come with me."

Ethan followed Roger to John Hamishaw's office where they entered without knocking. John was not there.

From outside John's office door, Roger yelled out to Nina.

"Nina, have you seen John Hamishaw?"

"No," she advised.

"Let me know if you do." Legion then turned to Ethan and told him, "Maybe later, Ethan."

Ethan acknowledged his comment and both men walked back to their offices.

Legion decided that he would no longer be reactive to any events. His success had always come through his proactivity.

CHAPTER 48

On Alex Road in Oceanside, not far from the Oceanside Municipal Airport and State Route 76, Tom Christopher sat waiting in his rented Chrysler 300 watching a lone building sit idle in the middle of a large lot.

The lot was approximately 4 acres in size and a chain link fence ran around the perimeter of it. There was only one entrance into the lot and it was gated. On the property, you could see one security guard's car, parked near the gate.

The building was four stories high, ten thousand square feet on each floor, made of brick, with a wooden structure underneath. The windows on the upper floors were not clear, but rather made of stationary, six-inch by eight-inch glass blocks to allow light in, but masked the view looking out of the window. The building was the former home of O-side Auto Parts.

As Tom fiddled with the radio to find an acceptable rock music station, Marc and John Christopher pulled up behind him in a U-Haul rental truck with a twelve-foot box. Marc and John exited the truck, walked up to the car, and got in.

John wore a red, Ralph Lauren, golf shirt, black Dockers pants, and black New Balance walking shoes.

"What do we have here?" Marc asked with interested zeal.

"I saw one security guard," Tom informed. "He must be in on it, because he opened the gate for them. On the back of the building are a couple of overhead doors. The guard went inside the building through the front door, then he opened the overhead door, the van pulled in, and the overhead door closed."

"They better keep Mrs. Legion alive long enough to get her husband over here," Marc postulated. "All right. John, check the signal strength on everybody's walkie-talkie. Then, check the cell phone reception strength. We can boost it, right?"

"We can use the truck as a hot spot," John suggested.

"Can we tap cell phone calls in a localized area like this?" Marc quizzed.

"As long as there's no interference from the airport, it shouldn't be a problem."

"Why don't you get going on that. I'm gonna go in and then I'll come back and unlock the gate," Marc apprised. "Tom, you bring the car in up to the front door."

"Why don't I back you up?" Tom asked.

"No. It's not necessary," Marc told him. "Did the security guard have a gun?"

Tom thought about the question for a moment.

"Wait, I think, ah, he didn't have one."

"You think he didn't have one or he didn't have one?" Marc demanded a response.

"I'm pretty sure he didn't have one."

"What you have to do, Tom, is pay attention to detail. I didn't see the guy and I know he doesn't have a gun. If he had a gun, the car would say 'Armed Response' on it and it doesn't. This is why on every job we've ever done, either John or I have had to pull your ass out of the fire. It's that kind of detail that can get one of us killed."

Tom merely looked at him.

"Do you want me to get you a rifle or a pistol out of the trunk?"

"No. How far would you say the distance is from the road to the doorway?" Marc quizzed.

"A hundred fifty feet?" Tom replied.

"If a car passes and sees either you or me with an automatic rifle in our hands, what do you think they're gonna do?"

"Call the cops."

"Yeah. And you don't know this, but the Oceanside Police Department Headquarters is right down the street, so they'd be here in about two seconds."

"So, I'll wait," Tom spoke and shrugged his shoulders.

"I wish our parents would have named you after one of the Evangelists like they did with me and John. Instead, they named you after the apostle who questioned Jesus after he returned from the dead."

Marc was referring to Matthew, Mark, Luke, and John, the authors of the New Testament of the Bible. The comment brought a smile to John's face.

"What do ya want?" Tom answered with disdain.

"Put your earpiece in and get ready," Marc advised, directing his comment to Tom.

Marc opened the door, stepped out of the car, and walked down the street toward the gate. The Christophers were about to storm the castle.

CHAPTER 49

Roger Legion perused new lawsuits received the day before and the facts of one of them was so odd, it was funny. A female, adult entertainer, who was the star of a number of pornographic films, claimed that she received an injection from a dermatologist and it resulted in a dimple on her butt cheek. Her claim was that the dimple reduces her value as a pornographic actress.

Roger shook his head in disbelief and planned to assign the file to an attorney in the firm named Luke Cordel. He was recently married and Roger knew that Luke did not have a wandering eye.

As Legion attached a Post-it note to the front of the file, his cell phone rang. The name on the Caller ID was 'Debby,' his oldest daughter, who was a licensed attorney, but also a stay-at-home mom.

"Hello," Roger answered.

"Hi, Daddy," she replied.

"Hi, honey. How are you doing?"

"Good. Have you talked to Momma today?"

"No, but that's not unusual," he told her.

"Well, I had a dentist appointment today and she was going to watch the kids. When I went home she wasn't there. Lupe said she didn't return from church. I've been trying to call her, but she doesn't answer."

Lupe was the maid at Roger Legion's home who lived on the property.

"Well," Roger thought for a moment, "I know one day a week, she goes to a meeting at church for the Women's Christian Fellowship."

As Legion spoke, he looked out the window and the wheels in his mind began to spin.

"I talked to her last night and she said she wouldn't forget," Deborah's voice echoed concern.

"I have to come up there anyway. I'll stop at church and see if they know anything. Don't worry. I'm sure she's fine," Roger advised with a calm, even tone.

"Okay, but I'm not going to say anything to Sarah. She loves the drama," Deborah cautioned. Sarah was Roger's other daughter.

"All right," Roger told her. "I'll have Momma call you as soon as I get a hold of her."

"Thanks, Daddy. I'll talk to you later. Bye."

"Bye, honey."

Legion lowered his cell phone to his desk and wanted to immediately dismiss any thoughts of retaliation against him for the failed attempt on his life. Then, his office phone rang.

"Yes," he responded to Nina.

"Glenn Edgarian is on line 4," she disclosed.

"Put him through."

The phone rang again and Roger picked up the receiver off the cradle and pushed the blinking button.

"Glenn, how are ya?"

"Good, Roger, how about you?"

"I'm fine."

"I talked to the people at Hennessey's. Both your boys were there: Hamishaw and Larkin. I'm told they met a third guy that you might find interesting."

"Who?" Roger posed a serious inquiry.

"Jim Roth."

Glenn's response was followed by a pall of silence.

"All right," Roger told him as his mind moved into overdrive.

"Do you still want me to collect some information on that guy?" Glenn wondered.

"No. Let it go. Send me your bill. Add a thousand dollars to it," Roger instructed him.

"Roger, that's not necessary," Glenn expressed to him.

"No. I say it is. E-mail the bill to me and I'll get it paid today."

"Roger, thanks a lot. You're the best. Take care."

"I'll be in touch. Take it easy."

With that, the call was concluded. Roger then called his wife's cell phone. Her number was on speed dial. The call went to voice mail and he redialed again. Again, to voicemail.

Roger placed his cell phone in the inside breast pocket of his suit coat. He left the office and his gait continued to pick up speed. By the time he reached the elevator, he was sprinting like prey being pursued by a predator.

CHAPTER 50

When Artie Clexx drove his 1978 Econoline van into the former O-side Auto Parts building, it was as if he went through a time portal back to the early 1970s. The dust and cobwebs were thick, portraying everything in the building with a brown hue. Natural light poured in, but the glass block windows prevented any view of the exterior.

As soon as the van was within the building, Tizoe pulled down the overhead door. The interior of the building was lit by free-standing, commercial halogen work lights that received their power from a Honda generator.

Around the perimeter of the first floor were various boxes, trash, and it appeared some fires had been set. Homeless people had taken up shelter in the building at one point and the City of Oceanside demanded that the owner of the building take precautions to avoid loss of life, so the owner hired a security company, whose primary responsibility was to keep trespassers out of the building.

The first floor of the building was the garage level used for intake and the center of the floor was totally empty and relatively clean. The ceiling of the first floor was open to the second floor. The second floor had a walkway around its interior perimeter for access to the former offices. At one end of the floor was a freight elevator and at the other end was a metal staircase that allowed access to all four floors and the roof.

The first floor was the only level with the standing lights. The rest of the floors had sufficient natural lighting.

Artie opened the sliding side door on the van and Lisa Nastasi and Valerie Legion sat across from each other, each sitting on a wheel well of the vehicle. Valerie was calm, but looked anxious. Lisa held the gun pointed at Valerie with her hands resting in her lap.

"Let's go," Artie told them.

The women exited the vehicle. Then Artie gave some direction to Lisa.

"Give me the shotgun." Lisa complied and handed the weapon to him. "Grab her purse." Lisa again complied. "We're gonna take a walk."

After the van pulled into the building, Tizoe immediately went outside, because he wanted to make sure there were no interruptions for the plan.

Artie, Valerie, and Lisa made the trek up three flights of stairs to the fourth floor of the building. This floor was much brighter from natural sunlight pouring in, but it was also warmer. The wooden floor was creaky and, once again, the perimeter of the floor was scattered with trash, empty boxes, and some old cleaning supplies. In one corner was a small area surrounded by two chain link walls from floor-to-ceiling, creating a small cage, approximately ten-feet by ten-feet. There was also a chain link door that allowed access to the interior of the caged area.

"This is gonna be your new home for a little while," Artie proclaimed. "I'm going to call your husband and tell him you're all right. Once he pays us, you go home. Real simple."

Valerie didn't respond. She watched Artie and Lisa's movements. Artie pointed inside the cage and she knew what he meant. She calmly walked in, but turned to speak to him.

"Can I take this thing off my wrists? It really hurts."

Artie closed the door, placed a chain on it and secured it with a padlock. He then took out a black, folding knife, with a four-inch blade, from his pocket.

"Come here," he told her. "Turn around."

Valerie complied and Artie cut the zip tie.

"What now?" Lisa asked.

"Look in her purse. Get her cell phone," Artie requested and turned back to Valerie. "Your husband got a nickname for you?"

"What?" she quizzed, not sure if she heard him correctly.

"What does he call you at home? I want him to know that we have his lady and that we're serious."

"Val-e."

"Okay, Val-e, sit tight, this will all be over soon. I apologize for the accommodations. I'm sure you're use to much nicer," Artie asserted. "Do you want something to drink?"

"Do you have water?" she wondered.

"Yeah. We got a cooler down in the truck. I'll get you one," he disclosed and turned to Lisa. "Stay and watch her."

Lisa showed Artie Valerie's cell phone.

"Check the signal strength, then shut it off," he ordered.

Artie placed the shotgun in a standing position against the closest wall and then began his trip back to the first floor.

Outside of the building, Marc Christopher unlatched the chain link gate at the property of the former O-side Auto Parts, entered, and relatched the gate. He cautiously walked up to the building and made sure to walk along the side of Tizoe's security vehicle to look inside. He saw nothing but magazines and a police-style hat.

On the eastern side of the building, far from the front door and the overhead door in back, was a fire escape/staircase that ran the entire height of the building except for the first floor. The fire escape system was supposed to have a ladder to climb down from the second floor, but it was broken off.

Tizoe spent most of his time on the eastern side of the building because people could not see what he was doing from the street. He would smoke cigarettes and occasionally play handheld video games to pass the time.

Marc reached the building and walked along the side of it. He turned the corner and still no sign of the security guard. He then slowly made his way across the side of the building with overhead doors and could see cigarette smoke lightly wafting from the eastern side of the building. Marc then fidgeted with both of the sleeves of his suit coat. He continued on his path to the eastern side of the building.

"Hey, how ya doin'?" Marc called out to Tizoe, who was surprised to see him.

"Can I help you?" Tizoe asked.

"I'm with a land management company," Marc conveyed, "and we're thinking about buying this property. Would I be able to go inside?"

"Sorry," Tizoe thought and answered fast. "I got strict orders. No one goes in without my boss giving the okay."

"All right," Marc added with a serene tone and a smile. "Do you know if they're going to knock down the building?"

"They were supposed to do one of those implosion things," Tizoe responded, "you know, like they do in Vegas. But somebody ran out of money. I don't know what the deal is."

Marc nodded and looked to the roof of the building.

"What's your name?" Marc inquired.

"Why you need to know that?" Tizoe quizzed.

"I just like to know," Marc replied with an eerie calmness.

"Tizoe."

"Thank you, Tizoe." The serenity of Marc's voice seemed to make even the wind stop.

Marc turned to walk away and Tizoe called out to him.

"What's your name?" Tizoe queried.

When the question was asked, Marc had his back to Tizoe, walking away. In one motion, he pivoted and at the same time hurled an eight-inch balanced throwing knife at Tizoe's neck. The blade was so sharp, it penetrated adjacent to his Adam's apple and the tip of the knife came out the back of his neck. Within a millisecond, he threw a second knife at him, with an underhand swing, hitting Tizoe near the center of his chest.

Tizoe's shock caused him to convulse and he dropped to the ground. Once he hit the ground, his life force left him quickly and his movements were negligible. Marc knelt down on one knee next to him and made the Sign of the Cross on Tizoe's forehead with his thumb while he spoke.

"Remember man that thou art dust and unto dust thou shall return."

Marc stood and put his earpiece in for communication with his brothers.

"Tom, bring the car in."

Marc looked at Tizoe and figured they could place his body next to the building and pile trash over it.

Then, it would be time to take over the interior. The body count had begun.

CHAPTER 51

When Roger Legion pulled into the parking lot of St. Elizabeth Seton Catholic Church, the first thing he saw was his wife's S550 Mercedes-Benz. Other than her car, there were only two other cars in the lot.

He pulled in the slot next to hers and exited his car to quickly examine Valerie's car. Nothing looked out of place in the vehicle and the doors were locked.

Roger moved quickly up a short flight of stairs to the church piazza area and then directly into the building. There was no one in the narthex or vestibule area and he moved directly into the church.

St. Elizabeth Seton Catholic Church was an extraordinary example of fine craftsmanship coupled with spiritual reverence. The cherry wood, stained glass, and carved stone were the result of a synergy of artisans whose work placed the visitor in awe.

Legion's wife always told him that she felt at home in this building and she was not alone in that opinion.

When you first walked into the church, there was a baptismal font, built of black slate and concrete that allowed the visitor to obtain a touch of holy water to bless themselves in a cross formation, known as the Sign of the Cross.

As Roger entered, he saw three women walking toward him from the alter that sat approximately one hundred feet ahead of him. The women were Nancy Bucsis, Ellen Price-Reardon, and Patricia Halderson. Nancy was 79 years old, with jet black hair and a permanent smile. She gave off a calming, maternal instinct.

Ellen was also 79 years old with white hair and used a walker. She always listened intently and her intellectual prowess was evident. Patricia was 66 years old with nicely coifed gray hair and perfect posture. The women were members of the Women's Christian Fellowship, a Church ministry devoted to bible study and loving fellowship. Valerie Legion was a member of this group.

All three ladies were engaged in heavy conversation, but Nancy redirected the conversation when she recognized Roger.

"Hello, Roger," Nancy said with an ebullient tone, somewhat surprised to see him.

"Hello, Nancy," Roger responded. "Have you seen Valerie?"

"You know, I haven't. She wasn't at the W.C.F. meeting. She was supposed to give a treasurer's report."

"I didn't see her at church this morning," Ellen added. "She always sits next to me."

"But I saw her pull in the parking lot," Pat told them. "She waved to me."

"Is anything wrong, Roger?" Nancy asked.

"No. I think one of my daughters picked her up. I was just checking on the car," Roger advised them wanting to avoid or minimize any potential panic.

"Tell Val, we all say 'Hello' and we'll look for her in church tomorrow," Ellen relayed.

Roger shared good-byes with the ladies and they continued on their path out of the building. Before leaving, Roger touched the tips of his fingers into the holy water at the baptismal font. Before making the Sign of the Cross, he looked at the far off alter and, in particular, a crucifix that sat on a pole situated several feet behind the alter.

In a soft, low voice, Legion uttered, "Don't punish her because of me."

He then turned and left the building. Roger Legion would not find solace in prayer; he would find it when he placed his hands on anyone who may have touched her.

CHAPTER 52

Outside the abandoned O-side Auto Parts building, Marc Christopher had his brother Tom back their car up to within six feet of the entrance door to the building.

"Pop the trunk," Marc called out to Tom. Tom joined Marc at the back of the car.

"You take the M-4," Marc informed him. "Follow me in, back me up. I don't want anybody getting killed right now."

Marc was referring to an M-4 carbine submachine gun. This rifle fired 5.56mm caliber rounds and could fire at a rate of 850 rounds per minute. The magazine for the gun held 30 rounds. Marc used one of these weapons during the Utica assault.

Marc continued to review the trunk items and picked up a Smith & Wesson M & P 45 semi-automatic handgun and pushed the slide back slightly to make sure there was a live round in the chamber. He then placed it behind him in the waistband of his pants. This gun was a .45 caliber and held ten bullets in the magazine and one in the chamber.

"Watch your fingers," he told Tom and slammed the trunk closed. "You come out in a little while and put the car back on the street." Just then, he heard his brother, John's voice in his ear.

"Somebody's making a phone call," John disclosed.

"Pipe it through, so I can hear it," Marc instructed him.

Moments earlier, inside the building, Artie returned with a bottle of water.

"Man, that's alotta stairs!" Artie declared, out of breath and fatigued by the ascent. He walked over to the caged area and handed Valerie the water through the bars.

"Smile," Artie expressed to Valerie. "It will all be over soon."

"When are we gonna call?" Lisa asked him.

"Get me her phone," he commanded to her and she complied.

Artie browsed the call log.

"Who's Debby?" Artie asked Valerie and she remained stoic and her countenance displayed uncomfortableness with the question. "She really wants to talk to you." Valerie continued to remain silent. "I'll call her and find out."

"No!" Valerie's response was sudden and jarring. "She's my daughter."

"See how easy it is. You comply and it moves the process along. Your old man only called you twice. I hope he's not gonna be a slacker about this thing."

With every sentence that he spoke, Artie's prowess as a criminal became more defined and focused. He was in command of the situation and he enjoyed it.

From Valerie's call log, Artie pulled up the last call record from Roger Legion. He pushed 'Call Back.'

Roger Legion was traveling southbound on Interstate 5 near Del Mar Heights Road when the Bluetooth allowed the phone to ring in the car.

As the telephone rang, all three Christopher brothers were listening in on the call. Roger answered on the second ring.

"Hello, Val-e," Legion's voice was rushed, but he was excited at the thought of hearing her voice.

"I have something that you're looking for," Artie spoke slowly and with authority. His enjoyment with the situation was growing exponentially.

"Who is this?" Roger's voice echoed desperation.

"That's not important. Don't you want to talk to your wife?" Artie asked with a ghoulish tone.

"Put her on!" Legion demanded.

"Listen, asshole," Artie declared with a short fuse. "I'm running the show. Now, apologize to me for being an asshole. I can wait."

"I didn't mean any disrespect," Roger spoke with a slight grind of his teeth.

"Next time you do it, I'm gonna hang up. I am going to go over the ground rules. Number one: no cops, no FBI. If you do, she's dead. Number two: I want you to stay in your office until I tell you differently. Number three: This is the last call I'm going to make from this phone. So, answer all the calls that come to your cell. I've got a tracker on your Cadillac and I know your movements. I've got one of your lawyers on the inside helping me out. Now, do you still want to talk to her?" Artie inquired with a smart-alec tinge.

"Yes, please," Legion's words were measured.

"Sorry, time's up." With that Artie ended the call and turned off Valerie's phone.

"Do you really have somebody on the inside at his law firm?" Lisa wondered in amazement.

"No, just rattling his cage," Artie told her. "And I don't have a tracker on his Cadillac."

Both Marc Christopher and Roger Legion were digesting the information shared by Artie. Marc concluded that the kidnappers were not professionals and Roger was further flummoxed by the events. Artie had rattled Roger Legion's cage and inside, a beast was awakened.

CHAPTER 53

Marc and Tom Christopher entered the building and Marc's mind worked like a computer assessing how it could be used to his advantage and the evident drawbacks to such a structure. He saw the open center of the first floor that allowed for a full view of the walkway perimeter of the second floor.

The area around the perimeter of the first floor was darkened, which may provide an advantage if cover was needed.

"Stay here," he told Tom. "Watch the entrance door. Don't come up unless I call you."

"All right," Tom acknowledged.

Marc began a stealthy trek to the fourth floor with his semi-auto handgun out and ready, where he could hear Artie and Lisa discussing travel arrangements out of Los Angeles for Charleston, South Carolina. As he arrived at each floor, he conducted a visual scan through a doorway to determine how the particular layout may benefit his ultimate plan of assassinating Roger Legion. When he observed the third floor, there was no garbage like the other floors. It was totally empty, except for a broken down Raymond forklift that looked like it had been chopped for parts.

Marc slyly made his way to the fourth floor and caught glimpses of the activity through a small square in the upper portion of the door that once had glass in it. He saw Artie and Lisa and Valerie in the cage.

Marc then looked around on the landing and saw a broken plastic milk crate. He threw it on the staircase and as it tumbled, it filled the building with a clamorous reverberation, loud enough to be heard by the occupants of the fourth floor.

"What's that?" Lisa inquired curiously.

"Must be Tizoe," Artie responded. "I'll check it out. Watch her."

Artie walked through the door to the stairway and pushed it open. On his second step out of the doorway, Marc took his left arm and with lightning speed flung it around Artie's neck placing him in a chokehold and with his right hand pressed the barrel of the gun into his temple.

The door had closed behind him, so neither Lisa nor Valerie saw the events outside the door.

"Tell me your name!" Marc demanded in a cruel and bloodthirsty tone.

"Artie," he said hardly having enough air in his lungs to pronounce both syllables.

"If I let go, you're not going to do anything stupid, are you?" Marc devilishly inquired.

"No," Artie answered, frozen by fear.

Marc released his vice-like grip and Artie stood while coughing slightly. Marc continued to keep his handgun aimed at Artie's head.

"Who's your lady friend in there? What's her name?"

"Lisa," Artie responded at first thinking Marc was a cop or an FBI agent based on his clothes.

While looking at Artie, Marc spoke into his earpiece.

"Tom, come up to the fourth floor," Marc ordered and Tom arrived in less than thirty seconds carrying his M-4 rifle. "Watch him. If he tries anything, kill him."

Tom leveled his rifle at Artie's waist. Artie looked at Tom and then back to Marc.

"Call her over here," Marc demanded and pointed to the small, broken-out glass opening in the door. Artie moved closer to the door.

"Lisa, come here. I need you."

Lisa picked up the Rexio .38 caliber revolver and walked toward the door. As she approached, from her diminutive angle, she could see Tom's blond hair through the window of the door.

"Artie, come in here," she called out.

"I can't. I twisted my ankle."

"Then drag yourself back in here," Lisa insisted.

Lisa aimed the gun at the door, ready to fire.

"Lisa, please," Artie pleaded with her.

"No," was her cold, lone response.

In a flash, Marc immediately put Artie in the same chokehold, pressed the muzzle of the gun into his temple, and kicked the door. Lisa was slightly stunned and her hands began to shake slightly as she aimed the gun at Artie and Marc. Tom entered the room and drew a bead on her as his target.

"Put the gun down or he dies and you're next," Marc informed her.

"NO! NO! NO!" she screamed with histrionic flare. "KILL ME! SHOOT ME! GET IT OVER WITH! I want my son back and I'm going to get him back. I'm not going to let these cops stop me. Where the hell is Tizoe and all his gangbanger buddies?"

"Tizoe didn't make it," Marc told her. "This is the last time I am going to tell you: Put. . .the gun. . .down."

Lisa eyed Marc and Artie, then turned her gaze to Tom. She despised the thought of surrender. Lisa tossed the gun to Marc's feet. Marc released his hold on Artie and shoved him toward Lisa. Then he picked up the Rexio gun and eyed Lisa.

"I know 492 ways to kill a person. Looking at you, I could probably blow hard on you and you'd drop dead. I admire your brazenness. It serves you well in a criminal enterprise."

"What do you want?" Lisa posed her inquiry.

"That's not important right now. Where's her cell phone?" he queried, pointing to Valerie.

Lisa walked over to Valerie's Michael Kors purse and retrieved the phone. She tossed it to Marc.

Tom varied the aim on his rifle from Artie to Lisa. Marc walked over to the chain fence enclosed area.

"How are you, Mrs. Legion?" Marc asked sincerely.

"Are you a police officer?" her voice pleaded desperation.

"No, I'm not."

"Who are you?" she asked continuing to hope for a savior.

Marc raised one of his index fingers and motioned her to come closer to the chain link.

"You go to church every day?" Marc quizzed.

"Yes."

"So do I. I admire that. I guarantee you that you will not be harmed this day."

Valerie took solace in his words, but still she wanted an answer to her question.

"Can you please tell me why you're here?" Valerie locked eyes with him as she hunted for the answer.

"I'm an assassin, sent here to kill your husband."

Valerie's eyes changed from crying out for help to viewing a monster. She looked at him with an open mouth as he smiled at her and walked away.

"Do you have zip ties?" Marc asked Artie.

"Down in the truck," Artie told him.

Marc turned to his brother.

"Watch them all, Tom. Don't trust any of them." Marc then addressed the group. "Get comfortable, we're gonna be here for a while. We are going to call Mr. Legion back in a couple of hours. You better have that same pumped up voice you had for the first call. You understand?"

Artie shook his head in acknowledgement.

Marc left the room and calmly descended down the staircase. He now controlled the interior environment. Soon, the trap would be set.

CHAPTER 54

Roger Legion was a man on a mission. His destination was the Bagheria Bedda, the restaurant operated by Jimmy Flowers. Roger left the southbound Interstate 5 at the Sassafras Street exit and within two miles, he was double-parked in front of the restaurant.

Roger moved rapidly and he entered the restaurant like a whirlwind, immediately surveying the interior. The restaurant was nearly half full as the lunch hour was not in full swing.

Donnino, one of Jimmy Flowers' bodyguards saw Roger enter and walked up to him to determine the nature of his business.

"Can I help you?" Donnino asked with a stern visage.

"I need to see Jimmy. Now," Roger demanded.

"Donnino," Jimmy Flowers called out. "Let him in."

Jimmy Flowers wore a light, blue Ralph Lauren Polo shirt, black Haggar pants, and a buttoned, black sweater.

Roger rushed past Donnino, and the restaurant full of patrons, to bee-line directly to Jimmy.

"Let's go in my office," Jimmy told Roger.

Roger entered, followed by Jimmy. Rolf Adler, the man who prevented Roger's assassination at the law firm, was in Jimmy's office.

Rolf wore a blue, Corneliani, crossbred, houndstooth suit, with a white shirt, and a lighter blue, silk tie.

Roger began to speak as Jimmy was closing the office door.

"They took my wife," Roger uttered in despair.

Jimmy's concern was evident. The look on Rolf's face indicated that he was already trying to deconstruct the kidnapper's plan.

"Have you heard anything about this?" Jimmy quizzed Rolf.

"No."

"Let me make a phone call," Jimmy told Roger and swiftly moved behind his desk and began spinning a Rolodex.

"Did they call you on your cell phone?" Rolf inquired.

"Yeah," Roger answered.

"Let me see it."

Rolf took the phone and began scrolling through the call log and then looked at the various Smartphone apps on the phone. He then dialed a number on the phone while looking at the screen.

"Her phone is shut off. Does she have the same phone?" Rolf asked.

"Yeah," Roger told him.

"Come outside with me."

Both men proceeded to a black, 2008 Honda Accord. Rolf opened the trunk and removed the back of Roger's phone. He pulled out the SIM card or subscriber identification module card that stores information and can identify and authenticate incoming and outgoing calls.

Rolf placed Roger's SIM card into a machine in his trunk and pressed one button. He then removed the SIM, placed it back in the phone, and affixed the back of the phone. Rolf handed the phone back to Roger.

"This SIM card has a lock on it. When they call you, even if they hang up, you don't hang up. Then we can trace their location. Where were you when they called?"

"I was heading southbound on the 5," Roger explained. "I found my wife's car in our church parking lot up in Carlsbad. A person saw her pull into the lot, but she never made it to church."

"All right. Let's wait for a call," Rolf declared. He then pushed a button on his phone to place a call. "I need a SIM lock trap trace. Number 1-1-2-8-7. I'll let you know when we're in motion." Rolf ended that call and turned to Legion. "Let's go find out what Jimmy found out."

Legion and Rolf re-entered the restaurant and walked directly into Jimmy's office. Rolf closed the door.

"Diego Barranca – the man who ordered the hit on you – he's now ordered another team of guys, the Christophers, to finish the job. Nobody knows anything about your wife being picked up."

"I've worked with Marc Christopher before," Rolf advised. "This is not his M.O. He is old school all the way."

"I've hired him before," Jimmy mentioned. "He's very good. But he wouldn't pick up another guy's wife."

"You said you think she was grabbed at church?" Rolf wondered.

"Yeah," Roger acknowledged.

"Definitely not him," Rolf expressed. "He's very religious for a guy who murders people."

Roger rubbed his forehead, frustrated at his inability to do anything.

"Where do you want to wait?" Rolf quizzed.

"My office?"

"No. Let's go to Mission Valley, around the center of the county. We stay near the freeways. We can get anywhere fast."

Roger acknowledged Rolf's comments.

"Roger," Jimmy interjected as he started to open the door. "I give you my word that you'll get her back. Whatever you need Rolf, call for it."

Rolf and Roger left the restaurant to fill the car with gas and wait for a phone call. What troubled Roger the most was his inability to protect his wife.

CHAPTER 55

At the Kinney Drug Store, located at 164 Swanton Road in St. Albans, Vermont, Herschel Gordon, the man known as 'the Gringo' to the Barranca Drug Cartel, waited in line to pick up his high blood pressure medicine and diabetes medication. He was also picking up Zithromax, or a Z-pak, for his wife who was suffering from chronic obstructive pulmonary disease.

He had been waiting for nearly ten minutes in line and there were two people ahead of him. As he anxiously waited, his name was called out.

"Herschel," he heard from one aisle over. He looked and there stood Serge Stiroy, an associate who brought news to Herschel firsthand, so it would be dealt with immediately.

Serge waved his hand for Herschel to come to him.

"No," Herschel told him definitively. "You come over here. I'm not going to give up my place in line."

Serge acknowledged his command and walked over. He spoke in a hushed voice.

"It's about our friend down south. Somebody took the lawyer's wife. Our friend hired the Christophers to finish the job on the lawyer and told those guys Jimmy Flowers was next."

Herschel looked at Serge and shook his head at Diego Barranca's audacity.

"All right, Serge. I'll take care of this. You staying in town overnight? We'll go to lunch tomorrow."

"I really got to get back," Serge told him.

"No problem. I'll call you."

"You sure there's nothing you want me to do?" Serge inquired.

"No. I got this one," Herschel smiled and offered Serge a handshake, which he accepted.

Serge left the store and Herschel started to dial a number on his cell phone when it was finally his turn at the counter.

"Hi, can I get your last name?" asked a cute, petite pharmacy technician.

"Gordon," he replied with a smile and the technician began searching the bins for his prescriptions.

Hershel pushed the send button on the phone and waited for an answer.

"Is the first name Herschel and Aileen?" the technician wondered.

"My wife's name is Marilyn."

The technician went back to look at the rows of filled prescriptions and Herschel's phone was answered.

"Is the line secure?" Herschel inquired.

"Yes," came a voice.

"Operation Double E is a go."

"When?"

"Immediately."

With that, Herschel ended the call and again greeted the cute pharmacy technician. Hershel was always proud of his ability to multi-task.

CHAPTER 56

Tom Christopher cleared off trash on a countertop sufficient enough for him to sit down. He placed his M-4 submachine gun in his lap and stared at his three hostages.

Artie appeared obviously depressed. He would look at the floor and ceiling, but not at Lisa or Tom. Artie and Lisa now wore zip tie handcuffs and the only way out of the fourth floor was either through the door they entered or a fire escape door on the eastern side of the building.

Lisa peered at Valerie, not as a person, but rather as a lost opportunity. Lisa realized that was what she needed now – an opportunity. She walked over to the bars and peered in.

"Is your dress a Michael Kors?" Lisa asked Valerie.

Valerie was sullen, focused on the ground. She shook her head affirmatively.

"What about your shoes?" Lisa wondered.

"They're also Michael Kors," Valerie acknowledged.

"That stuff's expensive," Lisa conveyed. Then in a hushed voice, she added to her comment. "The padlock on this cage is a combination lock. The tumblers are on the bottom. The combination is all fours. We've got a shotgun under the boxes over there."

"So, what should I do with that information?" Valerie inquired sarcastically. "Help the people who kidnapped me?"

"Listen, sweetheart, the guy running the show here is crazy. He's going to kill all of us, including your husband. He just needs you alive long enough to get your husband here."

"I know my husband. He won't just walk in here."

Lisa surveyed her with disdain.

"You have kids?" Lisa queried.

"Three," Valerie responded.

"I have one. And I plan on seeing him again. I am not going to allow anything happening here today to stop me. You understand?"

"Good for you," Valerie told her in a derisive tone.

Lisa walked away to be alone.

On the first floor, Marc Christopher and his brother, John, inspected the raggedy structure. In particular, Marc was interested in a series of drilled holes within various support beams of the building.

"What do you make of all these holes in the beams?" Marc wondered. "The security guy said he thought they were going to implode the building."

"That's what they're doing here, but it's not an implosion *per se*," John advised. "Strategically placed explosives are set in load-bearing supports of the building. They're set off in a controlled sequence and gravity actually brings down the building."

"What kind of explosive do you need?" Marc asked.

"It can be done with dynamite," John explained. "That's what I got from Toomey."

Toomey was their Arizona connection who provided weapons, technology, and explosives.

"Is it a big deal to set it up?" Marc quizzed.

"No," John told him. "The wiring is in place. All I would need is a sequence detonator. It might be here somewhere. Otherwise, I can modify one of the detonators we have."

"Okay, get going on that," Marc requested. "I'm going to make a phone call to get this guy over here."

Marc darted up three flights of stairs to the fourth floor. As soon as he entered the floor, Tom hopped off the counter and was at attention ready for an order.

"Why so glum?" Marc asked the crowd as he clapped. "I've been to wakes that had more energy." He then focused on Valerie. "Mrs. Legion, how are you doing?"

"I find this all to be very depressing," Valerie noted.

"Life is like that," Marc opined. "You must find balance. Take solace in the Lord."

"Why don't you just let me go and we can forget this ever happened," Valerie pleaded.

"Your naivety is charming, Mrs. Legion. Don't worry, I promise you will be at church tomorrow morning."

Marc pivoted and peered at Artie and Lisa. He then shifted his focus to Tom.

"Tom, take her," referring to Lisa, "down to the third floor until I call you. If she tries to run shoot her. If you shoot her, be sure you kill her." Marc's words were cold and detached.

Tom signaled to Lisa to start walking and Marc focused on Artie.

"So, what was the plan?" Marc wondered.

"We were gonna ask him for money, but get it piecemeal, except for the last piece." Artie advised.

"How much were you going to ask?"

"Ten million. And get it a million at a time."

"Not bad. The better practice would be to ask for two drops of five million dollars and be satisfied with the first drop. You would also have to change out the bag it's delivered in on the spot and x-ray the money. Make sure there's no tracers or dye packs."

Artie looked at Marc like a defeated soldier and acknowledged his comments.

"Where's her phone, Artie?" Marc demanded in an all business tone.

"Her purse."

Marc retrieved the phone and turned it on.

"Now, Artie, I want you to have the same pumped up voice you used on the first call. You understand? If you try anything, I will end the phone call and beat you to within an inch of your life. And after you stop begging me to kill you, we'll try it again."

Artie knew that Marc's comments were not bluster.

"Mrs. Legion," Marc shared, "I'm going to let you talk to your husband. We will put him on speaker and I will hold the phone. If you start to say anything foolish, I'll end the call. All he is going to want to know is how you're doing."

Marc looked at both of them.

"Are we all set?"

Artie and Valerie acknowledged him and he pulled up Roger Legion's name from the call log on the phone. He pushed on the words 'Call Back' and the call connected. Roger Legion's phone was now ringing.

CHAPTER 57

Located twenty-two miles northeast of Lancaster, California is Edwards Air Force Base. It is the home of the 412th Test Wing and the second largest base in the Air Force. The 412th Test Wing is responsible for the planning and analyzing of all flight and ground testing of aircraft and weapon systems in the Air Force arsenal. The base covers 481 square miles and oversees day-to-day operations for over ten thousand military, federal civilian, and contract personnel.

In a small, windowless, conference room inside the Air Force Test Pilot School, nine men assembled, on short notice, to discuss a black 'op' operation deemed urgent. The men ranged in age from 32 years old to 44 years old. All the men wore green coveralls and walked in wearing a blue side cap.

Captain Paul Messina would provide all instruction on the matter. Captain Messina was 47 years old, 6 feet 2 inches tall with a slender build. He served in both Iraq wars and was considered one of the Air Force's foremost experts on aerial weapon systems.

"Gentlemen," the Captain began, standing in front of a white board, "thank you for making yourselves available on such short notice. You may recall our preliminary meeting regarding

Operation Double E. We have now received authorization to proceed with it.

"You men were selected based upon your proficiency with particular aircraft and weapon systems. I apologize for the covert nature of this mission, but that's just the way it is."

The Captain then drew a large square on the whiteboard. Below it, he drew two circles.

"This gentlemen," he said pointing to the square, "is the Palace of Barranca, located in the middle of the desert, down in Sonora, Mexico. The place is huge. It is mostly concrete. From the exterior, it looks like a prison. Protecting it are advanced radar stations located within three to four miles from the Palace."

As he spoke the last sentence, he pointed to the two circles located below the square on the whiteboard.

"The plan is to knock out the radar stations on the southern side of the Palace. That is the side from which you will approach."

"Bootleg," Paul pointed to one of the men, a Chief Master Sergeant and helicopter pilot. He was on the original team at Boeing Aircraft that designed all the current modifications to the Apache helicopter. "You and Smokey, and your co-pilots, will be part of an advance team flying Apaches. The ordinance on them will be AGM-122 Sidearm air-to-surface anti-radiation missiles."

The Apaches were Apache helicopters and the AGM-122 Sidearm missiles are used to degrade enemy air defenses, particularly ground-based radar, in the initial period of conflict.

"We call those AGMs 'Wild Weasels,' Bootleg told the group. "They'll take down a little more than just a taco stand."

The comment caused the men to chuckle.

"Why are we using Apaches?" Smokey wondered. "That's the Army's bird."

"We don't want our actions to be traced back to any particular branch of the military," the Captain told them. "In close quarters combat, we all know that the best airship to have is the Apache."

All the men agreed with Paul's statement.

"Drake, Billy Bob, you guys will pilot the F-15 Eagle attack jets, along with your weapons specialists. Whether or not the radar is knocked out, you're going to proceed. The ordinance on your jets are GBU-24 Paveway III missiles, otherwise known as a 'bunker buster.' As you guys know, they are laser-guided and have a thermobaric warhead. They will create an intense, high-temperature explosion that will be significant in duration. We believe that one bunker buster will do the trick, but, while you're there, you might as well give it a double tap."

The Captain was indicating that he wanted the attack jet pilots to drop two bunker buster bombs on the Palace.

"Does this Palace have any ground-to-air capability?" Billy Bob asked.

"That's a very good question," Paul advised. "Our intel is that there are Scud missile launchers on the property that have to pop up. If the radar is knocked out, you should be able to neutralize them before they are able to fire. If not, prepare for a firefight."

"Other than the Scuds, anything else?" Drake quizzed.

"Fifty caliber machine guns. The turrets pop up out of the ground. So, once again, it's important to take out the radar stations."

"Is this all going to be done under cover of darkness?" Smokey wondered.

"Twenty-one hundred hours. That's when the attack on the radar stations should commence. The jets will be less than one hour behind the Apaches. Once the jets drop their ordinance, they return to base. If we get all the wheels moving on this 'op' at the same time, it will be completed very quickly. Any questions?"

The Captain looked around the room and no one spoke up or raised their hand.

"Just a few final notes," the Captain wanted to add. "After the Apaches are done with the radar stations, they proceed to the Palace as a cleanup crew. We are dealing with a cancer here. The treatment for cancer is not to heal, it is to destroy. It is important to note that there are no friendlies involved in this mission. Everyone and everything is a hostile and will be treated as such. Another reason that the Apache was selected was because of its extraordinary night vision capability. If it moves, it is to be eradicated. If you see a pediatric ambulance or a busload of kids, it is to be removed from the face of the earth. If anyone is thinking about growing a conscience, let me know now, so you don't waste our time. The objective here is to turn the Palace of Barranca to dust and give it back to the desert."

The Captain gazed at the men with a proud smile.

"Gentlemen, we have a transport waiting to take you all to Groom Lake. That will be your point of origin and that will be your point of return. The men operating the Apaches will take a second transport to Fort Huachuca in Arizona. That's where you'll pick up your airship assets. Good luck and God bless America."

The men rose from their seats and exited the room in a single file formation. They were heading to a remote detachment of Edwards Air Force Base located in Nevada referred to by some as Groom Lake and by others as Area 51.

CHAPTER 58

Nearly two hours passed. Roger and Rolf drove around in Roger's late model, black, Cadillac CTS. Rolf presented different scenarios to Roger and continued to make phone calls in an attempt to determine who was responsible for kidnapping Valerie Legion.

Roger was driving eastbound on Interstate 8 through Mission Valley when the car signaled that there was an incoming call.

"Wait till we see the number." Rolf cautioned Roger, hoping for the slim chance that the Caller ID may provide some locate information.

The name that came up on the Cadillac's information screen was 'Valerie.' Rolf stared at the screen and it troubled him. Roger looked at Rolf.

"Answer it."

"Hello," Roger spoke the word in a rather subdued voice.

"Hello, Roger," Valerie addressed him.

"Oh, Val-e. I've been so worried about you. How are you?" Roger rushed his words because he wanted to hear her voice.

"I'm okay. I was supposed to babysit today," she expressed with melancholy.

"Don't worry. I spoke with Debby. I didn't tell her what happened."

"Good. Listen to me, Roger. Don't come and get me. Please don't come and . . ." her pleading was cut off.

"That's enough," Artie told her as Legion and Rolf listened in. "Right now, she's in a cage. Are you gonna do what I say, or should I put her in a box?"

In spite of his situation, Artie's voice exuded genuine glee.

"What do you want?" Roger demanded.

"Ten million dollars," Artie calmly shared. "How long will it take you to get one million together?"

"I can get that immediately. You tell me where you want it dropped off. I'll call ahead to the bank now."

"Do you know where the trolley station is in Chula Vista?"

Chula Vista was located at the opposite end of the County from Oceanside.

"Yeah," Roger answered.

"Bring it down there. Your attorney will tell me when you leave. Somebody will call you when you get there."

"Do we have to do this nine more times?" Legion wondered.

"You have got to ask yourself this question: Is she worth it?"

Artie suddenly disconnected the call. He looked at Marc awaiting approval that he knew what he was doing.

"Now, we leave the phone on and we wait," Marc conveyed to Artie.

"Aren't you worried that he might get the money and go to Chula Vista?" Artie inquired.

"Maybe, if I was an amateur," Marc disclosed while flexing his prowess. "He's on his way here right now and he's probably going to bring an army with him. I learned a long time ago, that when you're backed into a corner, you're capable of extraordinary things."

In Legion's Cadillac, Roger visualized his wife and could hear her sweet voice.

"Where we going?" Roger's voice was insistent.

Rolf opened an application on the phone and located Valerie's phone.

"Oceanside," Rolf spoke slowly and deliberately. "Alex Road. It's off the 76 near the Oceanside Airport."

Roger sped up to reach the Texas Street exit to allow for a U-turn back onto the freeway to begin a race to Oceanside.

Rolf remained contemplative.

"You said they weren't going to call you again on her phone. But they did. They want us to find her location."

"Why?" Roger wondered.

"It's a trap," Rolf opined with certainty.

Roger Legion did not care. He had an appointment with an adversary. As he was so fond of saying, it was time for actions, not words. The rubber was about to meet the road.

CHAPTER 59

The 2nd Avenue Sykoz (Psychos) were a group of eight African-American friends who met twelve years earlier in Oceanside High School and decided that a basic 9-to-5 job, and the lifestyle that accompanied it, was not for them. They started selling drugs for larger drug dealers and stealing or boosting cars for a chop shop located near the back-gate of Camp Pendleton.

The owner of the chop shop was Tizoe's brother, Snazzy, and he allowed the Sykoz to hang out in the shop, plan their criminal activities, and hopefully benefit from the fruit of their labor. All eight members of the gang had served time in prison for various drug-related and property-related crimes. The one thing they sought out, but could never achieve, was the big score that would elevate the group to a higher respect level.

The unofficial leader was a gangbanger with the handle of Bugs. He was 5 foot 8 inches tall and weighed 165 pounds. Bugs always wanted to come across as the wise sage, who shared his worldly knowledge with men who could not read on a fifth grade level. Bugs wore a new, Detroit Lions baseball cap with the price tag hanging off of it. He also liked to wear white t-shirts, washed by his mother, gold chains, and sweat pants. He wore sweat pants because he claimed his 'junk' needed to breathe.

Bugs also loved to tell stories about all of his 1-8-7 adventures (the California Criminal Code for homicide). He liked to brag about how he got away with murders and now someone else was doing time for them.

He liked to show the other men in the gang the proper way to hold a gun to appear the most intimidating and his weapon of choice was the MAC-10 machine pistol.

Bugs was the only one of the gang in the garage this day and he was waiting for a call from Tizoe regarding a big score. Tizoe did not give him any details, but indicated it was going to be a seven-figure payday.

Artie Clexx and Tizoe had worked out a plan for the 2nd Avenue Sykoz to be the pick-up men for the Valerie Legion ransom. In exchange, they would be given one of the ransom drops (a million dollars) for their services. Tizoe was also promised one of the ransom drops, then Artie and Lisa would take the remaining money.

When another member of the gang, named Stash, entered the garage, Bugs began asking questions immediately. Stash was 5 feet 10 inches tall, not an ounce of body fat, and continually smoked Kool Menthol Kings cigarettes. His diet consisted of cigarettes and malt liquor. He never wanted to eat. When he did eat, it was usually half of a hamburger with nothing on it, just meat and the bun and he would toss the other half away. He would drink malt liquor from the time he awoke until he went to sleep. He never appeared drunk because he had built up such a tolerance to it.

"S'up, mah nigga? (What's up, my Negro?)" Stash wondered.

"You hear from Tizoe?" Bugs inquired.

"Nope," Stash responded between drags on his cigarette.

"What's goin' on wit dat fool? He says somethin' big's goin' down and he ain't around," Bugs flared in frustration.

"Call his cell," Stash responded nonchalantly.

"What you think I been doin', Negro? Hittin' the crack pipe?"

"Why you trippin? Just chill. He'll show up or call."

"Go find him," Bugs ordered. "Tell him I'm tired a waitin' on his punk ass. He better be pimpin' and not gettin' some sugar off a coochie. You tell him, 'Mah nigga es bigga!'"

Bugs warned that Tizoe better be making money and not spending time with a woman. Stash looked at him and smiled.

"That's why they call you 'Bugs.' Cause you one crazy sum bitch. Where he at? Still at that old parts place?"

"Yeah," Bugs acknowledged.

"I got this one," Stash told him. "I'll find out why he's not callin'."

Stash turned and headed back to the door where he entered and Bugs called out to him.

"Pac was a cowboy!"

Bugs referenced the deceased rapper, Tupac Shakur. Stash didn't look back, but merely uttered a one syllable response.

"Word."

CHAPTER 60

The Grant Grill, located within the U.S. Grant Hotel in downtown San Diego, has been an institution of fine dining for more than sixty years. In particular, attorneys like to congregate there because of its quiet, yet palatial atmosphere.

It was once a 'Men's Only' restaurant and bar, until 1969 when a group of four female attorneys staged a successful "sit-in" that caused the restaurant to change its policy.

Jim Roth and Larry Larkin were discussing business over a few late afternoon cocktails, when a whirlwind, in the form of John Hamishaw, entered the restaurant and walked directly to their table. Both Jim and Larry stopped their conversation to watch him approach. Without stopping, John slid into their booth, sitting next to Larry.

"We have to talk," John expressed with urgent seriousness.

"So, talk," Jim told him in slightly dismissive tone.

"I walked out on Legion today," John stated with a bitter tone.

"Yeah, so?" Jim conveyed.

"You gotta make things right about our deal," John demanded.

"You didn't do anything for us, John," Jim retorted.

"What are you talking about? What about Cy 'the Guy'? I can take Legion down in court. I know his parlor tricks."

"Cy 'the Guy' had a massive stroke. He's brain dead. That case is over."

"No," John argued. "You substitute the estate in as the plaintiff."

"His wife would probably settle for fifty cents," Jim declared. "That case never had any traction. The only thing going for it was that discovery issue and Legion did what he had to do."

John immediately switched topics.

"Larry wouldn't be sitting here today if it wasn't for me. So, I should get a piece of his action."

"I'm the guy who did all the leg work with Legion," Larry flared. "After Legion said 'no' the first time, I'm the one who got him to reconsider."

"Listen, both of you," John replied focusing on both Jim and Larry. "Legion wants ten million dollars. Tell him you could only get eight million. Then give Larry a million and I'll take a million."

Jim stared at John in awe.

"Jim, I know when it was two million, you promised him a ten percent finder's fee," John disclosed.

"I don't think my guy will go ten million now. There's going to be one finder's fee. You deal with Larry," Jim told him.

"Let me tell you something, Jim," John's voice was slow and deliberate. "I'm not the guy you screw over in this instance. I'm the guy you pay off for silence. I bet your boss would like to know where the leaks are in the information pipeline."

"You don't know Diego Barranca," Jim replied in a cold, menacing tone. "If you were to get an audience with him, which you can't, he would listen and then he would have you, and your entire family, killed. It would be in a most brutal fashion."

John slid out of the booth and stood looking at both men.

"We'll talk about it," Larry spoke up.

"SHUT UP!" John's voice reverberated throughout the restaurant. He stared at Jim. "We'll see," he fumed.

John exited the restaurant at a brisk gait.

Jim and Larry watched him exit. Jim shared a revelation.

"He wanted a million dollars and his wife and his four little kids killed. What kind of animal is that? Maybe, he would get along with Diego Barranca."

Larry was horrified at Jim's disclosure. He didn't know what to think. Just then, Jim received a text message to return to the Palace of Barranca immediately. It was urgent.

CHAPTER 61

Legion's Cadillac slowly rolled by in front of the abandoned O-side Auto Parts warehouse, after driving almost 80 miles an hour the entire way, allowing both men a swift, visual inspection in their search for a point of entry. The building sat quietly on the plot of land with only Tizoe's security car in sight.

"There are exterior stairs for a fire escape on the eastern side of the building," Rolf observed. "There's an entrance to each of the three upper floors. If you could create a diversion, I can get in through one of them."

As they turned the corner, Roger saw a 1974 green Ford LTD stop near the entrance to the stone driveway of the building. Stash, who was sent by Bugs of the 2nd Avenue Sykoz to find Tizoe, stepped out of the car and opened the gate. He then drove his car up the driveway and parked alongside Tizoe's security car.

"This guy can be our diversion," Roger advised.

"Turn around," Rolf told him. "Take me back to the gate."

Legion complied and Rolf added a few comments.

"Mr. Legion, I know you won't listen to me, but I prefer you wait in the car. I'm not a hundred percent sure what we are facing here and I don't want to worry about you in there. If you would wait in the car, I'll have a team of men here shortly."

As Rolf spoke, Roger continued to analyze the building.

"You're right, Rolf. I'm not going to listen to you on that topic. As soon as this guy in the car makes a move toward the building, I'll be right behind you."

"All right, then listen," Rolf's tone was serious. "One of the tricks these guys do is dip their bullets in garlic. So if the bullet doesn't kill you, the blood poisoning will."

"Interesting," Legion noted.

"We find your wife, you get her outta there. You just get in your Caddie and go," Rolf's words were definite.

"All right," Legion said to appease him, knowing that he would never leave him if there was any degree of danger.

Legion and Rolf saw the driver's door open on the LTD and they followed suit in the Cadillac. They dashed to the eastern side of the building unnoticed and set up the broken step ladder to allow them access to the fire escape stairs.

Earlier, inside the building, John Christopher finished installing dynamite charges in the pre-drilled holes for the building's implosion. He also located the sequence detonator that needed a battery to make the device fully active. He found his brother Marc to report on his efforts.

"The place is wired to blow," John shared with Marc. "Twelve charges on the first floor and twelve on the second floor. We need a battery for the sequence detonator. We might have one, otherwise, should I go get one?"

"Yeah, we've got time," Marc approved. "I'm sure there's a drug store or grocery store right down the street."

As Marc and John spoke, Tom walked down a flight of stairs with Lisa Nastasi, to the landing between the first and second floor. Tom was able to view the entire first floor from his vantage point. He was waiting for Marc to finish speaking with John, so he could find out what Marc wanted done with Lisa.

When Stash exited his LTD, he had a Kool cigarette in his mouth and a cell phone in his hand.

"Bugs, he's here," Stash said into the phone. "I'm gonna go in and get him right now. Chill, I'll put him on the phone."

Stash moved directly to the front door of the building and pulled open the large, heavy, dilapidated wooden door.

Inside the building, Marc, John, and Tom moved to attention as the natural light began to flood in from the swift motion of the door opening. Marc reached behind his waist for his handgun. Before he touched his gun, Tom leveled his Colt M-4 rifle and took one shot.

The thunderous roar of the 5.56 caliber bullet reverberated through the building. The bullet smashed into Stash's chest, lifting him off his feet, and bashing his body into the doorframe. His lifeless, crumpled torso fell to the floor, near his Kool cigarette, which continued to burn.

"GET OVER HERE!" Marc screamed ferociously at Tom. Tom lowered his weapon and cautiously approached. "What the hell is wrong with you? If that was a cop, we'd be in a world of pain right now. Never kill someone because you can, kill them because you have a reason."

Marc looked at Tom in disgust.

"If you did it,' Tom told Marc, "you'd give one of your long, bullshit, philosophical reasons, according to your *maestro*." Tom uttered the word '*maestro*' sarcastically. "You're fulla shit. You kill because you can."

"We don't have time to debate this now," Marc ordered. "Take her upstairs and watch all three of them. I'll deal with you later."

Tom walked back to the staircase and began to ascend it with Lisa in front of him. His brother, John, left the building to see if the necessary batteries were in the truck. He would ultimately determine the need for a road trip to the Auto Zone and then to a Walgreens.

Back at chop shop, Stash's gangbanger compatriot from the 2nd Avenue Sykoz, Bugs, was an ear-witness to Stash's execution. He also heard the conversation between Marc and Tom Christopher.

Bugs gazed at the phone with a shocked look that turned into a grimace. The remaining five members of the gang were now assembled in the shop awaiting the details of Tizoe's big score.

"SYKOZ!" Bugs proclaimed like a zealous preacher coming off a coke high. The remaining five members surrounded Bugs to hear what was happening. "Our brother, Stash, has been sacrificed for our cause. The time for vengeance is now. I want everybody strapped-up. We got cleanin' to do."

Bugs instructed the five Sykoz to make sure they had a weapon. He walked over to a cabinet in the back of the shop and removed a Kryptonite lock. Bugs removed a MAC-10 machine pistol and placed a full clip into it. The men each grabbed a weapon and followed Bugs to a 2001 Ford Expedition. Bugs would be the driver.

These men had no idea about what awaited them. They had an appointment with destiny.

CHAPTER 62

When Rolf Adler heard the Colt M-4 gunshot that killed Stash, he used the opportunity to force the fire escape door on the third floor open. The door on the second floor was bolted closed, but the third floor door was rotting, which allowed him to rip off the hardware with his bare hands. He dashed in followed by Roger Legion. Rolf attempted to close the door, but it would not return to its original closed position.

Rolf surveyed the third floor, which was essentially empty except for a stripped Raymond forklift. In his waistband, behind his back, was a .45 caliber Glock 21 Gen4. This gun had thirteen rounds in the magazine and one round in the chamber, ready to fire.

He then turned to Legion and spun the gun around on his right trigger finger and offered it, grip first, to him. Roger shook his head indicating that he didn't want it.

Legion and Rolf heard Lisa Nastasi and Tom Christopher coming up the stairs.

On the first floor, Marc Christopher squatted down next to Stash and looked at him. With his thumb, he traced the Sign of the Cross on Stash's forehead and uttered, "Remember man that thou art dust and unto dust thou shall return."

Marc then pulled Stash's body further into the building, placed it along one of the walls, and covered it with various empty boxes and strewn trash. In the middle of covering Stash, he stopped as if he had heard something. He looked up to examine the second floor. He took note of the dilapidated railings that were rusted and broken, but he felt something was not right.

As Tom passed the third floor landing to ascend to the fourth floor, Rolf made a stealthy move into the stairway and placed his gun behind Tom's right ear.

"Stop," Rolf told him in a muted voice. "We're gonna go downstairs."

Rolf backed him up, took his rifle, and gave it to Legion to hold. He then put Tom's hands behind his back and placed a zip tie restraint on Tom's wrists.

"Don't do anything stupid," Rolf warned Tom. "I'm as good as your brother."

Rolf signaled to Legion to check out the fourth floor. Legion nodded his head and stared at Lisa. He knew by looking at her that she was not an innocent hostage.

Rolf and Tom descended the staircase to the second floor. Rolf carried Tom's rifle in one hand and his semi-automatic pistol in the other. They stopped to obtain a visual on the floor and the layout. From the second floor, Rolf looked out onto the first floor through the center oval opening to see if he could locate Marc. No noise was coming from the first floor.

Rolf returned to the staircase and they began their descent. He stopped Tom with his gun still aimed behind Tom's ear.

"Call to Marc."

Tom was hesitant. The cold barrel of Rolf's gun against his flesh persuaded him.

"Marc." There was no answer. "MARC."

Tom's voice bellowed throughout the building. Then a voice, sounding as if it was on the other side of the first floor filled the air.

"If I knew it was you Rolf, I would have charged more money," Marc advised, with his voice resonating through the first and second floors.

At first, Rolf aimed his gun out to see if he could lock on Marc's position, but all he could see was darkness, other than the circular area lit by natural light from the second floor.

"One of the things my *maestro* taught me was how to throw your voice. It's a simple technique and very effective."

The second time he spoke, Rolf knew the voice came from a different location.

"What was his name? Your teacher?" Rolf casually inquired.

"Fiero DeMasi," Marc proclaimed with pride.

"The best of the best," Rolf acknowledged. "What was his nickname?"

"*La Sorpresa*, the surprise," Marc's response had an eerie calm to it.

"I heard you could never prepare against him. He never repeated himself. So, you never knew what was coming."

"A little like life, wouldn't you say?"

As Marc uttered those words, he held out his pistol to line up a head shot on Rolf. Rolf immediately moved Tom into Marc's line of sight to block the shot. Rolf did not have a visual on Marc, but could hear the air move and smell the dust rustle.

"What if I was to tell you that Diego Barranca is dead?"

Rolf did not actually have confirmation of that fact.

"Not totally unexpected,' Marc conceded. "But he already paid me. I gave him my word."

"You can't just walk away?"

"I can't." Marc's tone was succinct.

Rolf knew he was not going to be able to negotiate his way out of this situation. There was not a lot of places to take cover and he did not know what type of firepower Marc had at his disposal.

As Rolf debated his options in his mind, the 2001 Ford Expedition pulled into the driveway, filled with the remaining members of the 2nd Avenue Sykoz gang.

CHAPTER 63

When Rolf Adler began his descent down the stairs with Tom Christopher, Roger Legion ascended the stairs, following Lisa Nastasi to the fourth floor. He saw his wife, Valerie, and raced over to her. Lisa moved swiftly to Artie, both still restrained by zip ties.

"Val-e," Roger joyfully announced. Her clothes were soiled from the dust and dirt of her surroundings. To Roger, she was a beautiful sight.

Roger grabbed the lock on the cage and looked at the bottom of it.

"It's all fours!" Valerie blurted out at an accelerated pace, wanting Roger out of there more than herself.

Roger took the lock off and opened the chain link door. Valerie and Roger engaged in one quick, tight hug, but both knew they were in a race against time.

"Who are these people?" Roger inquired to determine whether or not he would give them any assistance.

"They're the ones who took me," she told him.

Roger moved at warp speed and before anyone realized what he was doing, he was within striking distance of Artie. He threw a violent, walloping haymaker to Artie's jaw. The punch lifted Artie off his feet as he twisted around falling backward to the floor.

Legion then looked at Lisa with a disgusted scowl and decided not to touch her. Valerie grabbed her Michael Kors purse and Roger held her by the forearm as they careened down the stairs to the third floor.

Artie rolled over and tried to slowly stand up while shaking off the pain in his face. Legion's forceful pummel left his head in a fog.

"Lisa," he murmured with a slight slur, "get the knife out of my pocket. Cut the zip ties."

Lisa complied and she helped Artie stand. He continued to shake off the pain as he regained his anger and energy.

"Where's the shotgun?" It was more of a demand than a question.

She retrieved the nickel-plated shotgun from under the several discarded boxes that concealed it. She handed it to Artie and he pumped it once to place a shell in the chamber ready for firing. He took off after Legion and Valerie, with Lisa close behind.

Legion made it out onto the third floor fire escape, but he was able to see the six men from the 2nd Avenue Sykoz walking to the east side of the building and each man carried some type of weapon. He went back into the third floor where Valerie was waiting.

"We're going to go another way, Val-e."

"What's wrong?" she wondered as she was able to read his demeanor.

"Nothing. This other way is better. Stay close behind me."

Roger returned to the doorway of the third floor and could hear Artie descending the stairs. Artie did not think anyone would be on the third floor and planned to go directly down the staircase.

"Artie, check the third floor," Lisa demanded.

Artie looked quickly through the third floor doorway and planned to continue down the stairs. In that moment, Legion pounced.

Roger jumped out at Artie grabbing the barrel and the stock of the shotgun. Artie was caught off guard and it backed him up right to the edge of the next flight of stairs. A test of strength ensued with each man attempting to twist the shotgun away from the other. Lisa realized that Artie was not going to win.

"Noooooooo!" Lisa screamed and jumped on Legion's back. Instead of pulling him off, her weight leaned them forward and all three tumbled down the stairs to the next landing. The shotgun went through the railing of the stairs, landing on the first floor, not far from Rolf and Tom Christopher.

Outside of the building, the 2nd Avenue Sykoz began climbing the ladder to reach the fire escape. From the ground, they could see that the third floor door was open.

Roger and Artie were engaged in a street-brawl melee. They matched each other punch-for-punch with vicious power and bloodthirsty combat, each hoping to score a death blow.

The men were now on the second floor and both were looking for anything and everything to use as a weapon. Artie appeared to be tiring and both had cuts on their faces. Roger suddenly pumped up with a second wind and began a merciless series of blows to Artie's face. The fight moved into one of the offices on the second floor.

Lisa ran down to the first floor to grab the shotgun. Valerie wanted to help Roger, but worried about what Lisa might do. Then, the sounds of fighting in the second floor office silenced.

Artie lumbered to the doorway, like a boxer who just heard a bell for the round to end, with a drained look on his face. He took one more step and fell forward face down. In the center of Artie's back was his black, folding knife with the four-inch blade. The blade was completely sunk into his back.

Roger Legion then appeared; bloodied, but standing.

"NO!" Lisa screamed and leveled the shotgun to fire at Legion.

Valerie saw Lisa's reaction and went into motion. She took off toward her like a defensive end football player intent on mowing down an adversary. Valerie hit Lisa and the shotgun with a shoulder block and Lisa pulled the trigger on the gun. The power of the recoil of the gun pulled them both back and they crashed into a railing that overlooked the first floor. The section of railing broke away. Lisa, the shotgun, and Valerie went off the second floor perimeter walkway and took flight, before slamming into the concrete of the first floor.

The 2nd Avenue Sykoz heard the shotgun blast and they were initially investigating the fourth floor. All six men were now preparing for a firefight.

Roger Legion quickly peered over the area where the railing broke and saw the two women on the ground. He bolted down the staircase to the first floor to check on Valerie's condition.

"Val-e," Roger spoke at a rapid pace. "Speak to me, com'on, honey."

She opened her eyes and said, in a soft tone, "That's not the best way to get to the first floor."

Roger smiled and gave her a quick, tight hug. He helped Valerie stand. They both looked at Lisa Nastasi and the back of her skull was the first thing to smash into the concrete with the weight of Valerie Legion on her. Lisa's eyes were open as was her mouth and her head appeared to rest in a pool of blood that continued to grow.

Legion turned his focus to Marc Christopher and Rolf. They were engaged in a fight to the death with each using a steel bar to pound on the other.

Roger heard footsteps advancing onto the second floor. He motioned to Valerie to keep quiet and he backed her up into a darkened area of the first floor. The 2nd Avenue Sykoz had arrived.

CHAPTER 64

When Roger Legion, Artie Clexx, and Lisa Nastasi tumbled down the staircase from the third floor to the second, Rolf Adler and Marc Christopher found themselves locked in a stalemate. Marc stayed in the perimeter of the floor, not allowing Rolf to get a visual on him to take a shot. Rolf moved around between the darkness and the edge of the lit area moving around with Tom Christopher in front of him, not allowing Marc to lock onto a target.

"Rolf," Marc's voice echoed in the darkness. "Let's stop wasting our time. How about you and I go at it? No guns. Old school. What d'ya say?"

"How many guns does he have?" Rolf asked Tom.

"One handgun," Tom replied.

"Marc," Rolf amplified his voice. "Come out of the darkness and swear on your Savior, Jesus Christ."

Marc emerged from the darkness with his handgun held up.

"I swear on my Savior, the Lord Jesus Christ that I will not use any weapon other than what we agree upon."

"What do you have in mind?" Rolf queried.

"Bar fight." Marc walked back into the darkness and reappeared with two pieces of three-quarter-inch thick rebar that were approximately four feet long. At each end of the rebar, they were cut to a point, like a chisel. Marc threw them on the ground into the lighted area.

"I've got one condition:" Marc said, "If anything happens to me, you let my brother walk outta here."

"Done."

"On the count of three, we toss the guns and we each grab a bar," Marc proclaimed.

"One thing I've got to do."

Rolf brought Tom to the staircase and zip tied his restraint around one of the metal pipes that comprised the first floor bannister. Rolf also placed Tom's Colt M-4 submachine gun against the wall between Marc and himself.

Both men emerged from the darkness with their handguns held up in the air. They walked toward each other in the lighted circle and each picked up a piece of rebar. Marc tossed his gun to one side of the building and Rolf tossed his to the other.

As Marc and Rolf commenced their bar fight, Roger Legion and Artie Clexx were pummeling each other on the second floor.

Both Marc and Rolf placed their hands approximately twelve inches apart in the center of the bar and at first, they seemed to just strike at each other left then right. Marc took an opportunity to swing at Rolf with his bar, but quickly retained his center grip. Marc appeared more powerful, but it was only because Rolf was distracted by his concern for Legion's safety. He had no idea what was going on between Legion and Artie.

In one move, Marc pushed against Rolf's bar as hard as he could and then began to swing his bar around like an airplane propeller. Rolf was strategizing the best move to deflect Marc's bar when Lisa Nastasi pulled the trigger and the deafening sound of the shotgun seemed to shake the building.

Rolf looked in the direction of the shotgun blast, but Marc would not allow himself to lose focus. In the instant when Rolf turned, Marc stopped swinging his bar and impaled Rolf from front to back in the lower, left quadrant of his abdomen.

Marc did not smile. He took no joy in what he had done. It was a necessary task to complete the job. Rolf stepped back two to three steps into the darkness, near the center of the side wall, where he had placed Tom's rifle.

In the darkness, Rolf went down on one knee as his strength felt sapped and he fought to control his trembling. He grabbed the end of the rebar that stuck out from him and pulled it with all his might. The pain was excruciating and a new voice was now heard.

"Well, well, what do we have here? Looks like a white boy playin' cowboy."

The voice belonged to Bugs, the leader of the 2nd Avenue Sykoz. Around the perimeter of the second floor walkway, fairly equidistant from one another were the six remaining members of the gang, each with a different weapon aimed at Marc.

"Don't move, cowboy," Bugs warned, "'cause we's all got itchy trigger fingers. I got some questions and I bet you got some answers."

As Bugs spoke, Marc surveyed the perimeter and analyzed each man and their weapon. Bugs had a MAC-10 machine pistol and the man next to Bugs, named Freddy, had what appeared to be a .44 caliber revolver. Next to Freddy was a man named Devo, who had a short pump shotgun with a one-foot barrel that would only hold three shells. The next man, named Tram, had an AK-47 submachine gun and the last man, named Gee, had a .50 caliber Desert Eagle handgun.

All the men wore sunglasses, leading Marc to believe that they were recently imbibing alcohol or shooting up some type of drug. If he could stop the two automatic weapons, he believed that he could take the remaining four in a firefight.

The problem was that he did not even have his handgun.

"Somethin' big was goin' down here today. And it looks like you interrupted it. Now, where's my boy, Tizoe, and my boy, Stash?"

Roger Legion and his wife, Valerie, stayed covered deep in the darkness. Roger worried about Rolf's condition.

Then, almost at the edge of the darkness, Rolf appeared blood-soaked on his left side from his wound to his feet. In his right hand, he held the barrel of Tom's M-4 submachine gun and the stock of the gun with his left hand. Marc gave him a quick glance attempting not to stare at him, but acknowledging his presence.

Rolf then held up three fingers and mouthed the words, "Three shot burst." He was advising Marc that the gun was set to fire three bullets with every trigger pull.

"Sykoz!" Bugs proclaimed. "Looks like this cracka white boy gonna need some persua . . ."

Before Bugs could finish his sentence, Rolf launched the M-4 and it flew through the air perfectly into Marc's hands. Marc opened fire immediately to first stop the automatic weapons. A head shot took down Bugs and he then pivoted approximately 120 degrees and took out Tram and his AK-47 machine gun.

Marc moved with ballet fluency and military precision. Before the Sykoz fired their first shot, Marc had killed two of them. The remaining men opened fire and bullets rained down mercilessly on Marc. The Sykoz began to move to avoid being hit and Marc was also being hit. He was struck by the .44 magnum and then some buckshot from Devo's shotgun.

Rolf moved at high speed like he was not wounded at all. He climbed the flight of stairs three steps at a time, to make his way onto the second floor. He took two steps in from the doorway and was able to silence each shooter with one shot from his recovered handgun. He then walked around the perimeter of the second floor walkway and put an additional bullet into each member of the 2nd Avenue Sykoz.

Marc stood in the lighted circle of the first floor and made eye contact with Rolf. Blood dripped down from Marc's forehead where a bullet grazed his scalp and he had three other gapping wounds in his torso. He fell to his knees and then to his back.

Tom watched his brother go down unable to comprehend what had just happened.

CHAPTER 65

Roger Legion darted up the staircase to the second floor to find Rolf Adler leaning against a wall on his way to the ground. Roger had Rolf put his arm around Roger's shoulder and they ambled down the stairs.

Valerie was at the bottom of the stairs and she held up Rolf while Roger took off his suit coat, rolled it up slightly, and wrapped it around Rolf to use as a dressing for his wound.

"Com'on, Val-e. You grab that side. We'll walk him out of here." Roger then spoke to Rolf. "Stay with us, Rolf."

Legion put one of Rolf's arms around his shoulders and Valerie placed his other arm around her shoulders. At this point, Rolf's feet were dragging and he was starting to lose consciousness.

"Wait," Rolf said to them in a weakened voice. "Cut him free from the stairs." Rolf was referring to Tom Christopher. "There's a knife in my pocket." With each word, the volume of Rolf's voice diminished.

Legion took Rolf's knife and cut Tom loose from the stairway. He did not cut Tom's original zip ties.

Roger returned and placed Rolf's arm again around his shoulders and the three of them moved as quickly as possible out the front door of the building.

Tom slowly walked over and gazed at Marc. Blood ran down both corners of his mouth. Marc turned his eyes to Tom.

"Go," he said as he mustered strength to speak.

"Let me," Tom began.

"NO!" A moment passed. "Go."

Tom stood and peered at his brother for one last time. He then walked directly to the front door and out of the building.

With his last ounces of strength, Marc reached into his pocket and removed his earbud. He fidgeted with it to place it in his ear. He then called out to his brother, John.

"John, you there?"

"I'm in the truck, outside the building." John had just returned from his trip to purchase batteries.

"Tom's coming out. When he's in the clear, blow the building."

"Marc, what's wrong?" John's voice denoted urgency.

"You know the password for the money?"

"Yeah."

"What is it?"

"Jesus."

"That's right. Because he watches over it and protects it." Marc's voice was losing energy. "Tell my wife and kids that I love them. You watch over 'em. And you watch over Tom."

John did not know how to respond.

"Do you see Tom?" was Marc's final question.

"Yeah." John responded.

"Then blow the building." Marc finally uttered.

Marc reached for his earbud and removed it from his ear. He then raised his thumb and summoned the strength to draw a Sign of the Cross on his forehead. As he did it, he mumbled the following words: "Remember man that thou art dust and unto dust thou shall return."

John twisted a knob on the sequence detonator and the dynamite, placed strategically in the building within the load-bearing components, began to explode. The dynamite erupted in a circular pattern, first around the first floor, then in a similar pattern around the second floor. The third and fourth floors pancaked down and a mushroom fireball commenced turning the remnants of the structure into a blazing inferno.

Roger, Rolf, and Valerie reached Legion's Cadillac just as the detonation of the building commenced. Roger looked back and as the wind blew in his direction, he could feel the heat coming off the building.

Legion refocused and pulled Rolf into the back seat of his car. Valerie stepped into the back seat and kneeled down beside him.

"Val-e, keep pressure on his wound," Roger requested. "We'll take him to Tri-City Hospital."

"NO!" Rolf's weakened voice commanded. "Too many questions. Take me to Jimmy Flowers' doctor."

Roger knew that Rolf would not last the nearly forty mile trip. Roger and Valerie locked eyes.

"I've got an idea," Roger advised as he put the car in gear and squealed onto the road.

Rolf began to slip in and out of consciousness and within twelve minutes, Roger pulled into the parking lot of the Kisses and Tummy Rubs Animal Shelter. He drove to the back of the building, where there was an emergency entrance for ambulances and walk-ins.

Roger drove right up to the door. He exited his car, walked in, and began to give orders.

"I NEED A GURNEY NOW!" he wailed.

One of the attendants rushed to him with a gurney. They took it out to his car and the veterinary assistant began to speak.

"Sir, we only deal with animals here. This man has to go to a hospital. He can't come inside."

Roger Legion had begun to pull Rolf out of the car and stopped for a moment to face the young lady. His face projected a threatening menace.

"Go get Dr. Walsh now. Tell him Roger Legion says it is an emergency. RUN!"

Roger and Valerie returned to removing Rolf from the car and placing him on the gurney. Dr. Walsh came outside immediately. He was 58 years old, white hair, 5 feet 8 inches tall, wearing a lab coat.

"Roger, what's wrong?" the doctor asked.

Dr. Walsh saw Rolf on the gurney. He then looked to Legion.

"Don't you think," and then he stopped speaking. Roger's eyes locked on his and he knew he should not utter another word. He turned to the two assistants who were outside of the building with him. "Prepare Operating Room-1 for surgery. Stat."

Rolf was rapidly moved into the operating room. Roger and Valerie followed him into the building holding hands. Most of the employees were shocked when they realized that the person with Roger was Valerie Legion, the woman whose life-sized portrait hung in the lobby of the building.

Roger and Valerie sat outside Operating Room-1 looking dirty, tired, and beaten. Amidst the chaos, both were overjoyed to be sitting next to each other.

Valerie reached over to hold Roger's hand. He looked at her and smiled. Valerie would be at church the next morning and Roger would be at the law firm. They would never discuss this day again.

CHAPTER 66

Later that evening, at the Palace of Barranca, Jim Roth waited patiently for Diego Barranca to appear in his office for a late night meeting.

Jim wore blue Ralph Lauren chino pants with a yellow oxford button shirt and leather boat shoes without socks.

He looked around the room and the cleanliness of it was stunning. The same two swords, still in their sheaths, sat in the corner of the room as Jim could not recall ever seeing them in the cabinet. Mexican music played and the scent of jasmine filled the air, attempting to mask the smell of cleaning products.

Diego entered the room swiftly and Jim took a seat before the desk. Diego sat in his chair and leaned back. He wore an Yves St. Laurent blue plaid collar shirt, black jeans, and a heather gray, sleeveless, V-neck sweater.

"How are you, my friend?" Diego asked with ebullient energy.

"Good," Jim replied. "What's so urgent?"

"I received some news today that I found most distressing."

As Diego spoke, he leaned forward in his chair.

"Apparently, someone kidnapped that lawyer Legion's wife and they are blaming me for it," Diego's pumped up voice was slowly turning more sinister. "Now, I don't mind receiving credit when it's due, but I don't like being blamed for something I was not involved in." Diego again leaned back in the chair. "Do you know anything about this?"

"This is the first I'm hearing about it," Jim advised.

"You know, Jim, I like you. All business. Shrewd. Pragmatic. You are the face that I want for my organization. But the same people who asked me about Legion's wife, know that I hired the Christophers. You and I were the only ones who knew that piece of information."

Diego reached into his top right-hand drawer and took out a Sig Sauer 9mm semi-automatic pistol and placed it on the desk.

"Now," Diego slowly enunciated, "do you want to tell me something?"

"The Christophers have big mouths. The way everybody knew about that Utica job. They like to boast. And a $3 million score to kill one guy is like hittin' the jackpot." The men looked at each other. "I don't benefit from selling you out."

As Jim finished speaking, Diego's phone rang and he put the call on speaker.

"Yes," Diego answered.

"Mr. Barranca, there is unknown hostile helicopter activity at the southern radar station."

"Bring up the cameras, so I can get a visual," Diego ordered.

Diego turned and stood from his chair to see the two Apache helicopters from Operation Double E on the 52-inch monitor before him commence fire on the radar station towers.

"Shoot them down!" he demanded.

Diego focused on the screen like a laser. Then, there was complete silence. Blood, flesh, and brain matter sprayed the screen. Jim Roth competently held Diego's Sig Sauer pistol and ended Diego's life with a 9mm hollow point bullet to the head.

Even though Diego did not hear or see his execution coming, the two guards in charge of searching and fumigating visitors heard and saw the action.

The first guard entered Diego's office holding a small, MP5-K submachine gun. The first guard then signaled to the second guard to enter the office. The second guard also carried the same submachine gun.

The guards looked behind the desk and saw only Diego's lifeless body. They slowly moved toward the other furniture in the room. Jim popped up from the area where your legs would go under the desk. With lightning, quick agility, as he started to stand, he fired the gun twice and took out both guards with a headshot.

Then an air raid siren bellowed throughout the building. Explosions could be heard as escape tunnels were being blown up and collapsing. In Jim's waistband, under his sweater, was a Genus satellite phone. He called a number that he had on speed dial and a male voice answered.

"Three-seven-two-nine-six, echo, tango, whiskey."

"Is the line secure?" Jim asked without his usual carefree charm.

"Affirmative," the voice answered.

"This is Talon. The target has been acquired."

"Copy that, Talon."

"Can you have Operation Double E stand down?" Jim's words were fast because he knew what was coming.

"Negative."

"How can I get out?" Jim demanded.

"Try the tunnels on the west side of the Palace. They should still be operational."

"How long do I have?"

"Expect impact within seven minutes. Good luck."

Jim moved like a man on fire. From the corner of the office, Jim picked up one of Diego's swords and unsheathed it. He lifted the sword high in the air and brought it down, as hard as he could, into the side of the top of the desk. The blade went deep enough into the wood to allow the sword to stand by itself.

Jim then picked up Diego and placed his lifeless body into his chair. He wheeled the chair to the end of the desk and placed Diego's thumb on the desk where the sword and the wood met. Jim made sure the blade was on the joint were the thumb connected to his hand.

Jim placed one hand to support it like a fulcrum and with the other hand he grabbed the sword's handle and pushed down with all his might to simulate the action of a paper cutter. He was able to detach Diego's thumb from his body.

Still moving at warp speed, he wrapped the thumb with a cloth napkin. He placed it on the biometric pad and the door that entered into the Palace clicked. Jim exited Diego's office, carrying Diego's thumb and his Sig Sauer pistol.

Jim went through three sets of doorways and halls. All allowed entrance by use of Diego's thumb on the biometric pads. He followed the same path that he had taken once before when Diego had shown him the new girls that were abducted to be Diego's courtesans.

When Jim reached the room where the stage was located, he saw Isa Cabrera, the Etiquette Administrator of the Palace, appearing to clear out her desk. Jim ran toward her and began to speak.

"ISA! Where are the girls?" Jim ordered aiming his gun at her.

"Mr. Roth, I believe we are all dead already." Isa told him with a calm note of surrender.

Jim shot her squarely in the chest and she, and the chair, toppled backward to the ground.

"Be careful what you wish for," Jim told her as he moved to the next room. He saw twelve girls dressed in white and his goal was to save them before the bunker buster bombs of Operation Double E found their target.

Ten minutes later the first bunker buster missile struck at the base of the Palace. The concussive blast was a dirt and sand tsunami. It raised the ground level twenty feet in the air, turning the concrete to particulate dust, and then returning it to its original level. The second bunker buster quickly followed and anything that even vaguely resembled the Palace was completely decimated.

Part 4

CHAPTER 67

7 Days Later

Some degree of normalcy returned to Legion & Associates, as threats from drug lords, assassination plots, and kidnappings were a fading memory. But there were some things that Roger Legion would not forget.

The Cy 'the Guy' Valiant case continued, even though Cy was now brain dead, his wife was waiting for his extended family to visit before she pulled the plug. The case had a discovery schedule and Roger asked Larry Larkin to defend the deposition of the employee at Scripticon responsible for collecting and verifying information on all electronic prescriptions that went through their system. The deposition was set for 10:00 am that morning at the Scripticon offices in the Sorrento Valley section of San Diego.

Larry arrived outside the newer three-story building at approximately 9:40 am. He entered the reception area and walked directly to the receptionist.

"I'm here for a deposition," Larry told the 28-year-old, cute, plus-size, young lady.

She immediately was familiar with it.

"You're going to be in the third floor conference room. Take the elevator to the third floor. The elevator doors open right into the conference room."

"Thank you," Larry responded with a smile and walked directly to a waiting elevator.

When the elevator doors opened, Larry stepped out and saw a large conference room table that could easily sit thirty people. There was no court reporter and one man sat at the far end of the table. The man wore a Brunello dark blue and navy plaid suit with a blue and white striped shirt, and a silk blue with gray and brown diamonds tie. It was Rolf Adler.

"Are you here for the deposition?" Larry inquired. Rolf nodded his head. "Have you seen the court reporter?"

"No," Rolf replied.

Larry sat down across from Rolf and began looking around the environment. Rolf rolled his chair back and stood. He stared at Larry making Larry feel a little uncomfortable.

"Could I get a card from you?" Larry asked with a smile.

Rolf was not smiling. His countenance was cancer serious.

"Where's John Hamishaw?" Rolf demanded.

"Excuse me?"

Rolf immediately pulled his semi-automatic handgun from his waistband behind his back and pointed it at Larry's head.

"This is the last time I'm going to ask you: Where is John Hamishaw?"

"I don't know," Larry advised with his hands up, trying to maintain eye contact with Rolf, but being distracted by the gun.

"Call him," Rolf told him in a calm tone. "Find out where he is. Or better yet, have him come over here."

Larry then looked around the room and saw that in every doorway of the room, stood a well-dressed man, wearing sunglasses, with a semi-automatic pistol in their hand.

"Who are you guys?" Larry wondered with sincere concern.

Rolf walked around the table and in one motion, put his right hand around Larry's neck and lifted him out of the chair. Rolf then kicked Larry's chair away and slammed him back into the wall. The strength of Rolf's arm was immobilizing Larry. Larry grabbed Rolf's arm and it felt like a steel girder.

Rolf pressed his gun against Larry's temple and pulled the hammer on the gun back.

"All right, whatever you want," Larry blurted out with perspiration filling his face.

Rolf let go of his throat and Larry reached inside his suit coat to retrieve his phone. Rolf snatched it from him to review the call log.

"Call him, put it on speaker," Rolf ordered.

As Rolf spoke, a bell went off indicating the elevator doors were about to open. They did and Roger Legion stepped out wearing sunglasses, which he removed as he spoke to Rolf.

"Is he cooperating?" Legion asked.

"I think he's having a difficult time comprehending," Rolf shared.

"That's most unfortunate," Roger expressed to Rolf as he stared at Larry. "Find out what you need to know, then I'll let you know what to do with him."

Legion returned to the elevator and pushed the call button.

"Roger. Roger! ROGER!" Larry screamed as Legion entered the elevator and the door closed.

Larry suddenly remembered how Roger dealt with the Judge at the downtown courthouse, when he was so upset about Larry's tie.

He now learned that Legion's power far exceeded the walls of the courthouse and the law firm.

CHAPTER 68

Later that day, as the afternoon waned, Nina's interest level in answering phones was fading. More and more, she had become introspective on her future, wondering if perhaps happiness was more of an idea sold by Madison Avenue advertisers than something someone should experience.

Her fiancé had continued to remain distant and he had not returned a call to her in over a week. She thought about calling Glenn Edgarian, Roger Legion's premier private investigator to see if her fiancé was up to nefarious shenanigans, but it was something she could not afford, either monetarily or having people start to talk.

She looked down aimlessly at her telephone and her desktop. It was clean, but barren. She thought it was the perfect analogy for her life. With a moment of clarity, she realized that she could be replaced by anyone that could push a button and say 'Hello' within sixty seconds. It was a fitting ending to a bad day.

Then, without warning, Roger Legion appeared before her. It was wraith-like. She did not see him walk up to her desk. He was just there. The time was 4:45 pm.

Normally, she would have perked up like a private in the military being called to attention. But today, she was passive, wallowing in pity for herself and watching everyone else seem to have dreams come true.

"Hey," Roger told her, "it's pretty quiet. You can take off."

She thought Legion may have smiled, but she wasn't sure.

"Thank you," Nina uttered without emotion.

She collected her belongings, walked to the elevator, and pushed a call button. Roger was looking at some papers on her raised desktop. He turned and their eyes met.

"Goodbye, Mr. Legion."

The way Nina spoke the line hit Roger's ear in a funny sort of way. There was a type of finality to it. Roger wanted to say something, but he didn't.

"Goodbye, Nina. See you tomorrow."

She entered the elevator and the doors closed behind her.

Later that evening, Nina sauntered out of her bedroom, wearing nothing but a bathrobe and slippers. She entered the bathroom and turned on the water in the bathtub. Nina made sure that the stopper was in place to allow the tub to fill.

She then headed to her living room and plugged her phone into a speaker to allow songs to play. Nina only wanted to hear one song. It was called *All I Know* and it told a simple story of a girl who dreamed about her wedding day. She pushed a button and the song began to fill the air:

When I was a little girl,
I dreamed about that day.
When I wore a pretty wedding dress,
And danced the night away.

My friends would ask me how he looked
That groom within my dreams.

LEGION'S LAWYERS

I never could remember him
How odd that may seem.

All I know is that he said he loved me.
All I know is that he said he cared.
All I know is that he'd never leave me.
All I know is that we are a pair.

As the chorus of the song played, Nina walked into her kitchen and directly to her junk drawer. She moved items around and found the item she sought.

From the drawer, she removed a box cutter blade. It had a small piece of brown paper that wrapped the blade and she removed the wrapping and discarded it. Then she walked into the bathroom and, as the water continued to run, she placed the blade on the ledge of the tub.

Nina turned off the water and allowed her bathrobe to fall to the floor. She took a moment to look at the inside of her arms, particularly from her elbows to her wrists. Finally, she slowly allowed her right foot to touch the bath water to assess the temperature.

She wondered if the temperature made any difference for what she was about to do.

EPILOGUE

St. Elizabeth Seton Catholic Church
Carlsbad, California

One Year Later

On this Saturday morning, activity swirled in the narthex of the church as a wedding was set to commence in a few minutes. In a dressing room off the narthex, a maid of honor and two bridesmaids attended to every detail of the bride's preparation.

The bride wore an Oleg Cassini white, strapless ball gown with a sweetheart neckline and lace appliques. The bridesmaids wore a regency, or purplish, short mesh dress, right above the knee, with a sweetheart illusion neckline.

There was a knock on the door and the closest bridesmaid opened it.

"Hello, Mr. Legion," said Karla Mulry. She was 31 years old, 5 feet 7 inches tall, blue eyes with a slender frame. Karla exuded the beauty of a photo model, not sexual, but rather authentic. It was a pleasure just to gaze upon her. She was a former law clerk at Legion and Associates and was married to one of the attorneys, Luke Cordel. Two and one-half years earlier, she and Roger Legion found themselves on the Coronado Bay Bridge in the midst of a terrorist attack directed against the bridge.

Roger wore a black, tailor-made tuxedo, with a single button coat, white pleat point collar, black bowtie, and shiny, black, round toe shoes.

"Hello, Karla," Legion answered with a smile as he received a kiss on the cheek from her. "How's that new baby?"

"Driving Luke and I crazy, but we love it."

"Hello, Mr. Legion," the Maid of Honor greeted him with a salutation and a kiss on the cheek. Her name was Diane Abrams. She was 35 years old, with radiant aquamarine eyes, perfectly flushed cheeks, mauve lips, and brown hair that projected natural beauty. She also had a prosthetic leg. Nearly three years earlier, she was in an accident where her car was hit by a tractor trailer. Roger Legion settled her case with the insurance company for the truck in the amount $4.5 million. Legion refused to take any payment for attorney fees.

"Hello, Diane. How's your little one?"

"Getting bigger every day," Diane confessed. "And faster."

"Hello, Roger," the final bridesmaid said to him.

"Patty?" he said pointing to her, hoping he remembered her name.

"Give that man a cigar," Patty White told him.

Patty White was Diane Abrams' sister and was a major part of Diane's life since her husband had died. Patty was 39 years old, 5 feet 2 inches tall, 110 pounds, with short, well-coifed blond hair.

Diane Abrams' husband, Lester Abrams, was an attorney at Legion and Associates who was murdered in the parking garage of the law firm, presumably by, or on behalf of, a drug dealer. Lester was also on the bridge that day with Legion, Karla, and Karla's soon-to-be husband, Luke Cordel.

"Is the bride ready?" Roger asked. "It's time."

The bride turned away to face him and there stood Nina, in all her radiant splendor. She walked over to him and everyone in the room cleared the way. When she reached him, she took hold of one of his forearms and tugged on it, so he would bend down slightly and allow her to kiss him on the cheek.

"Are you ready?" he asked and she nodded.

He did an about-face and offered his forearm for her to embrace. They walked through the narthex and into the church to the position where they had rehearsed the night before.

The church was filled with nearly 400 attendees. Nina never thought more than twenty people would ever attend a wedding for her. The man who paid for everything at her wedding, including the rehearsal dinner, her gown, and the honeymoon, stood next to her and everyone Roger Legion invited, including the entire law firm, made sure they attended with a gift.

This was not the first time Legion paid for the complete wedding of a person who was not a family member. Eleven months earlier, he gave the same gift to Karla Mulry and Luke Cordel.

In both instances, his wife, Valerie, demanded the best of everything, as if these girls were her daughters.

As the wedding march commenced on the church organ, Nina tugged at Roger's arm to share one more thing with him.

"I always feel safe when I'm with you."

Legion looked at her and smiled. She gazed at him and peered down the aisle, past the fifteen rows of pews to the altar nearly 100 feet away. As they began their procession, Nina began to remember.

It was approximately a year earlier. The fateful night that Nina drew a bath and prepared a razor blade to deal with a lack of hope in her life.

When she determined that the water level in the bath was high enough, she shut off the water. As she was about to set her foot into the tub, there was a pounding at her door. She had a doorbell on her apartment door, so she wondered who was in such a grave hurry to speak to her.

Nina put on her bathrobe, walked to her door, and looked through the peephole. There stood John Hamishaw, looking disheveled, dressed as if he was coming from work, leaning against the door, and continuing to pound on it. She did not want neighbors seeing him there. She took the chain off the door and opened it in one swift motion.

"What are you doing here?" she asked him with disdain.

"I had to see ya, sunshine," John explained as he walked right in. Nina could smell the alcohol on his breath.

"Get outta here. You're drunk," Nina told him with no-nonsense flare.

"Come on, baby. Daddy needs a little sugar," he uttered and his words were starting to slur.

"Get out or I'm going to call the police."

"Do that and I'll call Legion and share some interesting information with him."

"Go ahead," she told him and immediately started to walk by him to her bedroom when he grabbed her right upper arm.

"Did you hear what I said, bitch?" he inquired in a menacing tone. "Get in there, spread your legs, and then, after you thank me, we'll talk."

"Let go of me," she responded trying to pull her arm loose. "You're hurting me, asshole."

"I'm a lawyer. In the courtroom, I am a god sent to destroy and prevail. And you dare to say 'No' to me, you ignorant pig!?"

Suddenly, Nina reached across with her left hand and scratched his face. The strike to his face caught John off guard and Nina went to the bathroom because the door had a lock and the lock on her bedroom door did not work.

John gave chase for the short distance and tackled her. She landed on the floor of the bathroom and he was half-in and half-out of the bath. He then tried to position Nina and himself, so that he could rape her. As he was trying to pin her down, she reached up to the ledge of the bathtub and grabbed the box cutter razor blade.

With all her might, she slashed at him twice: first in the throat and then on the cheek. John was stunned as he attempted to unbutton his pants. Drops of his blood fell off him onto the floor and on his clothes. In the moment that he realized what happened, Nina stood, intent on running out of the apartment. John was able to grab her ankle and wanted to twist it to bring her back to the ground.

"You little piece a shit," John asserted.

As he spoke, Nina took her other slipper-covered foot and kicked John in the face. He was stunned and she took off. Just as she reached the door, John reached her. He pulled her back and punched her in the face as hard as he could. The blow sent her back toward the kitchen and one of her hands knocked over everything that was on her kitchen island.

John walked back and stood over her, numbed by alcohol, with blood dripping down on himself and the floor. One of the items that was knocked off the island was a butcher block knife set.

John went down on one knee and grabbed Nina's shoulder to turn her around. As she turned, she grabbed the largest knife from the set, the one with an eight-inch blade. As she rolled over, Nina grabbed the handle with both hands, and with all her might, plunged the knife into John Hamishaw's chest.

John went back on his butt, in shock at what had just happened. Nina grabbed a second knife, a filet knife, and plunged it into his neck. He completely collapsed to the floor, but he was held up slightly by the handle of the first knife. His blood profusely poured out.

Nina looked at him as if she had just slayed a monster. She backed up and stood. Her bathrobe was covered in his blood as were the soles of her slippers. The floor filled with a copious amount of John's blood.

Roger Legion was at the Bagheria Bedda, Jimmy Flowers' restaurant discussing Rolf Adler's activity that day with Larry Larkin. Roger's phone came to life and from the Caller ID, he saw it was from Nina.

"Mr. Legion," she started to speak as soon as she heard his voice, crying, nearly hysterical. "I'm in trouble. Can you help me?"

"Where are you?" Legion asked, in a calm, meted tone.

"The Algonquin Apartments on Laurel near Sixth Avenue. Apartment 5-11."

"I know where that is. I'm on my way. I'm close by. I'll be there in less than twenty minutes."

Legion ended the call and turned to Rolf.

"You got time to take a ride?" Roger asked him.

"Sure."

When they arrived at Nina's apartment, Legion knocked at the door.

"Who is it?" Nina asked.

"It's Roger."

Nina opened the door slowly and her face peered around it. Her lower lip was cut and bleeding from John Hamishaw's punch and the area near her lip was starting to swell and turn blue. When she opened the door the entire way, Legion and Rolf entered quickly and they saw her bathrobe was heavily stained with blood.

"Are you all right?" Roger inquired with urgency.

Nina pointed to the area behind her kitchen island.

"Mr. Legion," Rolf spoke up, "watch where you step."

Both men walked the long way around the kitchen island and saw the lifeless body of John Hamishaw.

Roger looked up at Nina.

"He was drunk," she exclaimed. "He tried to rape me."

Roger then turned to look at Rolf.

"Young lady, what's your name?" Rolf quizzed.

"Nina."

"Nina, we're going to take care of this situation, but I am going to need your help. I am going to ask you to do a few things. I want them done exactly as I tell you. All right?"

"Yes," Nina replied sheepishly, first looking at Legion for his approval.

"I want you to take your clothes off, including your shoes."

"But I don't have on underwear," Nina admitted.

"Don't worry about it," Rolf spoke in a clear and concise manner. "Mr. Legion is going to go into your bedroom. Tell him where the clothes are that you want to wear. I want you to wear socks and shoes. You and Mr. Legion are going to leave here for a little while."

She nodded in acknowledgement and dropped her bathrobe to the floor. She also stepped out of her slippers onto a portion of the carpet that had no blood on it. She kept one arm over her breasts and the other over her pubic area.

As Nina directed Roger on the location of the various clothes that she was going to put on, Rolf made a phone call.

"I need a drop and mop team. The Algonquin Apartments. Apartment 5-11." He then waited a moment. "Occupied, one time."

Rolf was advising the person on the phone that there was one body in need of disposal.

Roger returned from the bedroom with Nina's clothes in hand.

"Do you think you can walk to the bathroom without stepping on blood?" Rolf had ended his call and directed his inquiry to Nina.

"Yes."

"I want you to go in there and wash your legs, feet, and hands. Wipe them with a clean towel. Then, come out here and you can get dressed."

Rolf then turned to Roger.

"Take her for a cup of coffee. I'll call when you can come back." Rolf then refocused on Nina in the bathroom. "Nina, what kind of car does he drive?"

"A brown Audi. He usually parks it in my carport, number twenty-four."

Rolf and Roger looked at each other, both realizing that John Hamishaw had visited Nina before.

Inside a Denny's, located east of Route 163 in the Mission Valley section of San Diego, Roger Legion and Nina sat in a booth, with cups of coffee before them, trying to make small talk without much success.

"Is he a police officer?" Nina wondered, referring to Rolf.

"No, just a friend," Roger responded and smiled.

"I like when you smile," Nina told him. "I'm usually always afraid when I'm around you. But I also feel safe. I don't know why."

"When I was in college, I read a book called *The Prince* by a guy named Machiavelli. I learned a lot from it and I go back to it often. It talks a lot about whether a prince, the leader of a principality, should be loved or feared and the actions they should take. Whether in a courtroom, or a settlement conference, or dealing with other lawyers, love is not the path to victory. To be feared is a powerful weapon. I realized that a law firm is like a principality. And I'm the guy who leads the army. I have to be cruel, because that's the only way I can command my lawyers' absolute respect."

Nina looked at him and began to understand him.

"But I can't do it alone," Legion admitted. "I need the lawyers. I need the support staff. I need you."

Legion had his hands clasped together on the booth tabletop and she reached over and put her hands on top of them.

"I was going to kill myself tonight. Larry Larkin asked me to marry him, but we were both afraid to say anything to you, because we thought you would not let us work together."

"Does he make you happy?" Roger quizzed.

"He does."

"That's what I want. You to be happy."

They both smiled at each other and a calmness came over Nina.

"You like ice cream or pie?" Roger asked.

"I like'em both," she admitted.

Roger waived the waitress over to their booth.

"What kind of pie do you have?"

"Apple or cherry," the waitress advised.

"You pick," Roger declared.

"Can we share?"

Roger nodded in agreement.

"Apple."

"Heat it up and put some vanilla ice cream on it. Two forks," he instructed the waitress.

Nina slept well that evening. It was the first time that she could remember that she did not need a glass of wine to help her sleep.

As Roger and Nina were reaching the end of the wedding processional, another attendee caught sight of them.

Jim Roth, compatriot of Diego Barranca, savior of Diego's captured women, and survivor of Operation Double E attended at the invitation of the groom. As Jim watched Legion, he began to remember.

After shooting Isa Cabrera, the Palace Etiquette Administrator, Jim used Diego's severed thumb to make entrance into the next room over where twelve women lived under the microscope and rule of Diego Barranca. All the women wore a white, one-piece housedress, so that they could be made ready for Diego at his immediate request.

Jim entered the room like a man knowing that the moment of judgment was upon him.

"*Señoras, vamos! AHORA!* (Ladies, let's go! NOW!)" Jim screamed and the women all moved to follow him.

He used Diego's detached thumb to go through two more hallways before he stopped in the middle of the second hall, where the floor and walls were made of marble. Once again, Jim placed the thumb on a biometric pad and part of the wall, next to the thumb pad, retracted in to allow access to another room. Within the room, close to the door, were fifteen, thirty-inch, large, aluminum suitcases, with wheels on the bottom and a retractable handle.

"*Señoras, todo el mundo recojan una maleta! AHORA!* (Ladies, everyone pick up a suitcase! NOW!)"

Each of the women wheeled out a suitcase and Jim wheeled out two of them. The group made their way to the western tunnel, where Jim had arranged for a special black 'op' military armored transport to assure his escape and the ladies who accompanied him. They escaped less than six minutes before the first bunker buster missile began to turn the Palace to dust.

Operation Double E was named as an homage to Diego from his days when he was excessively using cocaine. Those who knew him in those days said he had no soul. They called him 'Empty Eyes.'

Each suitcase that accompanied Jim and the women contained $1.5 million in cash. It was a little side plan that Jim had been working on for months. He left the Palace that day with fourteen suitcases or $21 million. He often wondered about the one suitcase that he had to leave behind.

Jim gave one of the suitcases to the twelve women to split. They were each given $125 thousand. Two suitcases, or $3 million, were given to Herschel Gordon, the man known as 'the Gringo,' for his assistance. Herschel would also provide assistance in laundering the remaining money. Herschel's foot soldier, Serge Stiroy, also received a slice of the $3 million for his competent work.

As Roger Legion and Nina reached the base of the altar, Roger turned to her, lifting her veil and folding it back. He smiled and gave her a kiss on the cheek. Legion turned to the groom, Larry Larkin, and they shared a firm handshake. Roger moved close to Larry's ear and whispered, "You better take care of her."

Roger stepped back to the second pew, where his wife, Valerie was standing. As he entered the pew, he caught the eye of Jim Roth, who gave Roger one of his trademark smiles. Roger stood next to his wife, looking forward, and his wife patted his right hand. Then, Roger began to remember.

It was the early evening of the day that John Hamishaw and Nina had their fateful rendezvous. When Legion reached his car in the America's Finest City Building parking garage, there was a Post-it note on the driver's door window that simply said, 'Check the trunk!'

Legion popped the trunk and saw two of the aluminum suitcases from the Palace of Barranca. There was a small envelope taped to one of them. On the outside of the envelope, it was handwritten, 'For your trouble! Jim Roth.' Inside the envelope was a key. He opened one of the suitcases with it and smiled at the contents.

Roger took one of the suitcases to Rolf Adler at the Bagheria Bedda restaurant. Rolf would not take any money from Legion, but he would take it from Diego Barranca. Rolf gave Jimmy Flowers $200 thousand as tribute to share the wealth.

As for the remaining suitcase, that money was donated by Valerie Legion to the Kisses & Tummy Rubs Animal Shelter. Even though she requested that her name be kept anonymous, everyone at the shelter knew the source of such a generous gift.

As for Rolf Adler, he was at the church, but sitting in the shadows. It was a place that he definitely preferred.

Legion's intent on the day he went to talk to Rolf was to authorize the elimination of John Hamishaw and Larry Larkin. Rolf determined that Larry was not involved in attempting to betray the law firm. He told Roger about John's request for a million dollar payday, in addition to wanting his wife and four children killed.

"You know what's got to be done," Legion assured Rolf.

Roger was always proud of the work product produced by his lawyers, but betrayal was something that could not be redeemed. If necessary, the other lawyers would learn the price to be paid for betrayal. Fortunately, he never had to give that order.

Now, time was about to put all these events into the past.

Roger Legion once said, 'Money is time.' He understood the value of time; its finite nature, and how it could enhance, or punish, a lawyer's performance. In addition, the entire economic basis of Legion and Associates was the billable hour. It evolves life and foreshadows death.

They say that the only thing a lawyer really has to sell is his advice. His hourly rate is an artificial number that is based on what he believes his clients will pay. It really has no relation to anything.

Most lawyers spend their day accounting for what they have done. When they wake up the next day, they start all over again. They are slaves on a modern-day plantation that is a pyramid scheme called a law firm. Those at the top of the pyramid, like Roger Legion, want to stay on top as long as possible. But there will always be a threat from those lawyers wanting to knock him down. As long as lawyers, like Legion, stay vigilant and greedy, they will do what it takes to stay at the top.

What they should realize is the thing that makes them rich is the one thing they cannot control. Time.

ALL I KNOW

When I was a little girl,
I dreamed about that day.
When I wore a pretty wedding dress,
And danced the night away.

My friends would ask me how he looked
That groom within my dreams.
I never could remember him
How odd that may seem.

> All I know is that he said he loved me.
> All I know is that he said he cared.
> All I know is that he'd never leave me.
> All I know is that we are a pair.

I waited for what seemed to be
A lifetime for that groom.
And when I thought he came to me
He brought me only gloom.

I knew that he was not the man
Who loved me in my dreams.
But I tried to love him any way
My fear was so extreme.

> All I fear is being old and lonely.
> All I fear is dying all alone.
> All I fear is never having memories.
> All I fear is love that's never known.

Well then one day he came to me,
By accident it seems.
He said that when he looked at me,
I was the girl of his dreams.

So when you see your man of dreams,
Keep him in your sight.
Never, ever let him go,
Love him with all your might.

> All I know is that he says he loves me.
> All I know is that he says he cares.
> All I know is that he'd never leave me.
> All I know is that we are a pair.

> All I know is that he says he loves me.
> All I know is that he says he cares.
> All I know is that he'd never leave me.
> All I know is that we are a pair.

All I know his ring I'm gonna wear.
All I know a life we're gonna share.

© 2014 Vincent F. Aiello

Available on YouTube® and Amazon.com

About the Author

Vince Aiello grew up in upstate New York before moving to Southern California where he attended California Western School of Law. He is admitted to practice law in both New York and California. *Legion's Lawyers* is his third novel. His earlier novels, *Legal Detriment* and *The Litigation Guy*, were both acclaimed bestsellers. Visit his website at www.vinceaiello.com.

ACKNOWLEDGEMENTS

I would like to thank the following individuals for providing support and, in some instances, the use of their name for a fictional character in *Legion's Lawyers*:

Diane Abrams
Ethan P. Aiello
Sarah Rose Aiello
Valerie R. Aiello, RPh
Nancy Barton
Nancy Buscis
John Christopher, DMD
Marc Christopher
Tom Christopher
Paul Clifford
Lisa Nastasi Clifford
Fiero DeMasi
Glenn Edgarian
Michael Eiffert, M.D.
Nina Eiffert
Vincenzo Fiorito

Angelo Garubo, Esq.
Troy Geisser, Esq.
Herschel Gordon
Patricia Halderson
Don Howard
Paul Messina
Sebastián Lorenzo Monje
Karla Mulry
Addie Pane
Ellen Price-Reardon
Jim Roth, Esq.
Javier Jimenez Sanchez
Maria Jimenez Sanchez
Lisa Leffort Reynolds
Mark Reynolds
Rolf Safir
Patty White

www.ingramcontent.com/pod-product-compliance
Lightning Source LLC
Chambersburg PA
CBHW071259170626
46809CB00001B/282